Now You Wanna Come Back 3

Now You Wanna Come Back 3

Anna Black

www.urbanbooks.net

Urban Books, LLC
300 Farmingdale Road, N.Y.-Route 109
Farmingdale, NY 11735

Now You Wanna Come Back 3

ISBN 13: 978-1-64556-459-1
EBOOK ISBN: 978-1-64556-460-7

First Trade Paperback Printing June 2023
Printed in the United States of America

10 9 8 7 6 5 4 3 2

This is a work of fiction. Any references or similarities to actual events, real people, living or dead, or to real locales are intended to give the novel a sense of reality. Any similarity in other names, characters, places, and incidents is entirely coincidental.

Distributed by Kensington Publishing Corp.
Submit Orders to:
Customer Service
400 Hahn Road
Westminster, MD 21157-4627
Phone: 1-800-733-3000
Fax: 1-800-659-2436

Now You Wanna Come Back 3

by

Anna Black

Chapter One

Devon stood and peered out the window of his condo, wondering how he went from being happily married to Leila to cheating on her with his coworker Michelle. Then he'd moved on to marry Christa, his next mistake, because he was still in love with Leila when he said, "I do," leading to another divorce. Then Janelle was the one, he'd thought, and he finally fell in love again, only to find out that she was married with two kids. He was starting to admit that he was lonely and wanted to find love again.

Leila was happily married to Rayshon, living in bliss, and his ex, Michelle, ended up marrying another partner at their office. She was pregnant with her first kid, and all the exes he cared for were married except him. Christa had recently announced her engagement to Isaiah, and he figured Janelle's husband forgave her, too. There he was, alone with no one.

All he had going great for himself was his fantastic career and his 14-year-old daughter, Deja. She, at the moment, was driving him crazy. She was ready to date, but he, Leila, and Rayshon had all decided she had to wait until she was 15. She had less than two months before she'd turn 15, and because of some boy at her school named West, she was begging for them to bend the rules. He thought about it for a moment, but when he met the pimpled-faced lad, he swore that there was pure lust in his eyes. He was damn near Devon's height, with long cornrows in his Puerto Rican waves, and his light eyes looked like Honey Nut Cheerios. He wore colorful braces. When he spoke with a baritone voice as deep as Devon's, bending the rules was a fuck no.

He wanted to change it to 18 at that moment. Still, they had already said 15. Plus, young West was an honor roll student in the same advanced classes as Deja, and he didn't have his pants hanging off his narrow ass. West may have been a good kid, but Deja would have to wait two months before she got his permission to go on a one-on-one date with him. They allowed group gatherings and outings, but they were solid at 15. On May 15, Devon would stop monitoring Deja's every move and start to look for a love of his own.

He had become so consumed with fatherhood and trying to keep his one and only daughter boyfriend free that he was allowing his life to pass him by. He chuckled lightly at the thought of dating again, and then he went to his wet bar and fixed a drink. After a couple of sips, he went for his phone and called Leila.

"Hey, Devon," she answered on the fourth ring.

"Hey, Lei, what's going on?"

"Nothing too much, just waiting for your child to come home."

"Oh, so she isn't there. I've called her phone five times, and it goes straight to voicemail. I thought she was on restriction again."

"No, but she will be if her ass does not walk into this house in the next five minutes. She was told to be home by nine, and I am trying to give her the benefit, Devon, but your daughter is trying my patience. She will end up in a body cast if she doesn't get her act together. I mean, all she ever talks about is that damn West, and she thinks we are going to change our minds about fifteen, but she is dead wrong," Leila vented.

"I agree one hundred percent, Lei. Where is she anyway this late on a school night?" he asked.

"She went to the mall with her li'l friend Destiny."

"Okay, just have her call me as soon as she gets home. I wanted to let her know that my boss is having his daughter for the weekend and wants us to join him for a little while for a father-daughter night. Ever since I took Deja over for dinner that one time, his daughter keeps asking him about her," he said and finished the whiskey in his glass.

"I'll let her know, Devon, but how I feel right now, she may be on restriction until her damn birthday. I am tired of fussing about the damn curfew. Nine means nine," Leila spat.

"I hear you, because I am tired of this dead-ass phone excuse. I got her ass a portable charger for moments like this. Getting her voicemail is a damn problem."

"Oh, here she is now. Do you wanna talk to her?"

"Yeah, put her ass on," Devon said with irritation. He understood that she was a teen, but she had to be more responsible than she had been lately.

"Here, it's your dad," he heard Leila say before Deja came on the line.

"Hi, Daddy," Deja chirped.

"Hello, D.J. What have your mother and I told you about missing curfew, and where in the hell is your portable charger?" Devon asked, trying to keep his voice from roaring into the phone. "I told you that I wasn't having the 'my phone died' madness from you, Deja, and I am losing my tolerance for this wack-ass behavior!"

"Dad, I forgot it, I swear. I was rushing because Destiny's mom was outside blowing her horn like a madwoman, so I rushed out and forgot it."

"Okay. Forget again and I promise you I'll forget to make your cell phone payment."

"Yes, sir," she said sadly.

Devon continued to fuss her ear off for the next five minutes about being responsible and doing better. Then he sprang the news on her about going to his boss's house that weekend.

"Awww, please don't make me go. Eeeeeewwwww, she is so weird, Dad, and I don't want to hang with her. She doesn't even know who BTS is, so please don't torture me."

"First, you will not call Ryan weird because you guys don't like the same things. That is not how we raised you. Have you thought about sharing some of the things you like and letting her show you some of the things she likes? She is a lovely girl, and you know her dad's place is new for her. Since her parents divorced, she has to be with him on an entirely different side of town with zero friends, so think of others, Deja, and try to be nice."

"This is so unfair," she mumbled.

"And so is life. You are like two seconds from being grounded for coming home late, so do your dad a favor and drop the attitude, because you are going," Devon said.

"Yes, sir," she said sadly.

Seconds later, Leila was back on. "Yeah, Devon," she said.

"Look, I don't know what is going on with our daughter, but she is going to have to straighten her shit up, Leila. Missing curfew and keeping her head down in all those damn gadgets is not what I want her constantly focused on. And this little attitude she has found, she needs to lose that shit quickly because I'm not raising a damn idiot."

"I hear you, Devon. I will talk to her."

"Yeah, because she doesn't want to live with me, because I'd shut all that shit completely down."

Leila laughed lightly. "Whatever, man, you are all talk. Deja will be fine. It's just teenage shit."

"Whatever, I have to go."

"For what? You finally got a hot date or something?" she teased.

He chuckled. "Nah, I'm gonna chill around the house, get caught up on some work."

"Devon, that is all you do now. How about you at least come over and have a few drinks with us? You haven't been with anybody since that married chick, Janelle. I mean, even Christa is engaged. When are you going to find a woman, old man?"

"Oh, so you are monitoring my love life now?"

"No, but Ray and I agree that you should get back out there. Everyone I know has somebody but you."

"Wow, thank you, Oprah. Tell your husband, Dr. Phil, that I am good. You two don't have to worry about my love life, okay? I have work and a hormonal teen in love with some pretty boy named West Ortiz to concentrate on. Love is not on my to-do list," he said.

"If you say so, Devon, and I must say bye now because not like you, sir, I'm getting some, and my sexy-ass husband just walked in the door," she said, and Devon heard what sounded like a kiss. "Hey, baby, your food is in the warmer," Leila said.

"Whatever, Lei, and tell Ray I said what's up," Devon said, going for another drink.

"Yo, ask Devon if he is up for Jay's," Devon heard Rayshon say. He figured she had him on speaker.

"Nah, I'm good, man."

"You sure?" she asked.

"Yeah, we meeting up Sunday to go to the game, so I'm good. Later, Lei," he said and then disconnected the call.

He refilled his glass and went to power on his laptop. While it powered up, he did a quick fridge check, but there was nothing he wanted to eat or cook. He opened his junk drawer, pulled out a menu, and ordered from a Chinese restaurant not too far from his place. He got to work, and then his phone rang. It made him jump because it was quiet other than the sounds of the keys on his laptop. He answered and gave the doorman permission to allow his delivery to come up. Within a couple of minutes, the man was at his door. He had cash on hand, so he paid and hurried to the kitchen after he had locked his front door. He grabbed a pair of chopsticks from his utensil drawer and decided to just eat from the containers. After three a.m., he finally shut his computer down and headed to bed.

After a long, hot shower, he was under the covers, his mind wide awake with thoughts of finding love again. He had messed up so horribly in the past that he hoped God would grant him another opportunity to have it. He wondered if he'd find someone to love him as deeply as Leila or care for him as much as Christa.

"God, I know I have a terrible track record regarding love, marriage, and wives, but I am a better man. Forgive me for how stupid I was. If you give me another crack at this love thing, I will be the best man I can be. I'll love the next one more and better than I loved Leila, Christa, and even Janelle. I'm ready," he prayed, and then he finally drifted off to sleep.

Chapter Two

"Hey, *chica*," Leila said and stood to greet Christa.

"Hey, Leila." Christa beamed. "I'd like you to meet Jaiden's mom, Janiece, and this is her sister, Janelle," Christa introduced them, and then they all took a seat.

"Nice to finally meet you, Janiece," Leila said. Leila glanced at Janelle again and wondered where she knew her face from.

"Well, ladies, as you all know, my first wedding was small and rushed. However, I want this one to be grand," Christa said, interrupting Leila's examination of Janelle. "And as the saying goes, 'What the bride wants, the bride gets,'" she said, and the ladies giggled.

"Yep, this is true," Leila agreed, and the server approached. "Before all the wedding talk, let us order some drinks, ladies." Everyone agreed, and they all ordered their cocktails. "Now that the drink orders are in, let's get down to the wedding business," Leila said and pulled out her tablet.

"Yes, and, Christa, whatever you do, please don't choose purple as your color. That was our color," Janiece said.

"Thanks for the advice, but I won't. I mean, I want like a black-and-white color scheme."

Janiece nodded and then went for the glass of water that the server had poured when he approached before taking their drink orders. "That sounds nice. I am sure Isaiah would like that. He is not hard to please," Janiece added. "Plus, I can't believe I am even going to be a part of my ex-husband's wedding," she said and swallowed.

"I got one better for you. I planned my ex-husband's wedding when he married this chick," Leila said, pointing to Christa.

"Hold on, Christa's ex-husband is your ex-husband?" Janelle asked.

"Yes, we were both married to Devon."

"Crazy, but I fell in love with Devon long after he and Leila were over. Unfortunately, that went to shit because I was so damn paranoid that he wanted her back," she said, pointing at Leila. "I had not stopped to think for one second that Leila was happy with Rayshon and didn't want his black ass back. Lord, shit was a mess back then," Christa said as the server approached again, that time with a tray of goodies. He managed to put the right drink in front of the right person, and then they ordered some lunch. As soon as he vacated, they dove right back in.

"Devon, Devon, Devon," Janiece repeated. "Why does that name sound so familiar?"

"Because I had an affair with him," Janelle spoke up, and it was like the table went still.

Leila's mouth opened. "I knew I recognized you. You are that Janelle," Leila said.

"Yes, I am," Janelle confessed.

"Well, damn, all y'all done rode Devon's dick," Janiece joked, and the ladies laughed loudly.

"Well, I guess you can say we all have," Janelle said, taking a sip of her drink.

"Shit, I'ma keep it real. That was some good dick, baby," Christa said.

"Hey, Isaiah got the good D too, baby," Janiece said.

Christa's head nodded up and down. "Indeed, in-fucking-deed, and I know you got K.P. and y'all all happy and shit, but, Jai, how did you walk away from it, girl?" Christa inquired.

Janiece took a sip, and the girls all got quiet. "It was just that my heart ached for K.P. more. I mean, Isaiah is a great man, a damn good father, and he was an awesome husband. Isaiah came into my life to help me walk away from a toxic situation at that time with Kerry and Kimberly. I mean, those days were rough. I don't know, Christa. When I thought Isaiah had died, K.P. was on time to help me through it all, and we reconnected. We bonded, and what can I say? I fell so deeply in love with him all over again. When Isaiah came home, I was so sad that I had given my heart back to K.P. I tried to return to what we had, but K.P. held my heart prisoner. I decided that I would rather leave and give him another chance at love than stay and resent him and live a lie, and then when he met you, I was like thank you, God.

"I was so happy when he found you, Christa, and I am glad that your sexy, beautiful, gorgeous ass came along when you did," she said, and they all laughed. Her words were heartfelt, Leila thought, listening to her reference to Christa being sexy, and they lightened the mood.

"Well, I do what I can," Christa teased. "Plus, it was so easy to fall for him. I mean, you've all seen him. Isaiah is the epitome of fine, and the dick—oh, Lord—the dick," Christa said, raising her hands in praise.

"We get it, Christa, damn," Leila said. "This is so crazy. We have this whole entire soap opera past," Leila said.

"Yes, indeed, and I am grateful that my husband found it in his heart to forgive me. I mean, I enjoyed my fling with Devon, but I knew that shit was wrong. I was so stuck on Gregory cheating and knew I was right, but I was dead fucking wrong."

"Gregory is a damn good man, and I love my brother-in-law for staying with your ass. I mean, I told you to shut that shit down," Janiece added.

"You did, but my mind was set, and when I met Devon, shit, Leila and Christa know what it is," Janelle said and sipped her drink.

"Oooohhhhhhh, honey, we do, we do," Christa said, and they all laughed. They returned to wedding planning and agreed that they should get together more outside of wedding stuff.

Leila drove home sober as hell, laughing to herself about the conversations she and the girls had shared. She needed to hit the wine fridge as soon as she got home because although the cocktails were delicious, they were weak. They all had their spin on the men they had once been with or were still with, and Leila knew she may have made two new girlfriends.

Chapter Three

Leila walked in and wondered where everybody was. She knew Deja was going to Devon's, but she didn't expect Ray and the kids not to be at home. Of course, Rayshon hardly ever got home early. She put everything down on the kitchen island and went for the wine cooler. She was exhausted with all of Christa's wedding ideas, and although the budget was grand and she had more time to plan, she hoped she could pull it all off.

After she poured a glass and swallowed some of the golden contents, she realized she had messages that she had not checked. She went to the counter where the flashing light irritated her, and pressed play. The first couple of messages were from bullshit-ass scammers. She wondered how telemarketing still even existed in this day and age. She just quickly deleted them. By the fifth message, her hand stilled when she heard the familiar voice of one of her daughter's teachers.

"Hi, Mrs. Johnson. This is Alicia Gray, Deja's English teacher. I am calling because the school year is ending soon, and Deja is not doing as well as before. I am not sure what is going on or where things went left, but if she doesn't get back to normal, she may fail my class or finish with the lowest grade since the year began. Can we meet on Tuesday at twelve forty-five so we can figure out what is best for her going forward?"

Leila instantly got an attitude. She was angry that her daughter was doing the most. She was even more annoyed when her calendar revealed she was unavailable at the time her teacher requested. She had an appointment at the florist with Christa. Although Christa wasn't paying her as much as she was worth, she was a friend to her, so she grabbed her phone and dialed Devon.

After a couple of rings, it went straight to his voicemail, and then she hung up, not bothering to leave a message. She figured he'd see her missed call and then call her back when he was free. She grumbled a few profane words from her lips, and then she headed over to the family room to take a load off. Before her next swallow of golden stress reliever, the chime of the alarm system sounded off. Her family was home, and she hoped that Rayshon had fed them because she was in no mood to cook, and there was also nothing quick to make.

"Hey, baby," her husband said gleefully as she stood. He tossed his keys onto the counter, and she made her way over to him to greet him properly. The kids barely spoke as they raced upstairs with their bags, and Leila did not stop them.

She gave him a few soft pecks and asked, "Where were you guys?"

"At the mall shopping for Shon. He has outgrown all of his damn sneakers. On top of that, RJ and Rave also wanted a new pair. I just dropped a grip on six pairs of the latest kicks, according to the jobless humans that we take care of daily," he said.

"Well, Shon is growing faster than a weed. He is only five now and damn near taller than RJ," Leila added.

"I know, right? Whoever Karen's donor was had to be big and tall, because she was petite as hell."

Leila gave him a look. "I don't need to be reminded of how petite the other woman was, Rayshon," she said, going for more wine.

He walked up behind her, embraced her, and then kissed her neck. "Baby, don't even get all up in yo' feelings over that shit. You know it's always been you."

She tilted her head over to the side and allowed him access to plant more kisses, and she smiled. "I know," she whispered. Through it all, she knew in her heart that her husband adored her.

"I love you, woman," he added.

"I love you too, man," she said, and he held her tighter. She then remembered the call from Deja's teacher. "Baby, I need a huge favor. Deja's teacher called about her grade slipping and wants to meet me on Tuesday at twelve forty-five, but I will be with Christa. Can you swing that for me?" she asked.

"No can do, love. You know Tuesday is just like a Monday for me. Tuesdays are impossible, especially at this late notice," he said, releasing his embrace. He went to the fridge and grabbed a beer.

"I know, but I just thought I'd ask. I'm sure Devon can do it, but he didn't answer earlier when I called. I just don't know what is going on with D.J. nowadays."

"West is what's going on," Ray said.

"Oh, my Lord, if I hear that kid's name one more time, I will scream."

"It is her first love or crush, or whatever the kids call it nowadays. I mean, I don't want to be that dad, but I am just not ready for our baby girl to be kissing and grinding and shit," Ray said, leaning back against the counter.

"Neither do I, but we can't just lock her in her room. I mean, what can we do? We said fifteen, and we can't go back on our word, but her decline in school is gonna make me overturn that decision. I mean, why are her grades falling?" Leila said, and her kids came into the kitchen.

"Mommy, can we have a slice of cake?" RJ asked.

"Sure," she said and then paused. "Wait, we must figure out dinner before cake, son."

"We already had our dinner, Ma. We went to Beggar's Pizza," Shon announced.

Leila shot Rayshon a look. "Oh, you did, huh?"

"Yes, ma'am, we did," Raven confirmed.

"And y'all didn't think to bring me a slice of my favorite pizza?" she asked, going for the cabinet. She grabbed a few saucers and went for the cake.

"Well, Daddy said you were having dinner with Auntie Christa before he ate the last two slices," RJ spilled.

Leila watched her husband put a hand on his forehead and move his head from side to side. His kids had ratted him out, and she laughed.

"Y'all talk too much. Didn't I say in the truck on the way home not to tell Mommy where we went?" Ray said playfully, putting Shon into a chokehold.

"It's cool, traitors. I did eat with Auntie Christa, and we had Portillo's!" she spat and then stuck out her tongue to taunt them.

Leila gave them pieces of her homemade red velvet cake and chatted with them about everything. When they were done and instructed to go up and bathe, she and Rayshon went to the sofa in the family room. Her cell rang as soon as she sat, and when she retrieved her phone, it was Devon.

She filled him in on the message from Deja's teacher, and after he agreed that he would go, he asked, "You are not working now, Lei. Why can't you go?"

"Because I have an appointment with Christa to pick out flowers. I am not working, but I am planning her wedding," Leila said and sipped.

"Really, she and this Isaiah dude are doing this? Christa is really going to marry him?"

"I'm afraid so, Devon. Are you good with this? Are you over what you had with her?" she inquired.

"I am, and if I were not, what would it matter? I wonder how they have dated for what seems like five minutes, and she is already getting married. Has it even been a damn year?"

"A little more than a year, Devon, and need I remind you that you didn't date Christa long either before you two exchanged vows," Leila reminded him.

"Yeah, whatever," he said, and Leila heard the uneasiness in his voice. "Listen, I gotta go, Lei."

"Not so fast. Until you speak with Deja's teacher, snatch up that phone."

"Already done," Devon agreed, and they ended their call.

She talked to her husband for a little while longer, and when he said he'd go up to shower, she informed him that she'd be in the basement working on some things for Christa's wedding. She grabbed her unfinished bottle of wine and headed downstairs. After about two hours, her husband came down.

"Hey, Lei, how much longer are you going to be down here?" he asked.

She looked up from her project, not wanting to tell him to go to bed without her. "Oh, baby, damn. I did not realize how late it had gotten. I was just trying to do as many of these centerpieces as I can tonight," she said, holding one up for him to see. "What do you think, baby?" she asked, hoping he'd give his honest opinion.

"Wow, baby, these are so amazing," he said, examining all the ones she had finished. "However, it is not what I think. It will come down to what Christa thinks."

"Yes, that is true," Leila agreed and started cleaning up her mess.

"Baby, you are actually good at this. This looks like something out of a magazine, and I am impressed. And thinking back on how you did Christa's first wedding in such a small window of time, she should be paying you top wedding-planner dollars, baby," he added.

"Wow, Ray, you think so?" Leila said, looking down at the pieces she had already completed. She had done a damn good job.

"Yes, and I also think you have stumbled into your next career move," he said with a nod.

"What do you mean?" she quizzed.

"Wedding planning, hell, not just weddings. Parties, events. You have put together epic events since the store closed. Christa's wedding and her one-year anniversary for her modeling agency. Everyone still talks about the promotion party you did for Devon and the baby shower you did at the gym for Catrice. My party earlier this year, and not to mention the big plans you have for Deja's fifteenth while planning Christa's wedding. Leila, this may be your next move, babe."

"Seriously, Ray, you think I am talented enough to do this professionally?"

"How could you think that you aren't? Just go back and look at the pictures of your work. People would hire you, babe."

"I think you are right. This comes naturally to me, and I enjoy it so much that it doesn't even feel like work. I truly love doing this just as much as I loved having my bookstore."

"So I say you should just do it, Lei. Find a great location or work from the house while you build clients, and maybe hire an assistant to help you so the kids and I don't have to," he joked. "Either way, this is what you were born to do."

"I agree, and I can do this," she cheered enthusiastically.

"You absolutely can. The first thing you need to do is get a business name and get on social media. Build you a dope website with the pictures of the brilliant work to get it crackin', baby."

"Baby, you really believe in me. You won't have any issues with me getting back in the work world?"

He pulled her in for a hug. "Baby, I support you in whatever you want to do. Your flair for events is beautiful, and your talents deserve monetary appreciation. You are good at what you do, so no more volunteer work. You need to get what you deserve for your hard work, and I support you and this business venture with everything."

"You are a great husband, and I am so lucky to have you."

"You are a wonderful wife, and I am so lucky to have you too," he returned.

"Are you?"

"I am," he answered and kissed her. "You are smart, talented, and an extraordinary woman. You have stayed and stood by me through my worst moments in life, without hesitation, with Karen and then her mother passing, you allow Shon to live with us, to give him a home. That makes you . . ." he said and paused. "I can't even think of a word worthy enough to describe you right now, Lei."

"Incredible is a word."

"Underrated, but a good try," he said and kissed her. He pulled her in closer, and she felt his erection between them.

"Are the kids sleeping?" she whispered.

"I don't know," he answered. "But I want to bend you over and slide in before one of them finds us down here."

"And I want you to, so let's stop talking and make this happen," she said and headed to the guest bedroom they had finally finished when they renovated their unfinished basement.

After she locked the door, they fucked with no interruptions or knocks on the door from the unemployed minors that lived in their home. After two rounds, they managed to muster up the energy to go to their bedroom.

The second floor was quiet, with Rav asleep, but Shon and RJ were playing a video game with the fancy headphones that Leila forbade Ray to get them. Since it was a Friday night, he and Leila decided to let them be.

Leila went to shower, and before long, Ray joined her. They lathered up, teased each other, and tackled their third round before falling into a deep, exhausted sleep.

Chapter Four

"Jai," K.P. yelled, and Janiece heard him.

She figured he was at the bottom of the stairs. She was in the new baby's nursery, but she heard him. She heard him the last couple of times he called out for her, but she was dealing with her baby girl, who was spoiled to death because she never wanted to put her chubby ass down, and she was on the verge of just letting her cry this one out. She made her way to the hall just to answer her husband.

"Yes, what is it?" she yelled back.

"Isaiah and Christa are here for Jaiden," he yelled back.

Janiece rushed back in to give the new addition a binky, and of course, she refused it, but Janiece said, *fine,* to herself and left the baby to cry it out with her chubby legs and arms swinging. She was fed and dry but fighting desperately not to take her nap. She went to Jaiden's room, grabbed Jaiden and her bag, and headed for the steps. When she made it to the living room, Christa and Isaiah looked comfortable on the sofa, glued to each other. *She is damn near sitting in his lap,* Janiece thought.

She cleared her throat, and immediately Isaiah popped up from the sofa to pick up his daughter and kissed Janiece.

"Hey, Jai, how is everything?" he asked kindly.

"Hey," Janiece responded dryly, unsure why she was so suddenly irritated with him and Christa sitting so damn close on the sofa.

"Baby, do you want a drink?" K.P. offered.

She figured he could see the tension on her face because she was sure her brows connected like a unibrow at that point.

"Since I am pumped, that would be good," she said with her eyes locked on Isaiah. She let her daughter's packed bag slide down her arm and hit the floor. She gave Christa a look and then took a seat.

"So how are you, Jai, and how is the new baby? Jordan, right?" Christa asked after giving Jaiden a high five. Since they looked cozy, Janiece told Jaiden to go back to her room until they were ready, and she was off.

"Jordan is good, Christa. A fussy baby and chunky as hell, but she is good."

"Are you still breastfeeding? Maybe it's the breast milk," Christa suggested.

"I am, but Jaiden had the breast, and she wasn't nearly as huge, but their genes are different, so they are different," she said, and they all laughed.

K.P. returned and handed her a glass.

"Well, kids are the last thing we are thinking of now," Christa informed them.

"I'm sure. How is the wedding planning going?"

"Great! Leila has everything under control. My stress now is the house hunting."

"House hunting?" Janiece questioned, shocked with vaulted brows.

"Yes, we are looking for a place in the city," she replied.

"Isaiah, you're selling the house?" she asked, confused. He loved that house. He always stood firm that that would be Jaiden's home.

"Yes, Christa thought it would be a good idea if we start our lives in something of our own," he said.

Janiece didn't give a shit about what the fuck Christa wanted. She wanted her daughter to grow up in that house. She loved that house. "But, Isaiah, you love that house. I mean, when you first saw that house, you refused to look at any other houses," she said. Both Christa and K.P. looked at her like they wondered why she was so concerned.

"I know, Jai, but Christa and I don't need a house that large. I only have li'l Jai on the weekends now, and since Christa doesn't cook much, we don't need a kitchen that massive."

"Yeah, we are thinking of maybe a condo or a loft," Christa added.

"That sounds nice," K.P. said, and Janiece shot him a look.

"Really?" she said to K.P. and then turned her attention back to Christa and the man she used to live in that house with. "So where is our daughter supposed to play? Condos don't have backyards."

"We still plan to have about three bedrooms, Jai, and Jaiden will have some space of her own. And I'm sure we'll figure out the backyard situation," he answered. Janiece looked at him like he had lost his entire damn mind.

"So having more kids is not in your marriage plans?" she asked out of curiosity. She knew this was all Christa's idea because she knew how much Isaiah loved that house. Plus, she knew Isaiah wanted more kids.

"Well, I don't know, Janiece, and why would that be any of your concern?" Christa asked.

"It isn't, but I know Isaiah wants more kids, and to be downsizing when you already have one doesn't sound like something that Isaiah would want," she informed the new woman in his world.

"Jai, listen, Christa and I got our reasons, and if we decide to have more kids, maybe we will move, but for now, this is what we've decided."

"And if that's what's best for you two, I say go for it," K.P. interrupted, giving his wife a look. "As a matter of fact, Janiece, let me see you in the kitchen for a minute," he requested, standing from the chair.

She hesitated but stood and went into the kitchen.

"What's with you?" he asked, lowering his voice.

"What do you mean?" she asked, giving an attitude.

"Why are you all up in their business?"

"I knew something was going to be wrong with the flawless heifer. She is transforming Isaiah into someone else," she said and gulped her wine.

"What are you talking about?"

"K.P., Isaiah loves that house. He hated condo living. The whole time we lived in my condo, he complained about not having a garage or a backyard, and Isaiah wants more kids."

"And exactly how do you know that?" he asked.

"Because when we got back together, he begged me to give him another child," she said.

The sadness in his eyes after she said those words made her wish she could take them back.

"I'm sorry, Kerry. I didn't mean to just say it like that," she said, rushing over to him, and she set her glass on the island. She knew that had to sting. "I know you never wanted any details about that time we were apart, and I am sorry," she said, touching his face, but he turned away. "Hey, hey, babe. I'm sorry," she said, touching his hands with hers.

"Okay, and it's fine. But whatever Isaiah and Christa have got going on has nothing to do with you. Go back and act like you're my wife, not his jealous ex-wife."

"Maybe I overreacted a little bit," she said and kissed him.

"You did, so get it together, Mrs. Paxton," he said and gave her another peck. He returned to the living room, and she first refilled her glass.

She paused, thinking about the spell Isaiah was now under with Christa. To change his mind about more kids and settling for anything less than a single-family home was mind-blowing. By the time she took her seat on the sofa, the subject was still on the move, and K.P. referred them to his Realtor, Cortez Brooks. K.P. scrolled through the phone to give his number to the engaged couple.

"Thanks, K.P., this could help because the house has been on the market like four months now," he tried to say but was cut off.

"Four months!" Janiece belted. It just jumped out of her mouth before she could catch her words.

"Yes, Christa and I made a decision about selling months ago," he said.

Janiece opened her mouth to question him, but she looked at K.P. and changed her tune. "You know what? That's great, and I hope it sells soon," she said, taking a huge swallow of her wine.

"Me too. He's been at my place so much lately he practically lives there. And one mortgage will certainly be better than two," Christa added.

"I bet," Janiece said sarcastically, with a fake smile spread across her face.

"Well, we better get going," Isaiah said, standing. He went over to the bottom of the steps and called for Jaiden.

"So where will you guys be tonight? At Christa's or the house?"

"Why, Jai?" K.P. asked.

"Because I need to know where my child is going to be since Isaiah practically lives there now," she said with her eyes on Isaiah.

"At my house, Janiece. When I have Jaiden, I stay home so that she can sleep in her own bed," he said, giving her the same energy. He reached for his daughter's hand, and they headed for the door. Once they were gone, Janiece walked back to join K.P.

"So you gon' tell me what that was about?" he said as soon as she sat.

"What, K.P.? Do you mean to tell me that you don't notice how Isaiah acts when she is around? It's like she has him eating out of the palm of her little, petite model hands. She has him under some kind of spell."

"And what's wrong with that?"

"Everything. For instance, at Janelle and Greg's annual barbeque, I went to fix Isaiah a plate, and Christa stopped me before handing it off to him, talking about Isaiah doesn't eat steak and brisket. I was like, 'Since when? Isaiah loves brisket.' And she goes, 'Since we stopped eating beef.' K.P., I had to slip the man a brisket sandwich behind her back. That's what I mean."

"Okay, Jai, and whatever Christa does or has done to him, he likes it. He proposed to that woman, so it has to be changes that he likes. Fuck! Stop acting like a jealous ex-girlfriend."

"Kerry, you know that I'm not jealous of her. I care about Isaiah. He is my daughter's father, and if his life changes, it will affect our child's life."

He blew out a breath and then looked up. She could tell he was either collecting his thoughts or about to shake her to death, and she hoped he did not decide on the latter. "Listen, do you remember how Isaiah would criticize everything I did when we got back together? Like everything I said or did, he'd be in your ear about how our lives would affect his daughter's life?"

"Yes," she mumbled with a nod. She already knew where he was going with this point.

"And what were your exact words to him?"

"'I have my daughter's interest at heart, and I would never make any decisions without considering Jaiden.'"

"So trust him to do the same. Isaiah is a grown-ass man who has survived fucking war, Janiece. He can handle his shit with Christa. Stop worrying about the choices that he makes with his life post you. Maybe he wants to move on and away from the dreams he had with you and make new ones with her."

"But she is—" she tried to defend herself.

"What, doing what is best for her and her man? Love will make you do things you can't imagine that you would," he said, looking her in the eyes.

"I've never tried to change you, K.P."

"No, but you asked me to let you go back to Isaiah for ninety days, Jai. As much as that broke me, I loved you enough to allow you to figure your shit out. I had to deal with knowing that you were in his bed every damn night and wondering every second if you were going to leave or come back," he expressed, and his eyes watered.

She hadn't ever remembered seeing her husband cry, and hearing his truth was fucking her all the way up.

"So please don't ever dare talk about a man being under a spell, because people do things they'd never ordinarily do for love."

She moved closer to him and wiped the tears that he finally let fall. "I am so sorry for putting you through that, baby. I know that was the most difficult decision that you ever had to make."

"You have no fucking idea," he said and then walked away.

She stood and waited for him to return, but after a few minutes, she realized he wouldn't be back to that conversation.

She went down the hall to look in on Jordan, and she was still sleeping. *A good cry and a deep sleep never hurt,* Janiece thought as she headed down the steps. She found him sitting out by the pool.

"Hey," she said softly. He looked up at her. "Can I sit with you?" she asked. He slid back, opened his legs, and let her join him on the chaise. She rested her back against him. "I know it was ninety days of hell for you when I went back, but I have to be honest. I am glad I did," she said, and he tried to push her forward. "No, no, no, baby, hear me out, please. Let me explain."

"I can't have this conversation, Janiece."

"Kerry, please, just let me talk to you so that you can understand."

It took him a few moments of hesitation, but he eased back and relaxed. "I'm listening," he said.

"I don't regret it because that time away from you showed me just how much I truly loved you. You said you never wanted details, but you must know where my head and heart were back then. When I first got back to that house, it was set up exactly the way I left it, and it felt weird to me to even be there, but for Isaiah and Jaiden, I had to try. Every single day I tried, but every single day I missed you more.

"Every day that went by I wanted to go by even faster so I could come right back to you. As painful as the separation was, I needed that to ensure my heart was yours. If I hadn't gone back, I would have been stricken with guilt and what-ifs. I am not jealous of Christa. I just for once want him to be as happy as I am. I never ever want to see him hurt again like I hurt him. He is a good man, a great dad, and finally over us. I just want something great for him."

"Thank you for that, and I feel you more than you know. I have had the same feeling for Kimberly because I know the damage I did to her. However, they are both grown and may go through heartbreak again or a failed relationship, but we have to stay out of it. We have our own marriage to worry about. Kim and Rodney, Christa and Isaiah are not our business."

"You are right, and I understand. I will worry about my husband from now on."

"Good. Now let's go inside so that you can take care of this dick," he said and kissed her neck. As soon as they reached the top of the steps, a crying Jordan put a dent in their plans.

Chapter Five

"Take your time," Cortez told his client as he continued to look over his menu. Cortez glanced at his watch again and wondered what was keeping Cher. She was ten minutes late for their meeting, and the server had come to their table twice for their orders. Cortez advised him that he'd signal for him when he was ready.

"Thanks, Cortez," Mr. Sanders replied, looking over his menu.

"So about the house. You've seen it a few times, and I know you love its location," Cortez said, eager to get a signature. He had the agreement in his briefcase, and all Mr. Sanders had to do was say yes. "I have the papers here with me now, and if you want this house, it is yours." Cortez was desperate to close on this property. This commission would be huge for him, and with the economy going as it had been, he hadn't sold a property in a couple of months. Cher, however, was closing deals left and right, but somehow he was trailing her.

"I know, but I'm still a little concerned with the closing date. I mean, I still have almost ninety days before my house closes, and to take possession of this new property in thirty days is a blow to my bank, and I'm really on the fence with that."

"I understand that, Terry, and I know that is concerning, but if you don't jump on this offer, it may slip right through your fingers," he said, and Cher approached.

"Hey, baby, I am so sorry I am late. I had to get C.J. over to Kennedy's, and the traffic was mad crazy," she explained as he stood to greet her. Terry also stood and gave her a quick hug.

"It's okay," Cortez said after they were all seated. "Cherae, this is Terry Sanders, and Terry, this is my gorgeous wife, Cher," Cortez introduced them.

"It's a pleasure," Terry said with a nod. "Gorgeous indeed," he added.

"Thank you, Terry." Cher smiled.

Cortez signaled for the server, and he was at their table in a flash.

"Are you guys ready to order now?" he asked politely.

"Well, I just sat, and I need a quick moment," Cher replied.

"Cher, babe, we've been here a million times," Cortez interrupted. "She'll have a merlot and the rib eye, cooked well, with steamed vegetables," he said, ordering for her, and Cher looked at him with disapproval.

"Hold on, baby, I think I need a moment," she protested and opened her menu.

"Yes, please, give the beautiful lady a moment to decide what she wants," Terry said. The server nodded and was off in a flash to service another table.

Blood boiling, Cortez smiled. "Okay, Cher, take a moment and look over the menu." He snatched up his drink and downed the contents. He kept his cool, but he'd let her know later how he didn't like her going against the grain. Oh, he'd let her know. "So, Terry, what can I do to make this home all yours?" he asked, getting back to business.

"Hold on, Cortez, relax. We have time for business. Let's kick back, have a fabulous dinner, and enjoy a few drinks. I know the papers are in your briefcase, so let's chill," he said, smiling at them.

Cher smiled back, and Cortez made a fist under the table before agreeing with Terry. Cher let Cortez know she was ready, and he waved for the server. They ordered, sipped, and conversed over a delectable meal.

After the table was cleared, the server offered them dessert, and everyone declined. The last round of drinks was on the table, and it was time for business. Cortez opened his briefcase and pulled out the contract, ready to go over it again and hopefully walk out with a signature.

"So, Terry, are we buying this house, or are you taking the risk of losing it?"

"Hold on, Cortez. This thirty-day thing still concerns me. Two months of the double mortgage still has me undecided."

"I know and—" he said, but Cher interrupted.

"Can I take a quick look?" she asked.

Cortez wanted to tell her to shut the fuck up and just look good so this bitch could sign, but instead he slid the papers over to her after letting out an annoyed breath. They sat for a moment chatting about the details that Terry loved about the home as Cher flipped through the pages. "Okay, so Mr. Sanders, what I am hearing is your concern about closing in thirty days. This is what we can do. We can ask the sellers for a forty-five-day closing, which I am sure they won't dispute since your offer is above asking. Your first mortgage won't be due for another forty-five days, so that will give you ninety days before this mortgage is due."

Terry smiled. "Now if that can be done, I'll sign right now," he said enthusiastically.

"Hold on, let me make a call and see what we can do," she said, grabbing her purse and stepping away from the table.

"Wow, Cortez, your wife is not only beautiful, she is brilliant," Terry complimented with a lustful eye and mischievous smirk that Cortez did not like, but he decided not to check his ass.

"That, she is," Cortez said, hoping Terry could not detect the anger he had brewing.

"And you are a lucky man," Terry added. Cortez agreed. They talked small talk until she returned.

"Mr. Sanders, you just bought yourself a house," she announced and took a seat. She filled them in on all the details, and after Cher assured him that she would email him the revised documents to sign, they left the restaurant.

Glad to have the sale, he calmed down a little, but not enough to make him let go of the humiliation she had caused him.

"I have to head over to Kennedy's to pick up our son, so why don't you go to the office to modify the contracts for your client?" she said as they walked toward her car.

"Oh, so now he is my client?"

"Huh, baby? What does that mean?" she said, stopping at her door.

"It means you never stop being the whore you are," he yelled.

"Cortez, I'm confused. What did I do this time?" she inquired and then felt a sting to the right side of her face that knocked her into her car door. "Why did you do that?" she cried, reaching for her face. You promised you'd never do that to me again," she cried, holding her cheek.

"Get your ass in this car and go home," he ordered and opened her car door. She quickly got into the driver's seat, hoping he would not strike her again. "Go home! I will go and take care of my client," he said, emphasizing "my client." "I will then go to Kennedy's and pick up our son." He then slammed her door.

She sat there and cried for what seemed like forever before she dried her eyes enough to see clearly to drive. Her face ached, but the memories of his beatings were not far behind. It had been two months since the last time, and the last ass whipping was so bad she didn't leave her house for three weeks.

She drove with shaky hands, and when she finally made it home, she called Kennedy.

"Hey, hey, hey," Kennedy answered.

"Hey, Kay, ummm, Cortez is going to pick up C.J.," she said, voice trembling. She wanted to tell Kennedy so bad, but she held on to her secret.

"Are you okay, Cher? You don't sound okay. Are you crying?"

"Ummm, no. I, ummm, had some bad chicken or something at the restaurant, and my stomach is so upset, and I just need to spend some time in the bathroom," she lied.

"Cherae Marie, you know I know you. What's wrong? Do you need me to come over? I can bring C.J. Just say yes and I'm there."

"Kay, I'm good, don't worry. I'll call you tomorrow. Love you," she said and ended the call. She knew Kennedy would do anything for her, but this mess with Cortez was too embarrassing, and she didn't want a soul to know.

As soon as she walked in, her phone rang, and she hoped Kennedy wasn't calling her back. She saw it was her sister, Katrina, so she answered.

"Hey, sis, what's up?" she answered, sounding like all was good.

"Nothing much. I was just calling to make sure we were still on for brunch tomorrow?" she asked.

"You know what, Kat, I am going to have to reschedule. One of my clients was supposed to show his house today, and he had an emergency, and now I have to show this property tomorrow. Normally, I wouldn't reschedule on such short notice, but you know every house we sell keeps a roof over our heads," she added.

"I know, sis, and that's fine. Maybe we can get together for dinner. Cordell can throw some steaks on the grill, and you, C.J., and Cortez can come over," she offered.

"Sounds good. I'll check with my hubby and let you know," she replied, knowing it was a no.

"Okay, sis, call me tomorrow. Good night."

"I will," she said and ended the call.

She was now standing in the family room of their five-bedroom home, wondering why she stayed. Their home was beautiful, and she had all she wanted in life until her husband went from being her sweet dream to a beautiful nightmare. She was a proud mom, a loyal and good friend, and unstoppable in the real estate market. She had been closing deals left and right, and somehow her husband's closings began to trail hers. She was selling more houses and getting referrals to wealthier clients. Cher just was a natural at it and was hitting back-to-back home runs.

Things were a bit tense, Cher could tell, but she'd always be supportive because Cortez was the one who had gotten her into the real estate industry. One night after Cortez had accompanied her to a housewarming party that one of her biggest clients invited her to was the first night he put his hands on her. That was about two years ago, and she since had to hide plenty of bruises. She was so proud to be out that night and was thrilled because that was the largest commission she had ever made, and she thought he'd be proud, but that was not how it felt.

Envy and bitterness were what he carried for her and expressed that night when he hit her the very first time. When they left the party, Cher had no clue that he was boiling like hot lava on the inside. When they walked into their home, he accused her of whoring around with her clients.

"So are you selling houses or pussy?" he had asked her bitterly.

She had turned to him. "What?" she asked, confused.

"You heard me. You parading around this nigga's house like you built the bitch, and he pulling you left and right, introducing you to folks like you're his fucking wife."

"Cortez, he was only introducing me to potential new clients, that's all. His commission is what kept us from losing this damn house!" she'd spat, and that was when she had felt a blow to her face that sent her petite body to the kitchen floor. Blood quickly dripped from her nose, but she was in a daze and couldn't piece together what had just happened. She tried to focus, but her vision was blurred from the tears that quickly sprouted from her eyes. She tried to get up, but it was impossible. She heard his voice blaring obscenities, but she focused on getting off the floor. When her efforts failed, she just rested against the lower cabinets and held her nose. "You see what you made me do," she'd heard him say, finally understanding what he was saying to her. Before, it was a bunch of "blah, blah, blah, bitch, bitch, and blah, blah, bitch."

She just cried, and the next time wasn't far behind the first. She got thank-you flowers from a client, and since they worked in the same office, there was no way to hide them. Cortez had snatched up the card before she could even reach for it. "'You are not only beautiful, but you are also brilliant. I love my house. Thanks for your patience, because I know I am very hard to please! Best wishes, Ron,'" he'd read aloud. "Hard to please, hard to please, hummm! That sounds like you did more than sell him a house to me."

"Cortez, don't, please. I can't defend myself today over a card from a client. This entire thing in your head about me sleeping with clients is ludicrous."

He had laughed and then walked out. That evening when she got home, he was already drinking. Her son was at a sleepover, and she was glad because that night, the argument led to not just one but a couple of punches to her face and head. Her head and face throbbed when she finally woke up the next morning. When she sat completely up, she looked around to find him sitting on the floor with his head down. When he looked up and saw her, he rushed over to the bed and begged her to forgive him for what he had done to her. He made many promises to her and begged her to stay, and for some crazy reason, she did.

Things were good for a while, but six months after that last episode, he did it again, and over the last couple of years, Cher had lost count of the shoves, slaps, and punches. That night he had slapped her in public, and she knew she had to let it go. Her husband had lost her for good this time, and she had to escape before it was too late.

Chapter Six

Devon got to Deja's school at a quarter of five. He was a little late and hoped she'd wait for him. He found his way to her classroom, looked into the glass, and was relieved Ms. Gray was still there. He tapped, and she turned and waved for him to come in.

"Ms. Gray, so sorry I'm late. I had a meeting that ran over, and I'm terribly sorry," he said, and she smiled.

"It's okay, Mr. Vanpelt," she said, shaking his hand. "Thank you for coming. Just let me get my grade book," she said, and Devon checked out her legs.

She wore a rose-colored sleeveless, low-cut blouse and a gray pencil skirt that defined her curves. Her legs were shaped to perfection. Devon didn't know teachers who looked like that still existed. She grabbed her grade book and glasses and asked Devon to join her at a round table.

"So this is the final quarter, and with only nine weeks left in the school year, I want Deja to finish as well as she has done before this quarter. She was doing well, Mr. Vanpelt, until about here," she said, pointing out her grades. "Now her grade point average is a C, but Deja is an A student."

"I see, and I will tell you, Ms. Gray, ever since this West Ortiz has become a factor, that is all Deja talks about and all she wants to focus on," he said.

"Oh, yes, West, I know him, and he is a cutie, but Deja has to get her mind off the boys and back on my class," she joked, and they both chuckled.

"I know, and trust that I will handle her and she will return to normal. It is difficult with teens. Deja is my only teen and my first experience. She has been my baby, and now my baby is growing into a young woman. I mean, I just want to dress her in a turtleneck and snow pants and lock her in a tower," he joked.

"Well, I know what you mean. My experience with my daughter was similar, but now she is a college student at Chicago State, and I'm just learning, myself, how to let go."

"You have a kid in college?" he asked because she didn't look old enough to have a kid in college.

"Yes, she is completing her first year. I moved here from Texas last year to be closer to her, and it took me a minute to cut the cord," she confessed.

Devon laughed. "Well, I'm never cutting the cord," he added, and they continued to talk about Deja and other topics that were not about the teen.

An hour went by, and Alicia noticed the time. She had to run. "Oh, Mr. Vanpelt," she said, getting up, "I must run. I am going to be late for my class," she said.

"Class? I thought school ended at three o'clock," he said, looking at his watch.

"It does, but I teach dance two nights a week, and I've got to get out of here before I'm late."

"Dance, huh?" he said and figured that was why her legs were defined like they were. "How long have you been teaching dance?"

"Well, I've been dancing since I was a little girl, and dance was my minor at Gardner-Webb University. I taught swing out classes in Texas, and now in the Chi, I teach steppin' and, of course, line dancing like Cupid Shuffle and stuff like that," she said, and Devon didn't expect to feel an attraction to her. "Do you dance? Maybe you should come to one of my classes," she offered.

"Well, I was born and raised here in Chicago, and in case you haven't heard, we learn to step before we learn to walk, so if I come to your class, I'll be teaching you a thing or two," Devon said with confidence.

"Well, here is my card in case you decide to come by," she said, going for her bag. She retrieved one from her purse and handed it to him.

He glanced at it, noticing her cell number, and put it into his jacket pocket. He helped her with her bag and walked her out to her car.

"Thank you, Mr. Vanpelt," she said with a smile.

"Devon. Call me Devon," he said and returned the smile.

"Okay, as long as you call me Alicia," she returned.

"Of course," he said.

"And can I expect my student to be back on her game?" she asked, returning to the subject of Deja.

"No doubt," he said, and she got in, and he shut her door. Devon watched her car pull away, and then he headed to his car.

He called Deja immediately and made it clear that if she didn't get her act together, she would not be allowed to date West after her birthday. He made it clear that her school year should end with A's.

When he got home, it was back to loneliness. He went into the kitchen and turned on the grill on his stovetop to grill the salmon he had seasoned the night before. He put three cups of white rice into his rice cooker and opened the single-serving veggie pouch from the freezer. He was cooking for himself again and wished he were cooking for two.

After turning on some jazz, he poured a glass of pinot and powered on his laptop, deciding to get a little work done while he cooked. He went into his room, undressed, and threw on some sweats and a tank. He settled at his desk and ate his meal while he worked, and when it was close to midnight, he decided to call it a night. He show-ered, ensured his alarm was set, and climbed into his bed alone. He tried to fall asleep, but he thought about meeting with Alicia, and he got up and got her card out of his jacket pocket. He put her card in his briefcase and wondered if it would be appropriate to call Deja's teacher.

He thought about her until he drifted to sleep. She was the first thing on his mind the next morning. When he got into the office, he fell into a busy day that distracted his thoughts from Alicia. When he got home that night, he was tempted to call her, but since she didn't give him the card to call her for personal reasons, he declined.

He took out the card and called the dance studio instead, and they told him that her class would be the next night at seven, so he planned to go. When he got to the studio, he was nervous and wished he hadn't just shown up. He changed his mind and decided to leave, but she was walking in as he was walking out.

"Devon," she said.

"Alicia, hi," he said nervously because she caught him trying to leave.

"You decided to join my class?" she asked.

"Well, I was, but I changed my mind," he said.

"Why? You're here now. Why don't you stay?" she asked.

"Nah, I am going to head out," he said.

"Okay, maybe next time then?"

"Yeah, maybe," he said and was about to walk off, but paused. "Say, what are you doing after your class?"

"Nothing. Why?"

"How about I meet you afterward?"

"Sounds good," she said, flashing him her winning smile.

Devon knew her class would be a couple of hours, so to kill time, he got in his car and pulled out a novel he was reading from his satchel by K'wan called *Eviction Notice,* and before he knew it, people began to come out of the building. He tossed the book onto the seat and got out. He stood by the door, and she finally came out.

"How was your class?" he asked, and they began to walk toward the parking lot.

"It was good. You should have joined us. I see that you paid. I saw your name on the new members list," she said.

"I was thinking I'd give it a try, but I'm a pretty good dancer, so I don't need any lessons," he said.

"Okay, then, let's see what you got," she challenged him.

"Right now, right here?"

"Yes," she said, doing a couple of dance moves.

"No, not here. Let me take you somewhere," he said.

"Where? I can't stay out too late. I have school in the morning," she said.

He took a look at his watch. "I won't keep you out too late. I have an early day myself. This spot, Jay's, has something good going on, and I think it will be fun," he said, and she gave in.

"Okay, but not too late," she said, going to her car. "I think it will be better if I follow you," she said, and that was fine.

They pulled up to Jay's and were greeted at the door by a familiar face, Julian. "Hey, Devon, man, what's good?" he said, and they shook.

"All is well. Man, this is my friend, Alicia. Alicia, Julian," Devon said, introducing them.

"Hello," Alicia said.

"Hey, Alicia, welcome to Jay's," Julian said. "Come on in, and I'll get you guys a table," Julian said, and they followed him inside.

They took a seat, and shortly after, Kennedy came over and greeted them, and he introduced her to Kennedy. They had a drink, and Devon finally took Alicia out on the dance floor.

"So where did you learn to dance so well?" she asked.

"My parents. You can't live here and not know how to dance, Alicia. That is a sure way to lose your Chitown residency," he joked.

She laughed. "Wow, I didn't know," she said and couldn't stop smiling. "Where is the ladies' room?" she asked, and he pointed.

As soon as she departed, Kennedy approached. "So who is the new girl?"

"What new girl? You sound like Leila," Devon said.

Kennedy laughed. "Okay, who is your new friend?" she asked and proceeded to clean off their table.

"She is one of Deja's teachers from school. We met a couple of days ago, and here we are," he said, giving her the short version.

"She is a sexy teacher," Kennedy added.

"Yes, and that is why I had to ask her out. You don't think that's inappropriate, right? With her being Deja's teacher?" he asked, getting a second opinion.

"Well, you two are grown, and y'all can do grown-up things. It's not like you are asking for her hand in marriage," she said.

"Yes, you're right," he said, and Alicia returned and took her seat.

They decided it was time to leave and said their good-byes. He walked her to her car, and she thanked him for a good time. Devon suggested that they get together again, and she agreed.

Chapter Seven

"So what do you think?" Christa asked Isaiah, and he looked up from his tablet.

"Christa, baby, I told you, either one. I like them both," he answered.

"I do, too, baby, but I don't know which one I should choose," she whined.

He decided just to pick one. "Okay, baby, the ivory ones."

"Are you sure? The rhinestones are so sparkly."

"I'm sure. We will have enough bling to illuminate a city block, so the ivory ones," he insisted.

"Okay, ivory it is. I have to call Leila to let her know," she said, and she thought about the number for Cortez that K.P. gave Isaiah. "Babe, did you call the Realtor?"

"No, not yet," he said and hated that the subject had come up. Isaiah didn't want to sell his house, and he didn't want to move into a loft or a condo. He enjoyed his garage, where he tinkered around working on cars, and he loved watching Jaiden play outside in the backyard. Even though Christa was not a cook, he was, and he didn't want to give up the vast kitchen he had.

"Why not, bae? The wedding will be here before you know it, and I want us to be settled in our new place."

"Christa, we have time, okay? Besides, I don't know about condo living. Janiece is right. Where will li'l Jai play if we give up the yard? I know we said not right away, but I want more kids."

"Please, let's not do this. I'm in too good of a mood to argue with you, so give me the number, and I'll call him," she demanded and went for her phone.

"No, Christa, I told you I would call. This is not an argument, honey, and trust I'm not trying to get into it with you. Listen, Chris, I love you, sweetheart, and I am down with this whole big wedding event that you are working your ass off to make happen, and I am not standing in the way of any of it, but you have to give a little. And you act like you don't hear me, so I will say it again. I don't know if I want to sell my house. And I don't mind waiting a while to have more children, but I want you to know I want more kids, and if you don't think you want those things too, maybe we are moving too fast with this wedding thing," he said, being honest.

"Isaiah, you mean to tell me that this house means more to you than me?"

"No, babe, no, that's not at all what I'm saying," he said and moved closer to her. "All I'm saying is that I want a home and a family, and I want a place for my children to play and room for me and my family to sit and eat dinner together, and condo living is for young couples who are not ready to have families and cook instead of ordering carryout."

"I do want a family, Isaiah, and I can't help that I have more restaurants in my Rolodex than recipes. All I know is I want you," she said, putting her head on his chest.

"I want you too, Chris, and I want to be happy, and I don't want to move," he said honestly.

"That's it?"

"Yeah," he answered.

She backed away. "Are you holding on to this house because you are holding on to Janiece?"

"What? Christa, come on. Don't start that shit again. I thought we were way past that madness. I am over

Janiece, over my marriage with Janiece, and the only thing I love about Janiece is the fact that she is my daughter's mother. I asked you to marry me. I am not Devon, and this is not the same, so don't, Christa!" Isaiah yelled.

"Fine, keep the house," she said and stormed out.

Isaiah shook his head and wondered why Christa was such a spoiled drama queen. With all her flaws, he loved her. He fought it because he didn't want to let Janiece go at first, but Christa was kind, considerate, and romantic, and even though she was a bit shallow, she always showed Isaiah true love and affection. She didn't cook, but she would order takeout and serve it as if she cooked it herself. She was a giver and catered to Isaiah just as much as he catered to her.

She was not motherly, but she did her best with Jaiden. She never once complained about Isaiah having Jaiden all the time. Even if he canceled plans because of Jaiden, Christa would take it cheerfully and always tell him that he was the best dad on the planet. The thing with Christa was she was extremely jealous. She always felt that Isaiah still had a thing for Janiece, just like she knew Devon had a thing for Leila. The difference was that Isaiah was totally over his marriage and relationship with Janiece.

He knew that he and Janiece were over before the ninety-day trial ended because he could not only see it, but he could also feel it. Even touching her, he knew she wasn't with him. He'd catch her daydreaming, and he knew she was daydreaming about K.P. The connection was not there when they made love, and what they shared pre-Iraq was gone. The time he was away allowed her to give herself back to K.P. Deep down inside, he felt that Janiece always belonged to him.

When Janiece didn't walk through that door that Sunday evening at seven, Isaiah wasn't surprised. At times, he felt she was counting down the days, and he'd wanted to tell her just to go a few times, but his heart was still holding on. As much as he hated it, he knew the day she was gathering her things that she wasn't coming back, but he had that shred of hope. After she was gone for a few days, it didn't even hurt anymore, and he found himself missing her less and less as the days went by. When he met Christa, she was in the gym pretending to be working out a couple of feet away from him for maybe two weeks straight. He waited for her to approach, but after a while, he figured she was the old-fashioned type, so he finally approached her.

She quickly agreed when he asked her to lunch, and they hit it off. When he finally told Christa the truth about everything, including losing a couple of body parts in the war, Christa turned into an angel. She understood and bared herself to him too, telling him all about her life. She told him about her gold-digging days, her early modeling days, and even when she was on drugs when she was mixed up with the wrong man. She told him about Devon and admitted that she knew what Devon felt for Leila before marrying her, but she thought she'd win him over. Christa became Isaiah's best friend. They decided to be honest about everything, and Isaiah was glad he finally decided to be honest and tell her that he didn't want to sell his house.

Isaiah picked up his phone to call his current Realtor to inform him that he wanted to take his house off the market, and it rang in his hand. He looked at the ID, and it was Christa. "Hello," he answered.

"Baby, I'm sorry," she whined.

"Me too. I should have said something before about the house," he said.

"Yeah, you should have, but I don't care about the house. I care about you, and I know Janiece is not a factor, and I know you are not Devon, so I'm sorry. I promise that I will never say that to you again."

"Good, now wherever you are, turn around and come back. I have two hours before I have to get Jaiden, and I want to spend those two hours inside of you," he said.

"Baby, don't talk to me like that when I'm driving. You gon' make me crash," she laughed.

"Just hurry. I'm going up to start the shower," he said and hung up. A few minutes later, he felt her wrap her arms around him while he was in the shower. He was happy she was back and wished he could have more than the little time he had left to be with her. Isaiah handled her like a good lover would and left her sleeping in his bed while he went to pick up Jaiden from Janiece.

Chapter Eight

K.P. arrived at his office and had five young ladies sitting in the lobby waiting for him. His assistant, Rose, was
leaving, and he had to find a replacement, and he had interviews scheduled that morning, and he was anxious
to get them over with. He hated that Rose was leaving
because she opened the office with him and knew everything that made K.P.'s life much easier. He hoped he'd
get someone in there just as good as her.

She was leaving in thirty days, so he needed to hire
someone immediately so she could show them the ropes
before she left. He called in the fifth candidate and got
started. She was gorgeous, and her interview went the
best of all. He gave her résumé to Rose and told her to
call and verify her references, and after Rose came
to him with a good report, he decided Robin Douglas
was the one who was most qualified for the job. He called
her four hours after her interview, and she expressed
happiness and gratitude through the phone. He verified
she'd be in at eight a.m. the next morning, and when she
showed up, he handed her off to Rose.

Rose gave her a tour of the entire office and then had
her fill out her new-hire paperwork. After, they headed
out to a nearby restaurant to have some lunch. Rose was
friendly, but Robin wished she'd be training with Mr.
Paxton and not her old ass.

"So how many kids did you say Mr. Paxton has?" she
asked.

Rose brows bunched. "Why does Mr. Paxton's family matter?" she questioned.

"I just want to get to know my new boss and what kind of man he truly is, and family tells it all."

"Four if we include his stepdaughter, Jaiden."

"Really?" she commented and decided to get to the meat of it all. "So how many women does he have on the side?" she asked.

Rose dropped her spoon. "None! Why would you ask that question? He and Mrs. Paxton are very happily married. Mr. Paxton has been in love with Janiece since God knows when. Since I've worked for Mr. Paxton, it's always been about his family, and he is the only man other than my husband I respect," she said and took a sip. "Why would you ask something like that?"

"Just curious. Every office I've worked in, the boss has been sort of a rolling stone," she said and giggled. "You know, more than a couple of women on the side," she added and winked. "I just want to know what kind of boss I'm dealing with."

"Well, that is not Mr. Paxton. He is a stand-up family man, and Mrs. Paxton has him on lock. I see beautiful women come in and out of his office, and I've never witnessed him doing anything remotely inappropriate. Mr. Paxton is one of the good ones, and you will enjoy working for him. You just have to be on your p's & q's because he is a serious man. Business always comes first. He is fun and will be a delight as long as you are doing your job well.

"I'm in the office at seven forty-five every morning, and hot water is ready for his morning tea. Mr. Paxton is a tea man, and he doesn't drink coffee. I keep the cabinet stocked with his favorite flavors, and I'll show you when we get back to the office.

"Lastly, you have to keep up with receipts. If you spend a dime, you have to have a receipt for it. Mr. Paxton makes sure every penny spent is accounted for. That is why, in my opinion, he is so successful. Organization is everything, so I suggest you stay organized if you want to survive because Mr. Paxton is that guy," she said sternly.

Robin was good with that because she wasn't afraid of hard work. She worked for his kind before, but after seeing him, her only interest was to make him her husband.

She had made the sexual harassment complaint a couple of times, and it paid a pretty penny because she always settled out of court, and Kerry Paxton was supposed to be her next target, she'd thought before seeing him. He wasn't the old CEO, who was horrible to look at whom she had encountered before. He was the fine "gotta have him for myself" kind of fine, and now her plans to get a harassment settlement turned into a plan for taking him for herself. He was definitely her type and had all the qualities on Robin's list. She was excited and couldn't wait until Rose was gone so she could be alone to entice K.P. and make him hers.

Finally, thirty days had passed, and Rose was gone. Robin arrived at seven thirty that morning because she didn't only want to make K.P. a fresh cup of tea, but she wanted to set up her desk the way she wanted it to be. She put up a picture of her fake boyfriend and knew men liked women who were already spoken for. Even though she and Rose went over the dress code, she had on what she thought was hot office-proper attire that day because Rose was no longer there to say something. Her hair, nails, and makeup were flawless, and when K.P. walked in at five minutes before eight, she greeted him with a cup of tea and a bagel with cream cheese.

"Thank you, Robin, but tea is fine. My wife makes sure I have breakfast every morning," he said.

She thought, *one of those,* because women didn't normally get up that early to prepare breakfast for their men. "Okay, no problem. I didn't know. I just thought you'd be hungry. The wives of most CEOs I've worked for didn't know what the kitchen looked like," she joked and laughed a little.

"Well, even if Jai is too exhausted, we have Phyllis, our housekeeper. They make sure I get a meal before leaving my house in the morning, but thanks, Robin, that was thoughtful," he said and proceeded to his office.

"You're welcome, and your first client's folder is on your desk. He will be here at eight thirty," she said and walked back to her seat before he entered his office, ensuring he got a view of her plump ass. She had on a tight skirt and a blouse cut slightly lower than Rose's attire guidelines. She told herself that Rose was gone. Now this was her office, and she could do what she wanted.

As the day progressed, things were going smoothly. Every time K.P. had a call and it was a female, she screened the call. She was sure she'd never transfer his wife to him because her mission was to take him, and a pissed-off wife who assumed her husband was cheating was an easier target to work with, she thought.

"Paxton Financial, this is Robin. How may I help you?" she recited on the phone.

"Hey, Robin, this is Mrs. Paxton. How are you?" Janiece said sweetly.

"I'm fine, Mrs. Paxton. How are you?"

"I'm great. Is my husband available?" Janiece asked nicely.

"Well, he is actually in a meeting right now. I can have him give you a call back," she said.

"Okay, that'll be fine. Better yet, just tell him not to forget Kayla's recital tonight at six. I forgot to remind him this morning," she said.

Robin smiled and said she'd make sure he got the message. She hung up and then got back to her "take K.P." list. She gave him the message when he walked out, but she also made another appointment.

"Mr. Paxton, I just wanted to tell you that Mr. Brinks called and asked if you could meet him at Lawry's The Prime Rib at six tonight because he has to go out of town," she said, lying. Mr. Brinks called that day and said he decided not to buy at this time and would be in touch. "And Mrs. Paxton called about Kayla's recital tonight."

"Awww, I forgot," he said. "Listen, call Mr. Brinks and tell him I'll be there, and I will call Janiece and let her know I can't make this one," he said and went back into his office.

A couple of hours later, he was getting ready to head out, and Robin pretended to be on the phone.

"You're going to cancel on me now, Eric? You know this month is tight, and I was looking forward to dinner. Forget it. I'll eat noodles. You do you," she said and slammed the phone down. "I'm sorry," she said to Kerry. "I've just been out of work for a little while, and getting this job was a blessing, you know, but I had to pay rent and, you know, get caught up with my last check, and my sorry boyfriend was supposed to take me to dinner tonight, and now he canceled," she said, getting up. "I'm just tired of noodles," she expressed.

"Well, I'm meeting a client, and you're my assistant, so you can tag along. Dinner will be on me," he offered, and she smiled on the inside.

"No, I can't impose, Mr. Paxton," she said with a fake sigh.

"You won't be imposing. It's a business dinner," he said.

She quickly grabbed her purse. "If you insist," she said, and they left.

By six thirty, K.P. was checking his watch every five minutes.

"I guess he's a no-show," Robin said like she didn't know the real story.

"I guess he is. Dinner is on me. I have to get to my daughter's school," he said and stood.

To protest would have been too much and too soon, so she just nodded. "Thanks for dinner, boss. See you tomorrow."

"Yeah, good night," he said and then paused. He pulled out his wallet and pulled out two bills. "Here, this should help. I don't want you eating ramen," he said and slid Robin $200.

"Mr. Paxton, what's this? I can't accept this," she said.

"This is the same thing I would have done for Rose. You don't have to eat noodles until the next payday. Just take it as a signing bonus."

"Thank you, Mr. Paxton. I'm not a charity case. It's just been hard since I lost my last job—" she tried to say, but he interrupted.

"It's cool, Robin. I am in a position to help, and I am supposed to help. My family and I live well, and I can't sit and just do nothing when I see someone who needs a little help," he said, and Robin was in love.

"Well, know that I appreciate this so much," she said, picking up the bills and pulling her hands to her breast.

"You are welcome. I'll give the server my card, and you can order whatever you like."

She smiled brightly. "Thanks, boss, for everything."

"You are welcome, and good night."

"Good night, see you tomorrow," she said, and he was off.

He then went to their server. He gave him his card and pointed to her table, and she figured he ran it when he took it and walked away. The server took Robin's order. She ordered steak and lobster and enjoyed her meal. She took the train home and wondered what she'd wear the next day. Mission "Get Kerry Paxton" was in full effect.

Chapter Nine

Kennedy was at one of their restaurants, and her cell phone rang. She grabbed it and didn't recognize the number, but she answered it.

"Hello," she recited.

"Kennedy Banks?" the voice said.

"Kennedy Roberson," she corrected him.

"This is Dr. Marsh at The University of Chicago Medical Center. I am calling about Kenneth Banks. Are you his daughter?"

"Yes, what's wrong, Doctor? Is my father all right?"

"No, he collapsed and was brought in. He had a massive heart attack, and you need to get here as soon as possible," he said, and Kennedy's eyes watered.

"I'm on my way," she said and grabbed her purse. She gave a few instructions to her manager on duty and dialed Julian as she headed to the door. He picked up on the second ring. "Baby, my daddy is at The University of Chicago Medical Center. He had a heart attack," she said, and she was now crying as she opened the car door.

"Oh, my God, baby, I'm on my way," he said.

"Just hurry, Julian, hurry please," she said.

She drove like a madwoman, weaving through traffic with her heart racing. After what felt like hours, she arrived at the hospital about thirty minutes later.

"I'm looking for Kenneth Banks. I'm his daughter. Dr. Marsh called me," she said, and a nurse called the doctor, and he came out to get her, and when Kennedy saw the chaplain, her knees gave out. "No, what's going on?" she cried, and he escorted her to another room to talk.

"I'm sorry, Mrs. Banks, but your father died. We did everything we could, but we couldn't revive him," he said.

All Kennedy heard was, "Your father died," and she couldn't believe her ears. "You've got to be mistaken. I just talked to my dad this morning, and he was fine. You've got to have the wrong person."

"Mrs. Banks," he said, and she snapped.

"It's Mrs. Roberson, and there is no way you can have the right man. My father is as healthy as a horse," she said, pulling out her cell phone and dialing her dad. "Pick up," she said, crying, and the doctor handed her a tissue.

"Mrs. Roberson, you can come with me and see your dad if you'd like," he said, and she nodded.

"Yes, let's get this cleared up," she said and dialed her dad again. "My daddy went to the gym this morning, and he is fine," she said, and when she followed the doctor into the room, she looked at the man they claimed was her father, and Kennedy broke down. She dropped everything she had in her hands and was on the floor.

"Get . . . get my hus . . . husband," she cried, and the nurse picked up her belongings, and the doctor helped her to her feet. "No, no, no, no!" she said and slowly approached her father. She touched him, and he was already cold.

"My God, no!" she screamed, covering her face, and the nurse had to hold her up. "Wake up, Daddy, wake up!" she yelled and shook him. "How did . . . how did this happen?" She was close to hyperventilating, and they helped her to a chair.

The doctor began to give her details of the incident, and Kennedy didn't hear a word he said. Within minutes, Julian walked in. He rushed over to Kennedy, and she lost it. After some discussion, the doctor gave her something to calm her down. Julian called her uncles, and within the next hour, Kennedy's relatives showed up one by one. Kennedy was finally sleeping in the chair from the shot the doctor gave her, and they took her dad's body down to the morgue.

Kennedy's uncle Keith told them what funeral home would be picking up his body the next morning, and they allowed Julian and Kennedy to have that room until Kennedy woke up. When she got up, she thought it had been a bad dream, but she realized she was still in the same hospital room. And she began to weep, and Julian held her. A few moments later, Cher and Cortez walked in.

"Awww, Kennedy Renee," Cher cried and held her, sobbing uncontrollably.

"Cherae Monique, why . . . why . . . My daddy is gone," she cried, and Cher gave Julian and Cortez a nod to leave them alone.

"Shhhhh, baby, it's okay, baby," Cher said, and she knew she didn't have any words of comfort for her best friend. She just held her and cried for what seemed like hours, and Kennedy finally lifted her head.

"My daddy, Cher, my daddy is gone. Just like that, he is gone," she said with a face full of tears.

"I know, but you're going to be okay. You are going to have to be strong, and we are going to get through this. Remember when Mom died?" Cher said, and Kennedy knew she meant her mother. Cher called her Mom too and called Kennedy's father Daddy Kenneth. "You thought that you'd die too, but it got easier every day, and you are going to have to find that same courage and use it one day at a time as you did back then, and I am going to be right here for you just like I was when Mom died. We have to be strong and support each other," she said, and Kennedy hugged Cher's neck tighter than she had ever hugged her before.

"We have to go home now and go to the funeral home tomorrow. Uncle Keith has started the arrangements, but we have to go, okay?" she said, and Kennedy nodded.

"Will you go home with me?" Kennedy asked Cher.

"Of course, darling, of course. I'm here, and we are going to get through this," she said, and she helped Kennedy from the chair because all of Kennedy's strength was gone.

She was weak and looked over at the empty bed and wanted to see her father one more time before she left. Julian and Cher went to the morgue with her, and when they pulled the sheet back, Cher and Kennedy both broke down, and Julian wished Cortez would have come down with them. Kennedy fell onto her father's body, and she planted several kisses on his cold face until Julian had to pull her back.

"Come on, Kay, you're getting too upset. Come on, let me get you girls home," he said, and Cher grabbed her hand.

"Okay, okay, okay," Kennedy said, touching her father's face one more time. "I love you, Daddy. I love you. I love you so much," she said, and Julian had to pull her away.

Cher and Julian held Kennedy up to take her out. That was the ultimate. Kennedy didn't even remember feeling that much pain when her momma died. She had forgotten the anguish of her momma's death. She thought it was because she didn't remember it being that horrible.

When they got to the waiting room, Cortez stood when he saw them. "I'm going to go to Kennedy's and stay with her tonight," Cher said, and Cortez gave her a nod of approval. They helped Kennedy to Julian's SUV, and Cher decided she'd drive Kennedy's Jag so it wasn't left in the hospital's parking lot. They helped Kennedy into bed at the house, and Cher and Julian went to the kitchen to make a pot of coffee. They sat and talked.

"Cher, what happened to your face?" he asked, and she hated that he noticed.

"What?" she asked, raking her hair over the bruise.

"The bruise you're trying to hide with your hair."

"Nothing. I was playing around with C.J., and he accidentally kicked me, but it's no biggie," she said.

"Cher."

"What?"

"Truth?" he asked.

"Come on, Julian, you know better. Cortez and I are fine. We are happy, and you know he is one of the good ones," she said.

"You don't have to be afraid to tell me the truth, Cher. You're my wife's best friend, and you're like a sister to us, so don't lie for him," he said seriously.

"Jay, come on now. We're good. My marriage is good. You know I'd leave his ass if he went there," she said, but Julian didn't seem convinced.

"I've noticed how Cortez is after a few beers or drinks lately. His behavior has been a little odd, so if something is going on, we got your back. You don't have to deal with no bullshit. You and C.J. are welcome to come here anytime," he offered.

"I know, and my marriage is good. We just have to worry about Kennedy right now. She's going to be a mess for a whole minute. She and her dad were super close, and to lose him so suddenly is going to be a motherfucker on her, Jay. When mom died, she had cancer, and we knew it was coming, but Daddy Kenneth was like, boom!" she said, and her eyes filled with water. "It's going to be harder," she said, crying.

"I know, Cher. Kennedy and I are going to need you more than ever. I don't know if I can help her by myself," Julian expressed.

"You know I'll be here. Kennedy is the closest person to me on this earth, and it hurts double time because Daddy Kenneth is gone and my best friend is hurt," she said, and she sobbed, and even though Julian wanted to be strong and not show emotion in front of Cher, he cried for his wife and father-in-law.

He went to bed, and Cher went and sat by the fireplace, just to think. "Lord, help us in this time. I know you know what's best for all of us, Lord, but please help Kennedy, Lord. You took Daddy Kenneth for your reasons, so help us, Father, to be strong and be okay. Lastly, Father, forgive me for lying about my marriage. Please fix it. I love my husband, so please make our situation better. Amen," Cher said and then went to the guest room. She got into bed and said another silent prayer for Kennedy before going to sleep.

Chapter Ten

Devon showed up at Deja's school, hoping to catch Alicia. He called her a few times, but she didn't answer or return his calls, and he wondered what he had done wrong. He stood out in the parking lot and waited for her to come out to her car. It was freezing cold, but he didn't care. He had to see her. He smiled when she walked out the doors, and he called out her name.

"Devon, what on earth are you doing here?" she asked with a pleasant smile.

"I came to talk to you. I mean, we went out a couple of times and had a great time, and things were going well, I thought, and then you stopped answering and returning my calls."

"I'm sorry, Devon, it's complicated and just bad timing. I have some other matters going on right now. I have a lot on my mind, and dating is not in the program right now," she said, looking him in the eyes.

"Wow, just like that, just, 'Dating isn't in the program right now?'" he asked, wanting more than that. He liked her, and he wanted to know if it was him. "Did I do something, Alicia? I mean, things were going great, so I don't understand. Be honest with me. What's really going on?" he asked. Up until two days ago, they talked a lot and stayed on the phone late even though they had early mornings, so he stood there waiting for an honest answer.

She hit the automatic-start button on her car, opened the door, and put her purse and bag on the front seat.

"Listen, I wasn't completely honest with you. I told you about moving here to be closer to my daughter, but I didn't tell you about my son and my ex," she said, and he looked confused. "My ex-husband has custody of him, and right before I met you, we talked about possibly working things out and getting back together," she confessed. "So I can't do this with you right now," she said.

"So you're thinking of returning with your ex-husband?"

"Yes, for my son's sake, and I can't go getting involved with anyone right now," she said, and Devon sighed and hung his head.

"Okay, then, I guess that means lose your number?" he asked.

"No, we can still be friends," she said.

He chuckled. "I have plenty of friends, Ms. Gray, and I am looking for more, and since the day we met, you're the only thing on my mind, but I'll stay away. Oh, and one more thing," he said. "Why didn't you tell me about your son?"

"I honestly didn't think we'd end up hitting it off so well, and since we have, I can't continue to see you when I know that this may not last."

"Okay," he said and didn't hold that against her. After all, they only went out a handful of times. He just had to let that one go. "You take care, Alicia," he said and turned and walked away because it was cold, and he had his answer. He went to his car and waited until she got in before he drove away.

He thought he was back to square one because there were no other prospects, and he really liked Alicia. He was grateful for her honesty but wished it had come before they hung out.

For the next couple of days, Devon tried his hardest not to think of her, but it was impossible. He was tempted to call her several times and take her up on her friendship offer, but he knew that wouldn't be enough for him, so he didn't break. A week later, he was shocked to see her number on the ID of his cell phone. He answered.

"Hey, Devon, how are you?" she inquired.

"Great," he said, wondering why she was calling. "How about you?"

"I've been okay, except for being unable to get you off my mind," she said.

He was pleased to hear those words but unsure if he should be excited. "Really?" he said, wanting more.

"Yes," she said, being honest. "I love my son and wanted him to be here, but I don't want his father back. I am just tired of battling him for custody. I want you," she added.

"Okay," he said, and she could hear the smile in his voice.

"Listen, I miss talking to you on the phone at night, and I also miss your voice in the mornings on my ride to work, and I'm sorry for not telling you about my ex and my son's situation in the very beginning. It has been a nasty custody battle, and it's an issue," she said, and she felt so good that he didn't hang up in her face.

"I miss that too, but I don't want to complicate your life, so you do what's best for you."

"I plan to, and that starts with you. I don't want my ex back, Devon. It was all about my son. Going back to him is not what I want. I want to get to know you. You are amazing, and I would like it if we could start over," she said, hoping he'd say yes.

"I'd like that," he said.

She let out a sigh of relief. "Great," she said.

"Do you have plans for tonight?" he asked. "I'd love to see you."

"You're in luck because I have absolutely nothing going on tonight." She smiled brightly.

"How about dinner?"

"Dinner would be great. I am starving," she said and gave him her address.

When he arrived, she hurried out because she was eager to see him.

"Where would you like to go?" he asked when they pulled out of her driveway.

"I don't know. I haven't gotten out much since I moved here, so I don't know what's good."

"I know a place." He smiled.

"So where are we going?" she asked because she didn't recognize the area they were in.

"To this Italian restaurant that I absolutely love called Spiaggia. Their food is amazing."

"Wow, I've never heard of it."

"You will love it, I promise you."

"Is that the place you take all your dates?" she asked, looking at him.

"Yep, I sure do, and they've all seemed to love it," he joked.

"Ha-ha, I guess I deserved that," she said.

"Yep, you did," he returned.

She smiled at him brightly. She liked Devon and everything about him. He seemed so sweet, and she liked his smile and style, so she had to ask. "I don't understand how you've been married twice already. I mean, you seem like a great guy, Devon. I might add that you're smart, funny, and fine as hell. I mean, what's the thing about you that drives women away? Because I already know what draws them in," she said.

"So I did draw you in?" he asked.

"Yes, to be honest, you did, so I want to know what you can do to run me off?" she asked.

"Okay, my first wife, Leila, Deja's mom, was like my heartbeat, my first love. We met back in college, and I worshipped the ground she walked on. We got married after we graduated, and I got on at AT&T and moved up the ladder quickly. Things were going great until I transformed into my own worst enemy. Leila gained some weight when her mom died, and she went through it and put on more and more weight. Then she got pregnant with Deja, and to put it mildly, I was an asshole to the tenth power to her. Put her down and made fun, and I became embarrassed of my own wife, the woman I truly loved. I don't know. She embarrassed me with her appearance, and I was ashamed to take her around my colleagues because, over the years, my wife was the only one who packed on the pounds. I met a woman at the office named Michelle. She was beautiful, and I cheated, moved out, and then played the in-and-out game with Leila because I truly loved her and didn't want her to leave, but I couldn't get past her appearance. Long story short, she told me to kiss her ass, she moved on, dropped the pounds, and when I tried to get her back, it was too late," he said, and she listened.

"Damn, I don't blame her for kicking your ass to the curb."

"Me either. I deserved it, and for a long time, I couldn't let it go. I met Christa through Leila and her husband, Rayshon, and I started dating Christa for selfish reasons. I still wanted Leila back, and I thought the Christa thing would make her jealous enough to come back, but I was wrong, and then I started to develop feelings for Christa. I decided to move on and let Leila go because she made it clear that she loved Rayshon and she'd never leave, so I gave Christa a reputable and genuine attempt, but she could tell that it was off and knew that there was something about Leila still holding us back, so she left me. I asked her to stay. Hell, I begged her to stay, but she chose to go," he said, and Alicia wanted to know if he was still caught in the Leila trap.

"So is there any part of you still longing for Leila?"

"No, not anymore, and for a long time, I never thought there would come a day that I could say that. Then a couple of years ago, I dated a woman I was falling for and found out a few months later she was married with two children. After that, I just sorta put my dating shoes on the shelf. I'd do a little casual dating and avoid anything serious, but now I'm ready to have someone in my life. I'm getting older, not a young cat anymore, and I don't know. I'm kinda tired of being lonely," he confessed.

"Wow, you've had some ordeals. My ex was just a plain old dog," she said, laughing. "I stayed with him through a lot of affairs, and when I look back on it, I was a dumbass, a big old fool," she said, laughing, and he laughed with her. "I just accepted it. I loved him, but not enough to endure what I endured back then. I'm just glad I woke up."

"So if it's not too personal, how did he get custody of your son?"

"It's not, and my son worships his dad, and he acted out and did all kinds of things because he wanted to go and be with him. At the time, he was doing poorly in school, and I felt that if he was so unhappy with me, I would let him go and live with his dad. Anthony was a terrible husband to me, but a good father, so I did what I thought was right then, and I wish I had done things differently.

"I miss my son more and more each day. I decided to take him back to court for custody, and it's been a nightmare, so when Anthony called me a couple of days ago talking about maybe giving it another shot, I thought about my son. I thought it would be best for me to be with him again, but seeing you in the parking lot, I realized I don't have to take two steps back. Anthony makes my stomach turn, and I can't see myself going back to that man, ever," she said, making faces.

Then they pulled into the restaurant. Devon parked and got out to get to her door.

They were seated, and Devon was right. She loved that place. The delicious food and the wine were lovely as the lovely ambiance.

They rode back to her place, and she asked Devon if he'd like to come in.

"If you'd like me to," he said, and she nodded. Once inside, Alicia offered him a seat, and she grabbed the remote and turned on some music. "Your place is nice," he complimented her.

"Thank you," she said and joined him on the sofa.

"So those are your kids?" He looked at the pictures on her coffee table.

"Yep, that is my daughter, Angel, and my son, Anthony. That was taken when he was here on the last break." She picked up the frame.

"You have beautiful kids," he said.

"Thank you," she said, putting the photo back, and they were quiet for a few moments.

"I'd better head out," Devon said.

"So soon?" She sounded disappointed.

"Yes. Listen, you are beautiful, Alicia, and I'm feeling you, and I want to kiss you, but I don't want to rush into anything."

"Ooookaaayyyy," she said, looking at him. "But you know you are allowed to kiss me, right?" she said and leaned into him. They kissed each other deeply and hungrily because it had been a while since she had sex, and she was on fire.

"We should stop," he suggested.

"Yeah, we should," she agreed, but then they went at it again. She was now on top of him, pressing her pelvis against his erection.

"No, seriously, Alicia, I got to go because this is torture," he said, and she understood. She wanted him but felt it was a little too soon.

"Okay," she said, standing. She walked him to the door and gave him the final kiss for the night. As soon as she shut the door, she ran to take a cold shower because she was hot.

Chapter Eleven

Christa was in the kitchen doing the unthinkable, cooking. She didn't know how to cook and never learned, but she decided to be a little more domesticated to show Isaiah she had it in her to do it all. She tried to follow a recipe, but everything was all wrong. Her pasta was mushy since she didn't drain the oil from the chicken pan. She had a mushy, greasy Alfredo disaster. In her efforts to repair the Alfredo, she forgot about the garlic bread in the oven. It was supposed to toast only five minutes, but it was a burnt mess fifteen minutes later. She took it out and wanted to cry.

Isaiah's kitchen was a smoky catastrophe, and she didn't have time to call for takeout to fake it. She opened the window and French doors to fan out the smoke from the burnt garlic bread, and Isaiah walked in.

"Baby, what are you doing?"

She knew he was shocked to see her in the kitchen in an apron and his kitchen in disarray. "I was trying to make you dinner," she said and poked her bottom lip out. "And it went all wrong," she cried, walking into his arms, and he held her.

"Christa, what possessed you to attempt to cook?"

"I wanted to surprise you, baby, and I ruined everything," she whined like she normally did.

"It's okay, it's fine, boo. I know you don't know how to cook, and I can live with that," he said, and she still had a sad face. "Baby, you are good at takeout. I mean, nobody orders takeout the way you do," he said, and she hit him with the oven mitt.

"That's not funny. I want to show you that I can also be a homemaker. I know Janiece used to cook all of your favorite meals, and I want to be able to top that. We are getting married, and I don't want your ex-wife to have nothing on me," she pouted.

"Christa, stop it, okay? I love you, baby, and I love you for different reasons than I loved Janiece. I've never compared you two, and I never will. I love you, for you. I know you can't cook. I know you've had a housekeeper forever, and, baby, I'm okay with you not being domesticated. I know what I'm getting into, boo, and if you want to learn to cook for us," he said, lifting her head, "I'll teach you, but don't ever think for a second that you have to compete with or top anybody."

"Baby, I love you so much. You are the epitome of sweetness. Thank you because this is a complete disaster," she said, looking at the mess she had made.

"Yes, it positively is, but we can handle this," he said and kissed her. "I'm going up to shower," he told her.

"Okay," she said.

A few moments later, she went in to join him. Not long after, her legs wrapped around his waist, and he bounced her up and down on his dick easily because Christa was light as a feather. Her breasts were nice but small, but her nipples hardened so well he could never move his mouth from sucking them.

"Baby, that's good," he whispered and returned to her erect nipple. He sucked even harder and exploded inside of her instead of pulling out.

"You are the best fiancé on the planet," she said, being herself. She was quirky, self-centered, and a pricey diva, but Isaiah loved her just as she was.

"Wow, that is an honor," he teased and gave her another kiss. "Let's finish up and clean up that mess in the kitchen. We can order some pizza," he suggested.

"Baby, you know I don't do greasy," she said because she still followed her model diet.

"Christa, baby, you don't model anymore. You can eat pizza. A slice or two won't put you on the big girl list. You are certainly not a cheeseburger away from being a big girl," he teased.

"You're right, baby. I still work out every day, so I guess I can this one time since I destroyed the kitchen," she said, and they got out of the shower.

They dried their skin, threw on loungewear, and returned to the kitchen. They looked around, and Isaiah cringed because she had stuff everywhere. They cleaned the mess she made before the pizza arrived. She said she'd go for it, but she picked all the toppings off and scraped off most of the cheese.

They were resting on the sofa, and then it hit her. "Oh, my God, did you pull out earlier?"

"No, baby, I didn't pull out."

"You know you're supposed to pull out when we don't use a condom," she said.

"I came so fast. I promise you I didn't do that on purpose," he said, and she wanted to punch him.

"Baby, that's no excuse. You know I'm not on anything. Really, Isaiah, damn, baby," she spat and got up. "I promise you, Isaiah, you better not get me pregnant," she snapped.

"Christa, calm down. This is the first time I've ever slipped, so just relax. We should be good," he said, and she looked at him.

"No, it's not. You remember you slipped a couple of months ago when we were at Rona's party in the bathroom?"

"I didn't slip that time. You told me to go ahead because I didn't have anywhere to release it," he reminded her because when he said it was there, they both looked around, and the only thing that was there they could use was tissue, and they didn't want to get semen in the bathroom, so Christa had said, "Just this one time," and he did. She got her cycle, and she knew they got lucky. "Relax, baby, we should be good," he said and kissed her shoulder.

"We'd better be, or that's your ass," she threatened and stomped off.

"Don't worry, baby, we're good," he said.

Christa calmed down a little. The last thing she needed was to get pregnant. Honestly, she didn't want to be pregnant.

The next couple of weeks passed with wedding talk, and she was on the countdown. It was four months away, and she couldn't wait to become Mrs. Lawton. Leila was doing an awesome job despite the work she was putting into starting her party-planning company. She had finally found a location, and she was still on schedule with Christa's wedding planning. Christa was afraid that her wedding would go on the back burner, but Leila had it all under control.

"Then you add the veggies," Isaiah said, giving Christa her third cooking lesson. They decided she'd be in the kitchen while he prepared meals, instead of being off somewhere in the house doing something else, because she wanted to learn.

"Wow, that looks so good, baby, but it smells funny," she said and kept making faces. "It's suddenly making me a little nauseated," she said, stepping away from the stove. She fanned the air and wondered why her jaws were swelling, and she dashed to the hall bathroom but didn't make it. Vomit spurted out of her mouth, and Isaiah rushed to see if she was all right.

"Baby, are you okay?" he asked, and Christa stood still because she didn't know if more was coming. She tried to hold it, but the smell made more come, so she went to the bathroom.

When she finally came out of the bathroom, Isaiah already had a bucket of water that smelled of Pine-Sol. He had on rubber gloves to clean up her mess.

"Are you okay?" he asked.

"I don't know. It's like I was fine one minute, and then the next, I was nauseated."

"What did you eat today?" he asked as he continued to clean up the mess. She took a seat on the steps.

"This morning, an English muffin with two egg whites, and a blackened salmon salad for lunch, and I had carrots for my snack. The usual," she said, and it hit her. She had been so busy with wedding plans and her agency and trying to become domesticated that she didn't have her period. "Oh, my God, Isaiah, I am going to kill you!" she yelled and ran up the steps. He ran up behind her. She grabbed her iPad and hit the calendar and began to count. She was nine days late.

"Baby, what is it?"

"I'm late, Isaiah. I'm fucking late," she said in a panic. She started to pace.

"How late?"

"Nine fucking days, Isaiah!" she yelled. "I told you that time in the shower, boy, if I'm pregnant, I am going to kill you. You got that?" she yelled and raced down the steps, and he ran down after her.

"Where are you going?"

"To Walgreens. I need a test," she said, looking for her car keys.

"Christa, relax. I'll go. Just calm down."

"I can't calm down, Isaiah," she said with tears. "I can't be pregnant. I can't be," she cried.

"Christa, relax. You don't know for sure, and why are you so upset?" he said, grabbing her arms. "If you are, it won't be so bad," he said.

"Isaiah, are you crazy? I'm not ready to have a baby. I am not ready to mother a child. I can barely scramble a fucking egg. How am I going to care for a child?"

"Hey, hey, hey," he said, pulling her close because she was sobbing. "Shhh, baby, it's okay. You are not in this by yourself. I am here, and you are not going to be a single mother," he said, trying to calm her.

"That's the thing, Isaiah, single or married, I . . . I don't want to be a mother," she confessed, and Isaiah stepped away.

"What does that mean, Christa? We talked about having kids," he reminded her.

"I know, but we talked about it. We never said when, and I don't want it to be now," she said.

"So what if you are? Then what?" He was shaking.

"If I am, I don't know," she said with her head down.

"You don't know!" Isaiah yelled. "You're kidding me, right?" he said, and she couldn't look at him. She knew he was angry when he stepped back and his face scowled.

"I'm going to go to Walgreens. Finish cleaning up the mess," he said and walked away.

Christa went down after she heard the door shut and went to the kitchen. She was glad he took the wok off the burner because the stir-fry would have burned. She went to finish the cleanup and waited for him to return from the store.

He went to the store to get the test, praying that Christa didn't mean what she said, and he hoped if she did feel that way, the test was negative. He'd rather deal with her not being pregnant than being pregnant and not keeping it. His head was in a whirlwind, thinking of what would happen if she was and she didn't want to keep it. Sadly, if that were the case, he'd call off their wedding.

Chapter Twelve

Kennedy couldn't get back into the swing of things. She cried every other minute and didn't know when the pain would disappear. They had buried her father two weeks before, and it felt like yesterday every moment, and she still couldn't believe he was gone. Her daddy meant so much to her. There were no words to describe the pain she was going through, and she was damn sure tired of people telling her it would be okay because it would never be okay.

"Baby, are you sleeping?" Julian asked her in a low voice, trying not to wake her if she was.

"No." She sniffled. She hadn't gotten out of bed for a couple of days, and she was sure that Julian thought it was time for her to get up, shower, and eat something.

"I came to see if you wanted to eat. Cher took the kids home with her, and the house is quiet. I thought you might want to come and have some lunch and get out of this dark room," he said, picking up the remote to open the black-out drapes.

"I'm not hungry, Julian," she said, and he came to her side of the bed and touched her face.

"Baby, I know you are in a bad place right now, and I'm not trying to make you do anything, but you are my wife, and I have to take care of you. That means I can't let you starve, and I can't allow you to dive into a depression. I know it hurts, baby, believe me, I do, but you are going to have to get out of this bed and get back to life," he said, wiping her tears.

She knew her husband was right, but she didn't want to move. "I can't," she sobbed.

Julian got up and reached for her hands. "Come on, baby, yes, you can. Come on and sit up." He began lifting her up. She sat on the side of the bed, and he sat beside her. "Listen, it is a bitter pill to swallow, Kay, but you are going to have to be strong. The kids ask about you every morning, and they are too young to understand why you cry so many tears," he said. He grabbed her hand, squeezed it tight, and kissed her gently to comfort her. "I want to help you get back to normal, baby, but you have to try," he said.

"Normal? Julian, there is no normal. The normal for me was getting up, getting dressed and heading out to work, and calling my dad to make sure he ate a healthy breakfast. Going over his plans for the day and calling him in the evening to let the kids say good night to their papa. Normal was going to my daddy's house to make sure he has clean clothes, and the housekeeper is doing her job and not getting over on him. Normal was saying, 'Daddy, when are you going to remarry? You have a lot of life left,'" she cried.

"Baby, I hear you, and I am not going to say that that wasn't the norm, but Dad died, Kennedy. It is life changing for us all. I know that you and your dad were close, but I loved him too, baby, and we are all hurt by the loss. But we are still here, and we must get back to as normal as possible. So today will be your first step to healing, okay? I'm going to run you a bath, and you are going to put on some clean clothes and come eat a little bit for me. After you do that, I will leave you alone, but I want you to get out of this bed for a few hours," he said, and Kennedy nodded in agreement.

They went into the primary bathroom, and Kennedy looked at her swollen eyes and mangled hair. She grabbed her toothbrush first, and Julian started the water. After she brushed her teeth, she brushed her hair up and put it into a ponytail. Then she took a hot face towel and put it on her face several times. When she turned to Julian, he smiled at her, and she smiled back. He moved over to her, pulled her nightgown over her head, pushed down the panties she had been wearing for a couple of days, and helped her into the tub. He added some bubble bath, and Kennedy just sat and watched the tub fill without words.

After the water was high enough, Julian shut off the water and went down on his knees by the tub. He grabbed her sponge and began to bathe her. "John Boomer called again," he told her, referring to her father's attorney. "He has rescheduled the reading of your father's will twice and needs you to come in."

"Why does he keep calling? I told him I'd call him when I'm ready," she said and relaxed back in the tub.

"Well, this is kind of time sensitive, babe. It is usually done a couple of days after the funeral, and it's been two weeks."

"I know, but it's like, who celebrates an inheritance from the person they lost and loved?"

"It's not a celebration, honey, and trust that a man down on his luck would be celebrating if he inherited something. Honestly, if we weren't doing well, we would probably be a little more eager," he said. "It's not about what you're getting, babe. It's about getting it done."

"I guess you're right," she agreed, and a little while afterward, she was out of the tub and putting lotion on her skin. She had to admit it felt better moving around than lying in that bed.

When she went to the kitchen, she saw that Julian had prepared lunch for her. She sat at the table, and he served her lunch, which smelled great. She hadn't eaten in over three days, so she took small bites. She didn't clean her plate like she normally would because she loved Julian's cooking, but she was satisfied with the portion she did eat. He cleared the table and tried to devise something to keep her from returning to bed.

"Listen, it's freezing outside, so let's go into the living room, and I'll start a fire and get you a glass of merlot and read to you. We stopped reading to each other after the kids were born. I suggest you grab your Kindle, and we go through the million and one titles you have, and I'll read something to you," he said, and she was cool with that.

She went for her Kindle, and he turned on the gas fireplace. He returned with her glass of wine and a Crown and Coke for himself. They got comfortable on the sectional as he read some titles to her.

"Just do a Brenda Jackson search, babe. Let's see what she has new," Kennedy suggested and took a sip of her wine.

"Okay," he agreed. He rattled off a few titles and then said, "How about *Breaking Bailey's Rules?*" He read the synopsis.

"Okay, let's try that one," she said.

He scrolled through to chapter one, skipping over the acknowledgment pages. He began to read to his wife, and about fifteen minutes into it, their home phone rang, and Julian paused to answer it.

"Hello," he said, put his hand over the mouthpiece, whispered, "It's John Boomer," and then paused for a few seconds. "Yes, she is right here," he said and handed her the phone.

"Hello," she said.

"Kennedy, hi. How are you?"

"I'm okay, considering," she replied.

"I know, and I'm so sorry for your loss," he said.

"Thank you, John. I guess this call is about the will?"

"Yes, it is. I need to reschedule this because other parties have a portion coming to them, and I would like to make sure everyone is taken care of as soon as possible."

"Well, my loved ones are not rushing me to have this will read. You sent a notice out to Cher, Kory, and Keith. Keith and Kory are willing to come back to Chicago when I am ready," she said.

"Well, Kennedy, I'm afraid you four are not the only ones who have gotten notice. Your father had another person in his will," he said, and Kennedy was confused.

"Like who? My mother died when I was fifteen," she said, puzzled.

"Unfortunately, Kennedy, I'm not at liberty to disclose that information over the phone, so how about we schedule another date for you, and you notify Keith and Kory? Then we can go from there. How is next Wednesday? I have an opening at ten a.m.," he said.

Kennedy took it without hesitation. She wondered who in the hell could be in her daddy's will she didn't know. As soon as she got off the phone, she dialed her uncle Kendell first, and he vowed he had no clue. Then she called Kory's dad, and he was just as clueless. Now Kennedy's mind was no longer on her loss but on who her daddy left behind whom she knew nothing about.

Chapter Thirteen

"That's perfect," Leila said after Rayshon straightened the picture on the wall in her new shop. She had quickly found a space to start her party-planning business, and Rayshon took a couple of days off to help her get set up.

"It looks good, babe. I must say this is a perfect spot."

"I don't know how I'm still standing, baby. I mean, with Kennedy losing her dad and Christa constantly calling about this, that, or the other, and I'm still planning Deja's party, the kids, the house, and you."

"Don't say me because it's been days since you took care of me. I think the last time I got some was when I advised you to open this place, and I feel like you owe me," he joked.

"Awww, baby, you're right, and momma will take care of you soon, but now I've got some calls to make, and then I'm going to go by Kennedy's to check on her, and then I'll get home in time to get dinner started," she said. She gave him a quick peck before he snatched her back into his arms.

"You can do better than that, Mrs. Johnson."

She smiled. She put her arms around his neck and gave her husband a more passionate kiss, and then Devon walked in.

"Ummm, excuse me. Is this Parties by Leila or Kisses by Leila?" he joked.

"Shut up," Leila said and greeted him with a hug and a quick kiss on the cheek like always. That thing with

Devon and Leila was old news, and there was no longer any conflict of interest.

"What's up, Ray?" he said as they dapped.

"Nothing, man, just trying to get some QT. This woman right here has been on the move, neglecting her man," he said.

Devon laughed. "Yep, sounds like when she opened the bookstore. If I wasn't a book, she wasn't interested," he joked.

"Hey, I'm right here. Y'all don't have to talk about me like I'm not in the room," she said, bringing up her computer.

"Well, this show needs to get on the road because Rayshon ain't gon' hear too many more lata's. You feel me, Lei?" he said.

"Look, Rayshon, go to work, and, Devon, what do you want? Did you come to help or slow me down?" she asked.

"I came to ask your opinion on something," Devon said.

"On that note, I gotta go," Ray said. He walked over to Leila and gave her a quick kiss. "Y'all talk about whatever. I got a client in an hour," he said, and they both said bye. He headed out the back and yelled to Leila, "Don't forget to lock this back door."

"I won't," she yelled and turned her attention back to Devon. "Okay, spill. I don't have a lot of time. I got phone calls to make," she said while looking confused at the computer.

"What's wrong?" Devon asked.

"It's this new program that I'm still trying to figure out," she complained.

Devon circled the counter to peer at the screen. "Let me take a look," he said. He clicked a few buttons and explained some things. Devon was very computer savvy, and after fifteen minutes of giving Leila a crash course on her new system, he got back to why he came. "So I came here to talk about Ms. Gray," he said.

"Deja's English teacher."

"Yes. We went out a few times, and I don't know, I am honestly starting to like her," he said.

"That's great, Devon," she said, pretending she didn't know he was seeing Ms. Gray. Kennedy had called and told her that Devon was out with Alicia the night they had gone to Jay's. She just hadn't known he had gone out with her again after that night.

"Yes, it is, but I'm worried about Deja," he said.

"About D.J., why?"

"Well, it's Deja's English teacher, and I don't want her to have issues with that."

"Well, Devon, school will be out soon, and Alicia will no longer be Deja's teacher, and I'm sure Deja couldn't care less," Leila said and smiled because she was navigating through her computer system with ease. If Alicia and Devon hit it off, then Alicia might be the one. Devon wouldn't be alone anymore.

"Wow, I hadn't thought of that. All I was thinking was how I would tell her that I like her teacher. I mean, when I say I like her, I really am feeling her," he said, and Leila saw his eyes dance.

"Mr. Vanpelt, are you in love already?"

"What? No, why would you ask me something like that? It's only been a handful of dates."

"Because I can see that look in your eyes, and I know that look all too well," she said because that was the look he had given her a long time ago.

"Listen, calm down, okay? I do like her a lot—okay, more than a lot—but I'm taking it slow, you know. Nothing serious until I'm sure," he said, and Leila knew what that meant.

"Oh, so you haven't hit it yet?"

"Leila, you gon' come out your mouth and ask me something like that?"

"Oh, I'm sorry. Is that too personal? Says the guy who hit it the night of our first date."

"Hey, that was back in college. I'm a grown-ass man, so I do grown-ass man things now. I have more control of my organs now, not like back in college," he said.

Leila laughed. "Well, I hope she is the one worth taking it slow with, and if you are in love, that is cool. It's nice to see you smiling about a woman. You deserve someone great in your life," Leila said, happy for him.

"It's still early, so don't be trying to plan my wedding, Mrs. Johnson. Not yet," he said and smiled.

"If this does go that well, I would be honored to do it for you," she said.

"Oh, no, my ex-wife planning another wedding for me will not happen. The last two weddings you planned ended in divorce," he teased.

"The last two?" she asked, confused.

"Ours and then my and Christa's wedding," he said, reminding her of their own wedding.

"Oh, shit, I forgot about our wedding," she said, cracking up.

"Yes, you are not allowed to plan another wedding for me. You will not put the spirit of Leila on it," he joked and then looked at his watch.

"Okay, you're going to regret that statement. I hope to be the hottest, most successful party planner Chicago has ever seen."

"I'm sure you will be, babe, but I gotta head back to the office. I'll see you this weekend when I pick up D.J.," he said, heading toward the door.

"Um, will you tell her about Alicia this weekend, Devon?"

"I don't know, maybe," he said and left.

Leila dove right into work and closed up to go by Kennedy's. She was happy to see her up and doing better than the last time she visited. They shared a glass of wine and talked, and Kennedy told her about the reading of the will coming up for her in a couple of days. She was still baffled about who the mystery heir was. Leila's guesses were as good as Kennedy's. No matter who they thought it was, Kennedy would still not know until Wednesday morning.

When Leila got in, she sent Tabitha home and started preparing dinner. Shortly after, Deja walked in, and Leila looked at the clock. It was seven thirty, and dance practice ended at six, so she wondered why Deja was late.

"Who dropped you off?" Leila asked.

"Destiny's mom," she said and put her bag down on the floor.

"Why are you late?"

"Because after Destiny's mom picked us up, she stopped by Jewel's to get a few things, and a few things looked like groceries to me, but since it's cold, I couldn't complain," Deja said, opening the fridge.

"So if I call Sheila, she will tell me the same thing you told me?"

"Yes, Mom, yes," she said, opening a soda and grabbing some chips from the pantry. She was about to head upstairs, but Leila called her back. "Yes," she said, coming back into the kitchen.

"How is English going?"

"Good," she said and opened her chips.

"So what do you think of Ms. Gray?"

"What do you mean?"

"I mean, do you like her?"

"Yeah, she's pretty cool. She dresses better than all of my other teachers and likes hip-hop. She's cool and teaches dance in the evenings at some dance studio. She is the only teacher interested in dance. I think she like majored in it or something like it was her second major when she was in college."

Leila was relieved that Deja liked her and had at least one thing in common with her. "Oh, okay. That's great." Leila continued to move around the kitchen.

"Why do you ask? Did she call you again? My grades are where they need to be, and I've even turned in extra-credit work. Mom, I'm doing better. I promise," Deja said in a panic.

"No, D.J. Calm down. I just wanted to know what you thought of her, that's all," she said, and Deja let out a deep breath.

"Okay, can I go now? I have to finish my paper for tomorrow."

"Sure. Look in on your brothers and tell Rave she better be cleaning that room. Her room is the worst in this house," Leila yelled after Deja.

"Yes, ma'am," she yelled back.

Leila was almost done with dinner when her husband walked in. "Hey, baby," she said, walking over to him and leaning in for a kiss. But he didn't want to stop. "Ummm, excuse me," she said, looking at him as he pulled his sweatshirt over his head.

"Not now, baby. Let me shower first. Today I went hard, and my deodorant didn't," he said.

"At least a quick kiss. I've smelled your funky pits before," she said, and he gave her a quick kiss before dashing away. "Hurry back. I gotta tell you about Devon and his potential new love," she yelled, and Rayshon kept moving without replying.

Chapter Fourteen

Cher was in the kitchen, cooking and talking to Kennedy on the phone. She and Kennedy had been talking about the mystery person since John announced it to her, and they were both anxious for Wednesday to come. They had two more days, and the anticipation was driving them crazy. Cortez walked in, and Cher looked up at him. She could tell he had been drinking, so she told Kennedy she'd call her back after she had dinner.

She poured the seasoned chicken into the frying pan to sauté it, and Cortez headed for their room. She sighed, glad he didn't say anything to her. He had been in a foul mood lately because she had been spending a lot of time at Kennedy's and no time at work, and he had her clients to take on top of his.

She finished cooking and called C.J. down to eat. Cortez walked into the kitchen after she had given her child his plate. "You want something to eat?" she asked Cortez.

"What do you think?"

"Well, I don't know. You've been out drinking. You could've eaten elsewhere," she said and put her plate on the table.

"Well, I didn't, so fix me a fucking plate," he shot.

She hurried to get it done. She didn't want him to do anything in front of her son. "Okay, Cortez, sit down, baby, and don't do this in front of C.J., okay? I will fix you a plate," she said, hoping that night wouldn't be another night of him losing it on her. She would stay with Kennedy a lot longer than Kennedy needed just to stay away from home. She couldn't stand to be around him.

"Fix yourself a plate. I'll take this one," Cortez said and took her plate.

Nervously, her 6-year-old just looked down at his food and tried to eat fast. He never saw Cortez hit his mom, but Cher knew that he had heard it before.

"Take your time, boy. That plate ain't going nowhere!" he yelled at C.J., causing his little eyes to well, and he slowed down.

"Cortez, don't, okay? If you're angry about something, baby, take it out on me, okay, not C.J.," she requested and then took a seat. He just looked at her, and his jaws flared.

"Momma, can I be excused?" C.J. asked.

"No!" Cortez roared. Cher quickly jumped up, snatched C.J.'s chair from underneath the table, and told him to hurry to his room. He ran up the stairs as fast as his little legs could take him.

"Look, Cortez, you are drunk and in one of your moods. Now I can take the bullshit you serve up, but please don't you dare fuck with my son!" she spat with fire in her eyes.

Full of anger and rage, Cortez jumped up and launched at her. "You want me to serve up my frustrations, Cherae, huh?" he yelled, grabbing her face. "You want me to serve you up some bullshit, huh?" he yelled and pushed her face. She fell back into C.J.'s chair. "Well, here ya go," he said, taking C.J.'s uneaten food and dumping it all over her head. She began to sob, and he didn't care. He reached for her plate since it was closest to him.

"No, no, no, no, Cortez, please don't," she cried, holding up her hands, and he dumped it over her head.

"You have just been served up some bullshit!" he said and slammed the plate onto the table so hard it broke.

Cher began to wipe her face and brush the rice, chicken, and vegetables from her head. Cortez had turned into a monster, and she knew she had to either leave him or kill him.

She stepped out of her clothes in the kitchen because she wanted less of a trail of food to clean up. She went to the bathroom on the main floor and started the shower. She got in, sobbing the whole time, and wondered why he had become so cruel. In the beginning, he loved her and forgave her for some evil things she had done. Now he was her enemy. He never wanted to see her happy and would find a way to ruin a happy moment if he could.

After she showered and shampooed her hair, she wrapped a towel around her body and ran downstairs to get something to put on from her clean-clothes hamper. After putting on some sweats and a tee, and quickly checking on her son, she went back down and cleaned up every drop of food from her husband's ignorant-ass actions. She took her baby a turkey sandwich and a drink box into his room because she knew he had to be hungry. He was in his homemade tent when she walked in.

"You got room for one more?" she asked, kneeling.

"Yes, but only for one," he said and sat up.

"Momma made you a sandwich," she said, handing it to him, and then she crawled in.

"Thank you, Momma," he said and took his drink. "You can have half," he offered, but she wanted him to eat.

"No, thanks, kiddo, that is all for you," she said.

"Momma, why does Daddy treat you so mean?"

"Wow, baby, Momma doesn't know the reason for sure, but your daddy doesn't mean to."

"Does he say sorry since he doesn't mean to?"

"Yes, he does," she said.

"That's why you keep forgiving him?" he asked, staring at his sandwich.

"I guess so, C.J.," she said and smiled.

"I know God says we have to forgive people when they say I'm sorry, but what does God want us to do when they don't stop doing bad stuff to us?"

"I don't know, baby. Momma asks God that every day, and when He answers me, I'll know what to do," she said. "Now eat your sandwich, baby," she told him, and he took a bite and then extended his hand to give her a bite. He shared his entire sandwich and drink box with Cher, and she lay in his tent with him until they fell asleep. The next morning when she went into her room to get ready for work, Cortez was passed out in the bed, and she didn't bother to wake him.

She didn't bother to alert him that she and C.J. were leaving. She went into the office and told their receptionist to give her both of their schedules for showing houses, and she went to work. She closed five deals that day and was delighted that three of them were deals that Cortez hadn't gotten anywhere with. Cher's mind went into gear, and she decided she would buy him out, put him out, and get the hell on with her life.

Chapter Fifteen

"Paxton Financial, this is Robin," she sang into the phone.

"Hi, Robin, this is Janiece. Is Kerry available?"

"No, ma'am, I'm sorry. He just began a meeting with a client."

Janiece decided she'd leave the message with her. "Okay, tell him that Kimberly called, and said she will be giving K.J.'s party this year, so we don't need to make plans."

"Okay, I will let him know, Mrs. Paxton."

"Please call me Janiece," she said.

"Okay, then, Janiece. I will let him know, and I look forward to meeting you," she said.

"Likewise," Janiece replied and then hung up. She immediately called Janelle.

"Hey, sissy, what's up?"

"Robin, K.P.'s new assistant, that's what's up. I've tried to stay away and give Kerry the benefit, but I'm going to have to dress and pop in," Janiece said, wanting to see this new office assistant of his.

"Jai, we've talked about this. K.P. knows better, and if he says she is harmless, she is harmless."

"I know what he said, Nellie, but for the last two weeks, he is never available when I call, and his cell phone is like always powered off now all the time, because my calls go straight to voicemail," she expressed. "I never had a problem getting a hold of K.P. during the day when Rose was there. Now he is always in a freaking meeting or on a call," she whined.

"Janiece, come on, if this chick is answering the phone, that means she's at her desk, not on your husband's lap, so relax," she said.

"I guess you're right, Janelle, but I still want to see her. K.P. was like, 'She aw'right. She's attractive, but I'm not checking her like that, baby. You're the only one for me,'" she said, imitating K.P.

"Janiece, I know you're not jealous."

"No. Well, yes . . . no . . . hell, Nellie. I need to do something. I'm in this house twenty-four seven with this spoiled-ass baby who won't let me put her little fat ass down. Girl, all she wants is to nurse, and I know I'm gaining weight because all my clothes are maternity or have elastic in them. Since Phyllis is here to do mostly everything, I feel like I'm turning into a boring old house-wife, and some hot assistant is teasing my husband," she vented.

Janelle was quiet at first.

"Are you there?"

"Yes, and K.P. adores you. He knows you just had a baby. Jaiden won't start school for another year, so you have to stay home to take care of your babies. You're not a boring housewife. You are a stay-at-home mom, and you have a gym in your house, so put down the ice cream when the girls are napping and hit that treadmill. Jordan will stay spoiled if you don't start letting her cry it out. Stop picking her ass up. Lastly, you have Phyllis there, a live-in. Get out of the house for a couple of hours to get some air. Find something to do. Hell, your husband is loaded. I'm sure you can find something to do for a couple of hours of the day with yourself.

"Don't fall into that slump, Janiece, where you're sitting at home pulling out your hair because you think your husband is sleeping with his secretary. K.P. loves you, always has, and that ain't gonna change," she said, making Janiece feel a little better.

"Yeah, you're right. I have no excuse not to work out, and I have Jordan spoiled as hell."

"Exactly," Janelle said.

"So I shouldn't worry about K.P.?"

"No, but if you wanna visit the new assistant and show your face, that couldn't hurt. You know, I'm just saying. She ain't no competition, and we want to make sure she never is."

"You damn right," Janiece agreed.

"No, seriously though, K.P. isn't on no craziness, and, trust, those thoughts of thinking your man is cheating, and he isn't, is just as damaging to your marriage. I know that firsthand," she said, reminding Janiece of what broke up her marriage.

"Yes, I know. I shouldn't be insecure, but I was K.P.'s mistress for five long years, so you know he is capable," she returned.

"Come on, Janiece, are you kidding me? This is the same man who gave up everything for you and allowed you to return to your other husband for ninety days, so give my brother-in-law some credit," she spat.

"Again, you never cease to amaze me. I remember a time there was not one good thing you could say about that man, but now he is like some kinda hero."

"He is because he saved my baby sister, and he loves you, so cut this bullshit out, stop worrying about this Robin chick, and trust yo' man," she suggested.

Janiece finally agreed but decided to pay Robin a visit. After she got off the phone, she ran up to her room and went through her clothes to see what she could still fit into. She found something decent, but the treadmill was unquestionably a part of her near future. She called her hair stylist to see if she could get in, but she was booked. However, the owner, LaGenia, had a spot open, and she was the best, so Janiece agreed to see her. She showered, dressed, and told Phyllis she'd be gone for a while.

At LaGenia's, her hair was shampooed, blow-dried, and styled because she was in a hurry. LaGenia insisted she let her shape her brows and touch up her makeup. LaGenia's was so upscale. They got you in and out fast, so after she agreed to a manicure, two people worked on each hand to get her out the door.

She got in her husband's Hummer and headed to his office. When she walked in, no one was at the receptionist's desk, so she proceeded to her husband's office, looking gorgeous, undeniably like Mrs. Paxton should look.

"May I help you?" a voice came from behind as Janiece was headed toward Kerry's office. She turned around to see who the voice belonged to, and her mouth almost dropped to the wood floors at the sight of Robin. She was more than "aw'ight." She was drop-dead gorgeous. Like classy gorgeous, not trashy-slut gorgeous. Her hair extensions or wig was slayed, not tacky, and hung to her bust line.

She had on individual lashes that didn't look like bat wings but were natural and pretty, and her makeup looked as if she had just applied it. Her size six, maybe eight if that, was an hourglass no doubt, and the hour was ten 'til hips, twenty 'til plump ass, and thirty 'til perky C-cup tits under her black pencil skirt, gray turtleneck, and four-inch black leather boots. When she got up close enough, Janiece got a lung full of her Skyler Vanilla Sky perfume.

"I'm sorry, you must be Robin," Janiece said, politely trying not to stare.

"I am," she said. The confused look on her face would never have guessed she was Janiece, so she wasn't surprised when she asked, "And you are?"

"I'm Janiece," she said, and the look on Robin's face was shocked at first, but she quickly smiled and extended her hand for a handshake.

"Oh, Janiece, how nice to meet you," she said, gently shaking Janiece's hand.

"You too. K.P. has told me so much about you," she said, but she was thinking, *he told me nothing about you, sexy lady*.

"Yes, Kerry has said a lot about you, as well," she said, and Janiece wondered whether she always called him Kerry, because Rose always called him Mr. Paxton, even in conversation.

"Did he?"

"Yes, and I'm so sorry I didn't recognize you. You look so different in the photos on Mr. Paxton's desk."

"Well, I think he has pictures from before the girls, so they may have to be updated," she said, and then his door opened, and he stepped out with another man in tow.

"Hey, baby, I didn't know you were coming down today," he said and greeted her with a quick kiss. "Marvin, this is my beautiful wife, Janiece," he introduced her to his client.

Janiece noticed the disdain on Robin's face as she flung her hair over her other shoulder. Was it because of her pop-up visit, or did something else provoke it? Although Robin thought she paid zero attention, Janiece caught that look she gave her as she checked out her body. Janiece saw right through Robin's fake-ass smiles.

After the introductions, Marvin left, and Janiece and Kerry went into his office and shut the door. "So, baby, what brings you by?"

"Ummmm, I just came by to visit. I wanted to get out of the house and get a break from the girls," she said, taking a seat.

"Okay. I've been in meetings all day, and I am tired and ready to eat," he said and loosened his tie. He sat on the other side of his desk and began to put away some papers.

"So why did you describe your new help as 'aw'ight,'" she said, using air quotes.

"What do you mean?" he asked and didn't look up from his files.

"When I asked you how she looked, you said 'aw'ight,' like she wasn't all that," she said, lowering her voice because she didn't want Robin to hear her.

"Well, she is."

"K.P., that woman is gorgeous. She could be a damn model if she wanted to," she whispered in a high-pitched voice, and K.P. looked at her.

"Come on, baby. I know you're not jealous. You know me better than that."

"K.P., I would be lying if I said I wasn't insecure."

"Baby, Rose was pretty, and you didn't act like this."

"No, Rose was attractive, not like the glamorous teen Barbie out there," she said, pointing with her thumb. "K.P., you look me in my eyes and tell me you didn't notice her enormous ass," she said, leaning in over his desk.

"Janiece, baby, stop. I'm not checking out her ass or any other body parts. I am a married man who is madly, truly, and deeply in love with my wife." He stood and came around his desk to get close to her. "So stop this foolishness, and give me a kiss."

Janiece smiled and kissed her husband.

"Now sit tight, let me put these files away, and we can have a nice, quiet dinner, just us two, and then I will take you home and show you how much I noticed your sexy ass," he joked.

Janiece took a seat, smiling, shaking her head. She trusted K.P., so she decided to let the idea of him cheating on her with Robin go.

Chapter Sixteen

"Are you enjoying your meal?" Devon asked Alicia.

"Yes, I am." She smiled. "You are an amazing cook."

Devon laughed because he'd heard that several times before. They were hooked as soon as he cooked for them, no matter who he dated.

"What's funny?" she asked.

"You're about the tenth woman who has said the exact same words from that same chair," he said honestly.

"Oh, this chair right here," she asked, pointing to her seat.

"Yes, that chair," he said.

She got up and moved to the other side of the table, taking her plate and glass of wine.

"Why did you move?"

"It's obvious that that chair is bad luck since none of them are still around," she joked.

He laughed again. "You got a point."

"Of course I do, and I will never sit in that chair again," she said and sipped her wine.

"So you plan to be around for a while?" he asked.

"Only if you want me to be." She smiled.

"That sounds like a good idea, Ms. Gray," he said and leaned in to kiss her.

She tried to get more kisses, but he encouraged her to finish her food. After they were done and cleared the table, Devon looked at his life and wanted to break the routine. Maybe if he did something different, his relationships would go different, so instead of him taking her to the couch, the spot he and his dates usually went to before the bedroom, he asked her if she'd like to dance.

"Right now?" she asked because she wanted to relax on the sofa. It was a Tuesday night, and she had school the next morning.

"Yes, Miss Dance Instructor," he said, going for the stereo. He scanned through his old CDs and came across Marvin Sease's "Lady," a steppers song, and he popped it in.

"Oh, so you want me to show you a few of my moves," she said and began to rock her hips.

"Yes, show me what you got, baby," he said.

She began to sway to the music. He couldn't resist moving closer and dancing next to her body. The song seemed like the extended remixed version because their dance wouldn't end. When the song was finally over, they stayed close, and she wrapped her arms around his neck.

"You are a great dancer, Mr. Vanpelt," she complimented him.

"So are you, Ms. Gray," he said and planted a kiss on her lips. Devon didn't want to rush her into bed, but his dick said otherwise. Their kiss got deeper, and he pulled away. "I think I should take you home," he said.

Her eyes widened. "Why, Devon?" she asked with a confused look on her face. "I wanna stay with you."

"Because it's late, and we both have early days tomorrow."

She looked at him for a moment, and then she just said, "Okay."

He went to the coat closet, got her coat, and helped her put it on. He put on his coat and grabbed his keys, and they left.

"Is there a problem?" she asked.

"No, why?"

"Because it's like when things get hot and heavy, you back down," she expressed. "I mean, what's wrong? I thought you cared about me," she said.

"I do, Alicia. That's why I'm backing up a bit. I want things to remain exciting and new and not rush. I just don't want to dive in feetfirst and then we don't work out."

"Okay, I can understand that, but we are not moving fast. We've gone out over a dozen times in the last month, and I talk to you on the phone more than my best girlfriend back home. I don't want to force anything, but I'm ready, Devon," she said, and he swerved.

His dick woke up again and told him to quit being a pussy and make it happen. "So you not gon' get my goods and start acting funny," he joked.

She swatted his arm. "No," she said, laughing.

"Okay, then I'm ready too," he said and stopped at a red light. He looked over at her, and she smiled brightly. "You are so beautiful, Alicia," he complimented her.

"And so are you, Devon," she said, and he leaned over to kiss her, and cars started honking because the light had turned green.

"Okay, okay, calm down," Devon said and proceeded. When they got to her house, Devon wasn't sure if she wanted him to come in, so he sat there.

"Are you coming in?"

"Only if you want me to."

"Yes, I want you to," she replied and opened her door. "When I said I was ready, I meant I'm ready," she said, but when they walked in, her daughter was lying on the sofa. "Angel, what are you doing here?"

Angel sat up. "Hey, I came to wash some clothes. Who are you?" she asked, looking at Devon.

"Devon, this is my daughter, Angel. Angel, Devon," she said and took off her coat. She then took Devon's coat. "How much longer are you going to be?" she asked, wondering how she didn't notice her car outside on the street.

"Why? I was going to stay here tonight and go back on campus in the morning."

"Tonight? You're planning on staying over tonight?" Alicia asked. She didn't want her to spend the night. She wanted Devon to spend the night.

"Yes, Mother, tonight," she said and headed for the steps to go down and check on her clothes, Alicia assumed.

Alicia started to laugh really hard.

"Baby, why are you laughing?" he asked.

"Because I'm a grown-ass woman being cock blocked by my nineteen-year-old daughter," she said. Devon did find that funny. "She wasn't supposed to be here doing her damn clothes," she said and continued to laugh.

"Yes, that is pretty funny," he agreed, and they went to have a seat. "So I guess it won't be tonight?" he asked.

"I guess it won't, but it will be soon," she said, giving him a gentle kiss, and Angel walked in.

"So, Ma, why is this my first-time hearing about Mr. Devon here?" she asked, taking a seat like she was Alicia's mother.

"Well, Angel, that is because I am thirty-nine, and I don't have to report to you," she quipped. "Devon, would you like something to drink?"

"Sure, I'll take a beer if you have one," he said.

"I do, and, Angel, be nice. Don't get slapped," she said and headed into the kitchen.

"So, Devon, are you a teacher?" Alicia overheard her ask him. She moved quickly because Angel was nosy.

"No, I am a senior partner at AT&T," he replied.

"Oh, so how did you meet my mom?"

"She is my daughter's English teacher," he said.

"Eeewww, isn't that like, weird?"

"No," Alicia said, coming back into the living room. "What makes it 'eewww'?"

"I'm just saying, back when I was in high school, a kid would get beat down if their parents were dating a teacher. They'd always think that that student got extra attention or better grades because of the relationship."

"Well, Deja is an honor roll student and gets A's consistently, not only in my class but in all of her classes, and just because I'm dating Devon, I don't give her any extra attention, and Deja doesn't even know we are dating."

"And you're keeping it a secret. Good luck with that one," she said and got up. "I'm going to go fold clothes. Nice meeting you, Mr. Devon. Ma, behave. No kissing on the couch," she joked, and Alicia threw a pillow at her.

"I think I should tell her," he said.

"Yeah, me too. I mean, this is serious. Do you want to be with me?" Alicia asked.

"You know what, Alicia? I really do," he said, and they kissed again. Within minutes Devon was on top of her on the couch, and they were kissing and grinding like teenagers until they heard the basement door. Devon jumped up, and she sat up like they hadn't been fooling around on the sofa. As soon as Angel went back downstairs, they went at it again, and this time, Devon was under her top, massaging her breast. She pushed his head down to suck on her nipples, and when it started to feel really good, Angel came back up again. "I think I should go," Devon suggested.

"Yes, because I need a cold shower," Alicia said.

"Ditto on that." Devon stood.

She went to get his coat, and he gave her the last kiss for the night. "Will I see you tomorrow?"

"Yeah, after your dance class, right?"

"Yeah," she said, smiling.

"My place or yours?"

"Yours, because now that my daughter has met you, trust, she is gonna be all up in the biz," she joked, and they laughed.

"Okay, and you might want to bring your toothbrush," he said, and she smiled.

"Ooooh, I love sleepovers," she said, ending their night with a final kiss because cock-blocking-ass Angel was back in the living room.

Chapter Seventeen

Kennedy and Cher sat holding hands at the oval table at the lawyer's office. They had arrived at nine thirty, and no one was there yet. Julian sat on the side and kept giving Kennedy a reassuring smile, and she felt like she could handle anything that day would bring, but she was dead wrong. The door opened, and it was Kory and Keith. They greeted Kennedy and Cherae with hugs and kisses, and they all sat and made small talk until John entered the room. Kennedy was even more eager to see who else would be showing up.

A young woman walked in with a man, and they sat down on the other side of the table, and Kennedy suddenly began to study her face. She looked familiar or had a familiar face, like her own. She was thinking and knew they had to be somehow related.

"Good morning, everyone," John said, and a few low "good mornings" returned. "I know we are all anxious to get started, so I will get right to it," he said and took a seat.

Kennedy kept eyeing the young woman, wondering who the hell she was and how she was related to her father, but she turned her attention to John to get her answers.

"I'm going to hand out copies so everyone can see exactly what I'm reading," he said and handed out the papers. They passed the papers around to each other.

"Come on, John, at least introduce us to this stranger sitting across from me. How is she related to my father?" Kennedy demanded because her patience had run out.

"Actually, she was related to your late mother," he said, and Kennedy was more confused.

"How so?" she asked, thinking maybe she was a cousin because with the resemblance, it was evident they had the same blood somehow running through their veins.

"She is your mother's daughter," he said.

Kennedy almost fell out of her chair. "No, no, this is some kind of mistake. I'm an only child." Kennedy looked at him, wondering who this con artist was. "Who are you, and who told you that you were my mother's daughter?" Kennedy jumped up and yelled at her.

"Mrs. Roberson, please take your seat. You will have time to speak with Kenya after the reading of the will," he said, and Julian encouraged her to sit.

He took the seat on the other side of her and held her hand until the reading was over, and Kennedy could not believe that her father had left this stranger $50,000 and half of her parents' home. Kennedy felt like she was on *Punk'd* because it made no sense to her. When everything was over, John offered Kennedy and Kenya the room alone, but both agreed that their husbands should stay.

They all sat silently for a few minutes, and Kennedy was the first to speak. "Where are you from, Kenya?" she asked.

"Here. I was born and raised here in Chicago," she replied.

Kennedy was trembling. "I have a million and one questions swimming around my head, and I don't know what to ask first. How are you my sister? Where have you been? Who raised you?"

"I know you have a million questions, Kennedy, and I also know that this is difficult for you because it is difficult for me too, and to explain would be too much right now, so maybe we should go somewhere, you and me, and talk. I will answer all your questions the best I can, and I hope you will answer my one question," she said with her eyes welling.

"I have a million, and you only have one?"

"Yes, because I know everything else. I just don't know one thing," she said, and from the way she spoke, Kennedy could tell she didn't want to ask in front of Julian and her husband.

"Okay, give me your number, and I will call you, and we can meet later," Kennedy suggested.

"That will be fine," she said, and they got up to exit the room, and Kennedy's mind was in a whirlwind of confusion.

In the car, Julian and Cher went over and over why it couldn't be true, but Kennedy knew it was. Kenya looked like her, and her mom and Kennedy remembered her mother telling her long ago that she wanted to name her Kenya, but her daddy chose Kennedy.

"She's not lying, y'all," Kennedy interrupted.

"How do you know that bitch ain't lying, Kennedy?" Cher spat.

"Yes, baby, your daddy would have never hidden that. Why would they give her up, and why would your father never tell you?"

"John said she was my mother's daughter, not my father's. And we both look like Momma, so don't act like you didn't see that, Cher, and for whatever reason, my daddy died with that secret. I don't know, but maybe she is," she said softly because she was drained.

When Kennedy got home, she changed and had a couple of glasses of wine. She took out her phone and called Kenya, and they agreed to meet at the house—the house they both inherited. Kennedy convinced Julian to allow her to go alone, and he finally gave in and let her, but she had to promise she'd call if she needed him, and she promised.

She talked to Cher on the phone all the way there, and she had to beg Cher to stay away. When she arrived, she walked up to the porch, which was strange now that her father wouldn't be on the other side of the door when she opened it. She turned on the lights and couldn't help but cry. Now both her parents were gone, and she wondered if Kenya would consider selling the house since she had inherited half of it.

Kennedy entered the kitchen because there was a horrible odor, and she realized the trash hadn't gone out, so she opened the back door and took the trash can to the dumpster. When she went back inside, she went under the sink, grabbed the Febreze, sprayed the place, and lit a few candles.

The house was clean, but the housekeeper hadn't been there since the day before her father's death. She had to go through the fridge before she left to take out any food that would spoil or that had already spoiled. She made a note to get some estimates for someone to come out and pack up the entire house. She told herself she'd spend a couple of weeks figuring out what she wanted to keep, like photos, heirlooms, and keepsakes. She was getting ready to head upstairs when the doorbell rang. It was Kenya, and she was anxious to see her.

"Did you find the place okay?"

"Yes, it was easy," she answered, coming in, and she took off her coat. "Wow, this is where you grew up, huh? It's very nice," she said, looking around. "This is massive compared to the house I grew up in," she shared.

"Yes, this is my folks' house. Have a seat," she offered, but Kenya went over to the pictures of their mom.

"Wow, Mom was beautiful," she said, and Kennedy didn't like that.

"Yes, my mom was," she said and took the picture out of Kenya's hand.

"I'm sorry, Kennedy," she said sincerely.

"It's okay. Let's sit and get past the hard part, and then maybe there will be an easy part," Kennedy suggested, taking a seat. "So the first question is, how old are you?"

"Thirty-seven," she said, and that didn't surprise Kennedy because she didn't look too much younger than she. "How old are you?" she asked Kennedy.

"I'm forty-two," she said, and they both figured she came along when Kennedy was around 5. "Who is your father?" Kennedy asked.

"Royce Ellis. He was the—" she tried to say, but Kennedy finished for her.

"The bass player for my momma's band."

"Yes, he was."

"Is your daddy still alive?"

"No, he died about five years ago," she said and looked down.

"I'm so sorry to hear that," Kennedy said.

"It's okay. It was hard at first, but it got easier," she said, and they went silent again, but Kennedy was anxious to get details.

"So tell me the whole story, Kenya. What did your father tell you? As you can see, my father didn't tell me anything," she said and sat back on the sofa to listen.

"Well, he said their affair started about three months after they went back on the road for a tour that your father forbade Mom to go on because you were young, but our mother did what she wanted and left. One month later, your dad told her if she didn't give up her singing career and come home and be a mother, he would be done with her, and giving up singing wasn't an option. Then the affair started.

"After she was gone for six months, my daddy said she couldn't take hurting your father anymore, and she missed you terribly. When she returned, not long after she was home, she discovered she was pregnant. She knew I was my father's child, not your dad's, and your dad was furious, but he loved our momma and told her to get rid of me. When Mom told my father, he begged her not to, and she went against your father's wishes and didn't do it. She carried me to term, and my father agreed he'd raise me and stay away, and I never got a chance to meet her. My mom helped my father take care of me financially, but she never once wanted to see or meet me. My dad said she didn't even look at me at the hospital but gave me my name.

"I begged several times to know who and where she was, but my dad never told me. I got older and decided to find her myself, and when I did, I learned she died of cancer when I was ten. Even after she died, your dad continued to ensure my daddy got a check. I didn't know until my dad was dying that I had a sister, and I gave him my word that I would never contact you. After your dad died, I got a letter from Boomer's office, and then I met you today," she said, and Kennedy figured that was the entire story.

Kennedy tried to think back really hard to when she was 5, and she didn't remember her mother being pregnant or even being gone for six months. She remembered her band when she was around 11, but by the time she was 13, her momma couldn't sing anymore because cancer had taken over.

"I have some pictures if you wanna see them," Kenya said, going for her purse, and Kennedy got up to sit beside her. She went into her purse and pulled out about twelve pictures. That was all she had of her mother.

Kennedy looked through them, and there was no denying that Kenya was her sister. She felt she looked more like her momma than she did.

"Wow, Kenya, I'm sorry." Kennedy felt bad. She wanted to be angry at her parents, but what would be the use? They were dead and gone and took that secret to their graves.

"It's okay, Kennedy, it's not your fault, and trust, I didn't want to meet you the way I did today at the lawyer's office, but your dad's instructions were for us to be there together, so I couldn't get out of it."

"I know. I was wondering why John made it so urgent," Kennedy said and remembered Kenya saying she had one question. "You told me earlier that you had one question for me," Kennedy reminded her.

"Yes, I do," she said shyly. "What was she like? How did her voice sound when she spoke? How did her hair smell? What was her favorite thing to do or eat? Could she sing as beautifully as my daddy said?" she inquired about everything, teary-eyed.

Kennedy thought, *that was more than one question,* but she knew she meant she wanted to know what it was like growing up with their mother.

"Wow. Mom was sassy, a sophisticated woman. She was voluptuous and alluring and carried herself with elegance and style. She was always on me about keeping my hair done and dressing like a lady at all times. Momma was strong, but she had this sweet, sensitive side that showered you with love and tenderness. Like Momma could cuss you out and then come back in the same breath and say, 'Ya know I love ya,' and wink.

"She cooked. Boy, she could cook. Daddy and I used to race to the table. She would clean house all day, cook, sit at her vanity, and get all dolled up for a show, with her drink and her cigarette," she shared, smiling at the memories.

"Wow, I wish I could have heard her voice or heard her sing, just once," she expressed, and Kennedy remembered she had cassette tapes and VHS tapes of her momma singing.

"Follow me," Kennedy said, and they went downstairs to where all of her momma's old things were. Even her vanity and chair were down there.

"Is this Momma's vanity?" Kenya asked.

Kennedy smiled. "It sure is," she replied.

Kenya began to touch everything. Kennedy found a tape, popped it in, hit play, and was amazed it still played and sounded okay. Kenya listened to it for the first time, and Kennedy listened like it was her first time. They ended up sitting and just listening to song after song, and both shed a few tears. They finally got to a song they both knew, called "Misty Blue," and began singing along. Kenya could sing, too, and Kennedy knew that was her little sister.

They continued endless conversation, and they noticed it was after one a.m. They called it a night and hugged tightly before they departed.

"Kennedy, I am so happy to have met you." Kenya smiled.

"Kenya, it was hard to accept you this morning sitting across that table, but I'm so glad that I met you too," she said, and they held hands.

"So I will see you tomorrow? We have so much more to catch up on, and I can't believe I finally get to be with my big sister," she confirmed.

"Yes, tomorrow, and I can't believe I have a little sister." Kennedy smiled, and they departed. As soon as Kennedy cranked the engine, she called Julian.

Chapter Eighteen

When Isaiah returned with the test, Christa was waiting on the steps. He handed her the bag, and she took it and went up the stairs without words. She opened the package, and there was a test with two sticks in it, so she grabbed a Dixie cup to catch some urine in it so she could take both tests to be sure. She pulled the cap off the first test, dipped the stick in, and replaced the cap, and as soon as it started to process, two lines appeared. She said that she'd wait the full time. Then she removed the other cap, dipped it, and replaced the cap.

She looked at her reflection, and she recognized that look of terror. She wore it many years ago when she was 15 and had gotten pregnant by the football team captain, Andre Wallace. He was a senior, and she was a sophomore, and he dumped her right after she gave up her virginity to him.

A month later, she found out she was pregnant, and when she told him, he laughed in her face and told her that the baby wasn't his. She was hurt and confused, so she went to her dad because her Korean momma would have had her executed for not only having sex but for getting pregnant. Her mom would always tell her in Korean that she would send her to her grandma in Korea to work on the farm with hard labor until she miscarried if she ever got pregnant, but her dad wasn't so vicious, at least not to her and her younger sister, Charley.

He took her to the clinic and handled it, telling her mother that she had appendicitis and had to stay home for a few days. He then hollered at some thugs from around the way to pay Andre Wallace a little visit on the football field, thus ending his football career.

That feeling returned, and she was doing what she did back then when the test was processing: praying that it would be negative. She looked down after five minutes of begging the Lord not to let it be, and it was. Both tests were positive, and she burst into tears. Christa loved Isaiah. She adored Jaiden but was terrified of motherhood. She loved other people's kids and never imagined having her own. What would she do with it? She tried to have a dog, which turned out horribly, so being a mom was never in her plans, and now Isaiah was going to hate her because she didn't want this. Maybe later she'd develop that maternal instinct, but now it wasn't anywhere to be found in her.

Isaiah tapped, and she jumped. She was terrified to open the door, but she did. She had to be honest with him, and it would not be easy. She opened the door, and her face was drenched. She just walked by him, and he went in to see the two positive tests. He followed her into the bedroom, and she sat on the bench at the foot of the bed and put her face into her hands.

"Are you seriously upset, Chris?" he asked, and she nodded up and down. "So what do you want to do?" he asked, irritated. "I know this wasn't in the plan, but we are getting married, and we'd have kids eventually."

"I don't know, Isaiah," she whispered.

"Well, Christa, here are the facts about this. If you even think about having an abortion for one second, we are done," he said with his temples flaring.

"Just like that? Are you not going to consider how I feel about this? You will throw away what we have if I don't want to keep this baby?"

"That is the point, Chris. If you want to abort my baby, we have nothing. You can't look me in the eyes and tell me or even give me a legitimate reason why you would want to terminate this pregnancy."

"Isaiah, I am not ready to be a mother!" she cried.

"Dammit, Christa, cut the bullshit!" he yelled. "You are fucking thirty-eight years old. You are not a fucking child. You made love to me and got pregnant."

"Because you came without a fucking condom, Isaiah. That shit wasn't my fault. I agreed to have one child after we were married. I don't want this right now, Isaiah. I wish I did, but I don't. I'm not ready to be a mother, and I can't keep this baby!" she cried.

"Then get the fuck out!" he yelled, and she looked at him like he was crazy.

She couldn't believe he was speaking to her like that and literally putting her out. "No, Isaiah, baby, wait, please, consider what I'm saying," she said, trying to grab him, but he snatched away. He went for her bag in the closet and started to pack her things. "Isaiah, are you serious? You're done with me?"

"Christa, right now, I can't even look at your ass, okay? So grab your shit and go. If you want to kill my kid, that is on you, not me. You answer to God on that." He rushed out the door and slammed it so hard pictures fell off the wall.

Christa slowly packed and gathered all her things. She double-checked when she was done to make sure she didn't forget anything, and she headed to her condo. She tried Isaiah several times, but he didn't pick up. She was hurting for the both of them. She understood how he felt, but she wished he understood that she wasn't ready to be a mother.

She was exhausted after bringing all her stuff in when she got home. Her place seemed foreign, because she stayed at Isaiah's most of the time since they decided to keep the house, and she missed him like crazy already. She called and called him, but he didn't answer. The next day was the same thing, and she took a chance and went by the house, and he wasn't home.

After a couple of days of trying to talk to him, she wasn't getting anywhere because she wasn't saying what he wanted to hear, and that was, "I want to keep this baby." She finally called, made the appointment, and told them she only missed one period, and she knew the date she may have conceived was only about three weeks ago, so they gave her an appointment one week from that day. She talked to Leila and could never get Leila to agree with what she was doing no matter how she explained it, so she stopped trying to convince her. She ended up calling Cher because she needed someone to pick her up. Although Cher didn't agree with what she was doing, she told her she didn't have to go alone.

The following week, Cher was there to pick her up on time, and Christa was shaking like a leaf. She was depressed that she had lost her fiancé behind her decision, but she figured she needed someone in her life who could love her for her, and Isaiah no longer fit that bill. They drove in silence, and Christa just stared out the window.

"Christa, do you wanna talk about it?" Cher asked.

"Why does it make me less of a woman if I don't want kids?"

"Wow, that is a tough question, Christa. In my opinion, it doesn't make you less of a woman, but women who have had children and have experienced the joy of being pregnant, and having this little, tiny blessing from God in their arms, may think that you're knocking it because you haven't tried it," she said.

"I don't need to try it to know I'll be horrible at it," she protested.

"Christa, what are you so afraid of? Be honest."

"That I . . . I won't be able to love it more than my freedom. Babies require so much, Cher, and I don't know if I'm ready to give up me for it," she said, being honest.

"Well, you asked me, and now I'm going to tell you the truth. That is some selfish bullshit, Christa. Babies are not a prison sentence. They are not a ball and chain. You have Isaiah, and us, and a support system, so you're not by yourself. If you want a mental mommy break, I'm sure Isaiah will give you that. Motherhood is not prison, and trust me, once you take one look at your baby, everything goes out the window.

"All the pain of labor, the gas, the swollen feet, all those memories of discomfort vanish when they put your baby in your arms. I'm not trying to change your mind, Christa, but if you are waiting for this maternal instinct to fall from heaven, stop, because God already gave it to you when He gave you a uterus. Trust me. It will kick in as soon as you feel your baby move inside your womb. There is absolutely nothing like it," she said, but Christa couldn't be persuaded.

"Well, when the time is right, I will have that experience. Now is not that time," she said, and Cher pulled into a parking space at the clinic.

"You sure this is what you want to do?" Cher asked.

Christa wasn't sure, but she knew it was best. "Let's get it done," she said, and they got out.

Christa filled out all the paperwork and waited nervously for them to call her name.

"You can still leave," Cher said, but she followed the nurse.

"I need you to remove your clothing from the waist down, and the doctor will be here in a minute. It would be best if you had the opening in the front because the doctor will have to do an ultrasound before the proce-dure," the nurse said, and Christa nodded. The nurse left the room, and Christa undressed and got on the table. Shortly after, the doctor came in.

"Christa, how are you today?" he asked.

"Good, considering," she sighed.

"I read your chart, and you say that you are about four weeks. Is that correct?" he asked and opened the front of her gown and began to feel around her abdomen.

"Yes, sir," she said, frowning because he was pressing deep. Christa's stomach was not showing at all, so the doctor was concerned because what he felt, felt bigger.

"Well, it feels a little larger than four weeks, so let's take a look. I'm going to listen to see if I can get a heartbeat first," he said, and Christa nodded. He squirted a little warm gel on her lower stomach area, and the heartbeat was strong, and he knew she was a little further than four weeks. "The heartbeat sounds great, and I think you may be further along," he said.

"No, because I had my period last month and the month before," Christa protested.

"Christa, some women experience bleeding after con-ception, even throughout the pregnancy, so just relax, and let us take a look," he said, and the nurse lowered the lights. Christa looked away from the screen because she didn't want to see anything. The doctor measured the baby, and Christa was approximately thirteen weeks.

"Okay, Christa, I think you should take a look so I can explain this to you," he said.

"No, Doctor, I don't want to look."

"Well, let me tell you what is going to happen here," he said, and she looked at him. "You are about twelve, maybe thirteen weeks. We have performed the procedure before this far along, but there are more risks."

"That's impossible. I only had unprotected sex once," she was about to say, but she remembered the bathroom love scene at the party. "Whatever, Doc, do it. I don't care how far along I am. I'm not ready to be a mom," she said again, but she couldn't resist looking at the monitor. The doctor looked at her and pointed everything out, and Christa's eyes watered.

"That's my baby?" she asked, and the tears rolled down her face, landing in her ears and hair.

"Yes, that is your baby, and in about two more weeks, maybe three, your ob-gyn should be able to tell you if it's a girl or boy," he said, and Christa could see the little heart beating, and the baby moved.

"Did it just move?" she asked in awe.

"Yes," he said, and it continued to put on a show for her. "I truly don't recommend termination of pregnancy at that stage."

"Why didn't I feel it?"

"Well, believe it or not, he or she is still too small for you to feel any firm movement, but in about four more weeks, you will feel baby movements," he said, and Christa didn't want to turn off the monitor.

"Doctor, I will pay you whatever you want if you just let me watch my baby for a few more minutes," she said, smiling.

"So I take it there will be no termination today?" he asked.

"No, I am going to be a mommy," she said with a bright smile.

The doctor gave her five more minutes and printed her two sets of ultrasound pictures before Christa got up and dressed. When she walked out with a long role of ultrasound pictures and wearing that dazzling smile, Cher knew she had changed her mind.

"I'm going to be a mommy!" she yelled in the waiting room with excitement, and she couldn't wait to tell Isaiah the good news.

Chapter Nineteen

It was the first weekend in May and two weeks before Deja's birthday party. Devon still hadn't told her about him and Alicia. They had finally consummated their relationship and had been inseparable since that night. It was a month before the school year would end, and Devon wanted to wait until the school year ended to make his announcement, but he knew it had to be sooner rather than later.

He and Deja pulled up to one of their favorite restaurants. Devon had taken her to upscale restaurants often since Deja was a small child to show her fine dining. She knew in what order to use her silverware, and she could read a menu in Italian, French, or Spanish because they went out often and even more during the summer.

"Daddy, what's going on? Who is she?" she asked after the hostess vacated their space.

"What makes you think a woman is joining us?" he asked.

"Dad, come on. You've been smiling the entire ride, and I can tell when there is someone special because you act all goofy and stuff like you did the last time you were in love with that woman Janelle," she reminded him, and he wished she hadn't said her name.

"Okay, truth," he said, and the server came over to get their drink order. Deja got her usual virgin strawberry daiquiri, and Devon got his scotch and soda. He offered them an appetizer, but Deja said the bread was enough.

"Okay, Daddy, your truth," she said, diving back in.

"Well, truth is I have been seeing someone, but it is someone you know," he said.

She looked at him, confused. "Someone I know? You're not kid patrolling, are you? That is like, wrong on so many levels," she said, making faces.

"D.J., get real. You know your daddy is not a perv," he said, and Alicia walked in and waved, but he gave her the "one minute" finger, and Deja looked over her shoulder and saw her.

"OMG, don't look that way. Ms. Gray is here, and I don't want her to see us," she said, and then Devon frowned.

"Why?"

"Because she is my English teacher, and she's been acting all weird. Lately, she is like . . . I don't know. She has to be head over heels for some guy now because she's just been acting all weird and super, extra nice," she said.

"Is that a bad thing?"

"Well, I guess not, but she just acts so differently now."

"Something like how you act when you are around West?" he asked, and Deja blushed.

"Yeah, sorta," she said, and Devon waved Alicia over, and he stood.

"Deja, this is my other date for the night," he said, and Deja was blinking a thousand times a minute.

"Hello, Deja," Ms. Gray said, and Deja got up and ran off to the bathroom.

Alicia and Devon just looked at each other. "Well," he said, "let's sit, and I'll order you a drink."

"I take it you didn't get to the part where you told her we were dating?"

"I'm afraid I didn't," he said, waved for their server, and ordered Alicia a drink.

After the drinks were out, Deja hadn't returned to the table, so Alicia volunteered to go to the ladies' room to talk to her. She stepped in and saw Deja's feet under the stall.

"Okay, Deja, what do you have to say?" she asked.

"I don't want to talk to you, Ms. Gray," she spat.

"Okay, I understand you're upset, but it would help if we talked about it," she said, and Deja unlocked the door and came out.

"Why didn't you or my dad tell me?" she asked with watery eyes. "All this time I watched you prance around the classroom, giving me extra smiles and help and coming to my dance performances at the games. It was all because you were seeing my father, not because you were interested in anything that I was doing," she cried.

"Deja, that is not true. At first, your dad and I were casually dating, so we didn't think there was anything to tell anyone. Now that we have gotten serious, we had to tell you because we really, really like each other now. I have been giving you extra attention, and it could be because of your dad. It's because everything he loves is what I'm starting to love, and, Deja, your dad loves you more than anything on this planet. Trust me, we wanted to tell you weeks ago, but we had to make sure that we were there before we told you.

"Your dad told me that he didn't want to introduce his daughter to another woman he wasn't serious with, and I respected that," she said, and Deja wiped her face.

"So you care that much about my dad not to break his heart?"

"Yes," she said.

Deja smiled. "I'm sorry I walked off. I was just mad. My dad has never kept a secret from me, but I want him to be happy, Ms. Gray, so don't break his heart," she said.

Alicia looked surprised because that sounded sort of like a threat. "I won't, I promise. Now can we go eat? A sista is hungry," she said, and she and Deja went and joined Devon.

Deja went straight to Devon and hugged him. "I love you, Daddy, and I want you to be happy," she said and gave her daddy a kiss.

"I love you too, baby, and I'm sorry I didn't tell you sooner."

"It's okay. Ms. Gray explained everything to me. I know you had your reasons."

"Okay, then, let us order some dinner. I'm starving," Devon said, leaning over and kissing Alicia.

Deja smiled. "So I see why mom asked me all those questions about how I felt about Ms. Gray. Dad, you told Mom about Ms. Gray weeks ago, didn't you?" she asked.

"I did when I knew that I was falling for her," he admitted, waved for their server, and then checked his phone. They ordered and had endless conversations. They ate great meals, and the night ended pleasantly. Alicia hated that she couldn't stay over because Deja was there, but Devon told her he'd come by and treat her to sexual dessert right after he got Deja settled.

When they got to school on Monday, Deja took her seat in Ms. Gray's class with a big smile on her face because she was the prettiest teacher she had, and she cared about her dad. Her dad had been heartbroken a few times, and she hoped Ms. Gray was the one to keep a smile on her dad's face.

Chapter Twenty

"Terry, thank you for taking my call," Cher said.

"Hey, it's a pleasure. How can I help you?"

"First, I want to thank you for your advice," she said, and he was lost.

"Which piece of advice was that?"

"That I don't have to stay in an abusive situation. I can leave," she said, and he was glad she called.

"Listen, Cherae, whatever you need, I'm here. I know firsthand, trust, so you're doing the right thing."

"I know, Terry, and that's why I'm calling. I want to buy my husband out of our business. For the last three years, I've turned over seventy-six percent of the profits, and without me, we would have closed months ago. I need to know what I need to do and where I need to start," she explained.

"I can help you, Cher. Can you meet me and bring me all and any documents to substantiate your profits versus his, like tax returns, bonuses, and any legal, financial documents you can verify that you've been the stability of your agency? I can get the ball rolling for you," Terry said.

"Oh, thank you, Terry. I will get whatever you need, and I wanted to know if you can refer me to a good divorce lawyer," she asked because divorce wasn't his field.

"You bet. Let me make some calls to a few friends, and I'll have a name and number for you this evening. How about my place, around seven?" he said.

"That's perfect, and thanks so much," Cher said, and they hung up. She began to collect all the info she could. A couple of hours later, she felt she had all she needed. She was about to head out of the office, but Cortez walked in.

"So where are you off to?" he asked.

"To Kennedy's, why?" she said nervously.

"Why? Because I got a call from Wanda this afternoon, and I know what you are up to, Cher, so don't play with me," he said, referring to their shared receptionist.

She was on his team because she worked for him as a receptionist before he met Cher, and they started their own business together. Cher knew her loyalty was with Cortez, so she wasn't surprised that the bitch ratted her out. She never wanted her and Cortez together to begin with, and Cher was sure she may have sucked Cortez's dick a time or two. In Cher's opinion, what stopped Cortez from being with her was that she was far from what she considered attractive. Smart as hell, but not too easy on the eyes.

"And she told me about your little plans to buy me out and divorce me, so where the fuck were you on your way to?" he asked again with more bass in his voice.

Cher backed up because she could see that he was furious. "Cortez, let me pass, okay? This thing we have going on here ain't working anymore. You are an alcoholic, and you will run this business into the ground if I don't take it over, and I can't take another ass whipping from you, Cortez. I've had it!" she yelled, backing up, and he kept coming in closer.

"You ungrateful bitch!" he yelled in her face and then backed her up against the wall. She was now shaking. He grabbed her face and pinned her head against the wall. "I made you, Cherae. You were a homeless, dick-chasing whore, and I took you back and gave you a chance after everything. I paid for you to go to school. I got you into real estate, and we started this company from nothing, and you think you can buy me out!" he yelled, squeezing her tiny face tighter with his huge hands.

"Bitch, you are not going to leave me with nothing. I took your sorry, whoring ass in with nothing, and you will not leave me!" he yelled and pushed the left side of her face hard, and she went down and hit the side of her head on the receptionist's desk.

He went to lock the door, and Cher was terrified. And she tried to go for the phone on the desk, but he pulled her back by her hair and pushed her onto the floor again. "Please, please, please, Cortez, don't do this, please. I won't leave. Just please don't!" she begged. He pulled her petite body up from the floor by her silk blouse.

"I know you're not going to leave me!" he yelled and backhanded her across the face, catching a clean hit across her nose. And her nose gushed blood, and she cried and tried to fight him off, but he wouldn't release the grip he had on her blouse, and he struck her again, that time with a closed fist, and she welled in pain.

"Cortez, please, no, no!" she pleaded, and he pushed her so hard she fell back into the desk again before hitting the floor.

"Don't beg now, bitch. You wanna divorce me? You calling on Terry to save your whore ass? Are you fucking him, too?" he yelled, and she tried to crawl into his office because that was the closest option to her, but he dragged her back and pulled her up by her hair, and Cher continued to scream as loud as she could, crying for help, and that made him angrier, and he put his hand over her mouth.

"Bitch, I will kill you if you don't stop screaming. Do you understand?" Cher was terrified. "Now when I let you go, you will get in your car and take your ass straight home. Is that understood?" he barked.

She quickly nodded yes.

He let her go with another thrust, causing her to fall forward onto the floor, and she sobbed.

"You didn't hear me!" he yelled because she didn't move fast enough. He snatched her up by her hair again, pulled her to the bathroom, and pushed her into the bathroom door. Her head hit the doorknob on her way down, and she grabbed her head and screamed in pain.

"Didn't I tell you to stop screaming?" he said, and she tried to muffle the sounds with her other hand as he snatched her up and opened the bathroom door. He pushed her petite body so hard she landed face-first into the toilet, and he shut her in, and all she could do was sob.

She thought he beat her badly before, but she was so beat down that time it hurt to move. She stayed in the bathroom for close to an hour, scared to open the door, but she finally did. She staggered out to the front, and there was no sign of him. She searched for her phone, but he must have taken it, because she couldn't find it. The only thing she could think to do was call Jay's because she didn't have any numbers memorized. She grabbed the phone book from the receptionist's desk, found the number, and Tony answered.

"Jay's, you got Tony," he said.

"Tony," she said so low he barely heard her.

"Jay's," he said again, and she had to push the sound out.

"Tony, Kennedy," she said.

"Kennedy isn't here. Who is this?"

"Julian, please," she said, and he put her on hold.

"This is Julian," he said a couple of moments later.

"Julian, this is Cher. Help me," she cried. Her lips were so swollen he could barely understand.

"Cher, is that you?"

"Yes. Help me. I'm at my office. Please come now," she cried, and Julian heard her clear enough to know she was at her office and needed help.

"I'm on my way," he said and rushed out.

When he arrived, he parked in the fire lane and barely put the car in park before opening his car door. He burst in the door, finding Cher on the floor with the phone in her hand. Her face and clothes had so much blood on them that Julian didn't know if she had been shot, stabbed, or just beaten. "Hang on, Cher. Hang on, sis," he said, picking her up from the floor.

"Julian, thank you," she murmured.

He grabbed her purse from the floor and helped her out the door, not caring about locking up her office. He put her in the front seat and hurried her to the closest hospital. He called Kennedy and told her that Cher had been attacked in her office, and Kennedy raced to the hospital to see what had happened.

The doctor looked at her, and there wasn't any severe damage, but she had to get four stitches in her head because the doorknob broke the skin. The doctor gave her some pain pills and told her she could go home, but she didn't want to face anybody with her face looking like a monster, so Kennedy suggested she go to her parents' house. It was the last place Cortez would go to look for her. He knew absolutely nothing about it.

Julian was furious and knew he would whip Cortez's ass when he saw him. The cops came, and Cher pressed charges, so they headed to pick him up, but Cher knew her son would be home with the sitter, so Julian took any reason he could to go and visit Cortez. Kennedy confirmed with her husband that she'd take her to her parents' house and return as soon as Julian came home to look after the kids. No one wanted her son to see her face like that.

"Kennedy, thanks so much," she mumbled through her swollen lips.

Kennedy had to ask, "Cher, how long?"

"What do you mean?"

"How long has he been putting his hands on you?" Kennedy said bluntly.

"Too long," she answered, and the tears rolled down her swollen face, and Kennedy held her.

"Once they take him into custody, I'll take you home with us," Kennedy said, and Cher nodded. "You did the right thing by pressing charges."

"I know. I didn't want to, but I'm tired, Kennedy, and I just want out," she said.

"I know, Cher, and you are going to be okay," she said, gave her one last hug, and left.

While driving, she wanted to call Julian and tell him not to hurt Cortez, but she knew it would be useless. She called her sitter and asked if she could stay late because Kennedy felt she'd have to bail Julian out soon.

Julian got to Cortez's before the cops made it, and he leaned on the doorbell until Cortez finally opened the door.

"Julian, what brings you by?" he asked with a stupid grin like he was clueless.

"Are you serious, ma'fucka? Step yo' bitch ass outside really quick!" Julian yelled in anger.

Cortez laughed in his face. And before Cortez knew it, Julian snatched his ass out of the doorway and threw him to the ground. He was so drunk he could barely stand, but Julian punched him with a right hook, knocking him backward, and Cortez laughed as if it didn't faze him, trying to get up, and Julian hit him again. That time he knocked his ass out cold on the lawn. Julian headed inside and called for C.J., who came to the top of the stairs.

"Uncle Julian." He looked happy to see him.

"Hey, little man, come on, you're going over to our house for a few days," he said, and C.J. ran down the steps toward him. Julian hurried to get C.J. out of the house before the cops came.

Julian put him in the truck and saw his dad lying on the lawn.

"What happened to my daddy?" he asked, clueless about what was happening.

"He just had a little too much to drink, little man, don't worry," Julian said, hoping C.J. wouldn't ask any more questions, and he didn't. As Julian was pulling out, the cops were pulling in, and he didn't bother to stop.

Chapter Twenty-one

Christa called Isaiah over and over, but he still didn't answer. She didn't want to text him with the news, so she decided she'd go over and talk to him face-to-face. He wasn't home, so she texted him that it was urgent and to please call her, but he didn't reply or call. She got into her car and decided she'd find him.

Her first stop was at his parents' house, and they claimed not to know where he was, so the next stop was Iyeshia's, and sure enough, that was where he was. She saw his truck, so she parked on the street and retrieved one of the framed ultrasound photos from the back seat. She used the spare remote she still had on her key ring to unlock the door to his Tundra, put the framed picture on his seat, and returned to her car.

She parked a few feet away and hit the panic button on his truck. He came out and looked around, not seeing anyone, so he hit the button to cut it off. Two minutes later, she hit it again, and he came back out, and since he still didn't see anyone on the street, he hit the button to turn it off again, and then she turned it on again. Isaiah came down the steps to see what was going on, and she watched him open the door and pick up the photo. That was when she hurried out and approached him.

"It's our baby's first photo." She smiled.

He let out a sigh of relief. "Really?" he asked with a smile.

She could see that he needed confirmation by looking at her with desperation in his eyes and wrinkles on his forehead. "Yes. I couldn't do it. I saw our baby move, and I couldn't do it," she said, walking into his arms, and he hugged her tight.

"Oh, my God, Christa. We are having a baby!" His excitement couldn't be contained.

"Yes, I am going to be a mommy," she said, and she was so happy to be back in his arms.

He looked at the picture, and his eyes just welled. "I'm going to have another child, and this time I'm going to be here for everything," he said.

"Yes, and it turns out the shower wasn't the time," she said, and he looked confused.

"What? What do you mean?"

"It was the bathroom at Rona's party. I'm about thirteen weeks," she said, and it was unbelievable. She didn't even have a pouch or a bump on her stomach. She had been looking at her stomach since leaving the doctor's office, wondering how the baby had room because her stomach was still flat, but she then noticed it was hard.

"So that means you'll be a little over seven months on our wedding day," he said, and she didn't want that anymore.

"Umm, can we go? Because it's cold, and we need to talk about this wedding thing," she said, and he agreed. He was about to run upstairs, but she stopped him. "Isaiah, wait. I have something for Iyeshia," she said. Going to the car, she came with another framed ultrasound picture.

"Christa, you can't be serious. You are not giving these out to people?"

"Well, you were the first, but I had one for all of our friends framed yesterday," she said, smiling.

"Christa, baby, no one gives out framed ultrasound photos."

"Well, this is our baby's very first picture, and I want to share it with our family and friends," she said, and all he could do was kiss her.

"You know what? You are special. Go get in the car, and I'll be right back down," he said, laughing his ass off at her. It was corny, but that was Christa. He went inside and showed the photo to Iyeshia.

"What the hell is this?" Iyeshia asked Isaiah, rubbing her pregnant belly. "Why are you giving me a framed picture of my fetus?" she asked. She was having her first baby with a man with whom she had a one-night drunken fuck fest. They started dating after she told him about the mishap, and she finally had a life and a man of her own to worry about.

"That is not your fetus, retard. That is my and Christa's fetus," he said, and she laughed.

"Your fiancée framed the baby's ultrasound picture, Saiah?" she asked, laughing hysterically, holding her belly with her free hand.

"Yes, and I know it's bizarre, but that is why I love her. She is always surprising me," he said, set to leave.

"So this is it. No more dreams of you and Janiece. Christa is the one?"

"No more Janiece dreams. Christa is the one," he said, and his sister hugged him.

"I'm happy for you, big bro." She smiled. "I'm glad she did the right thing, and I hope this lasts forever for you. Janiece and I are cool now, thank God, but I knew she wasn't the one. Christa is different. I see that love in her eyes when she looks at you, and I wish only the best for you two," she said.

"You, too, sis. I know your situation with Craig is not traditional, but he's a decent brother, and for some strange reason, he loves your crazy ass," he teased.

She slapped his arm. "Get out," she said, and he had to go anyway.

He gave her one more hug and left. He looked at Janiece's old door, then looked out at Christa's car waiting for him in the parking lot, said goodbye to his past, and hurried down the stairs to his present and future.

When they got to Isaiah's house, Christa talked nonstop about the baby, and she was truly excited. Isaiah was so happy to see her celebrating her pregnancy instead of wishing it away like she did the night they found out.

After telling Isaiah she didn't want to have a wedding at seven months pregnant, they agreed to move the date up. When Christa called Leila with the news of moving it up, Leila told her that she'd have to scale back on some things if she wanted to move it up because with her new planning business being open, she had other obligations. Christa quickly agreed, and Isaiah couldn't have been happier than that moment.

He reflected on his relationship with Janiece and how happy he had been about marrying her and becoming a father. Still, the feeling with Christa was different, and he felt that even though their courtship was short, she truly loved him, and there were no feelings deep inside her for anyone other than him. He could admit to himself that he was happier with Christa than he was with Janiece. There was no tug-of-war or struggle to have Christa, and he knew her heart truly belonged to him, and although he never saw the day that he could no longer feel romantic love for Janiece, it had finally arrived, and he planned to give Christa the life he wanted to give to Janiece.

Christa lay in his arms, and he held her tight.

"This is no ordinary love. I've never loved a man enough in my life to want to give him children, and I realize my love for you is much deeper than the love I've had for any man," she confessed. "You are the one my heart has been waiting for, and I'd give you ten babies if that would make you happy."

"Are you okay? I hear you, but I want to make sure you mean the words you are saying," he said.

"Yes." She smiled, looking up at him.

"I love you, Christa, and I am glad you chose our family."

"I am too, Isaiah. Seeing our baby on that monitor and seeing his or her heartbeat just let me see life inside of me. And I am so happy knowing that I'm going to have a part of us, and I love us so much."

"Me too, baby. Beneath your beautiful exterior, you have a genuine heart, and I'll do whatever it takes to make sure you're happy," he said.

"Same here, love. Well, the baby is starving," she said, and he laughed.

"Really?"

"Yes, and we'd like food."

"I can do that," he said, getting up. He stepped into his sweats and gave her a gentle kiss.

"Thank you, baby," she said, and he headed for the kitchen.

Christa stood and went to the mirror to look at her stomach again. There was nothing to see. She rubbed it and honestly couldn't wait until she would start showing. She smiled to herself as she admired her glowing face, happy with her entire life and situation. Meeting Isaiah was the best thing that ever happened to her, and she looked forward to becoming his wife and the mother of his child and/or children.

Chapter Twenty-two

Robin sat at her desk, watching the clock, waiting for K.P.'s meeting to be over. She would normally be on her mission to seduce her boss into a trap that got her a nice settlement, but that was no longer the operation. She wanted him and knew the money came with him, so she had to find a way to get in and Janiece out.

Her first tactic would be the woman in distress. Men always felt the need to help a woman in need of maintenance because it made them feel manly and in charge when women needed them to do things for them. A damsel in distress usually set the stage, and she had just the plan to get the ball rolling.

As soon as she saw his office door open, she began to flip through the manual of a wall unit she had purchased. She gave a friendly smile to the client, and he got on the elevator to leave. She waited until K.P. was a few steps away from his office door, and she asked, "Mr. Paxton, do you know what this means?" she said, holding up the manual, and he went over to see what she was talking about.

"Let me take a look," K.P. said, and she stood, moved close to him to point out her questions, and gave him a whiff of her perfume while K.P. examined it. He read a couple of lines and then explained it, but she still pretended to be clueless, and he could tell she had no idea what he was saying. "Still not making any sense?" he asked.

"Yeah, and no," she said and laughed.

"It's really easy," he said and tried to go through it again.

"Okay, but I'm sure once I get home, I will be stuck," she said, returning to her chair. "My stupid boyfriend is just a joke. He promised me he'd put this thing together weeks ago, and I'm tired of looking at the box, and I want to put my things away," she said, hoping he'd offer.

"It's not complicated, Robin. Don't be intimidated by a few instructions. It is much easier than it looks," K.P. replied.

"That's easy for you to say. I took it out of the box, and this thing has a million pieces," she cried.

"Listen, I'm done for the day, and if you'd like, I can assemble it for you," K.P. offered, and that was exactly what she wanted to hear.

"Are you sure, Mr. Paxton? I don't want to bother you with my entertainment unit. I mean, my stupid boyfriend will get it done, hopefully before hell freezes," she joked, and they laughed.

"Listen, it's cool. I don't mind at all. Just let me call Janiece and let her know I'll be a little late, and we can go and put this thing together," he said.

She smiled innocently in his face but smiled a devilish one inside. "Oh, thank you, Mr. Paxton. You are a life-saver," she said, thinking, *step one: check.*

They finished up in the office and headed out, and since she normally rode the train to work, she rode with K.P. in his Benz, feeling like his woman as she warmed Janiece's seat with her plump ass. She knew it was too early in the game to plant objects in his car, but she made sure her scarf fell to the back seat floor when she got out. When they got inside, K.P. was impressed to see her place was nice, and he could tell she had expensive taste.

"Wow, Robin, your place is very nice. Am I paying you too much?" he joked and took a seat.

"Ha-ha," she teased and put her things down on the chair. "No, you're not paying me enough, and my place is compliments of my old man. He bought it and furnished it for me, and everything was all good until he married his new wife, Jaren. She is my age, and now she is his new princess, and somehow I was disowned by the royal family," she said, taking off her shoes.

That was the lie she told all the men she was after because she couldn't tell anyone that her expensive taste was supported by her settlements for sexual harassment. She never even knew her dad. Her mother died over ten years ago. That was how she ended up doing her sexual harassment scam. She had expensive taste and never desired to be with any of her victims, until now. K.P. was the ultimate exception to the rules.

"Wow, are you serious? I have three daughters, and I wouldn't let anyone come between my girls and me, ever," K.P. said.

"Well, that was how my daddy and I were before Jaren. When my mom died, my dad and I grew really close, but about three years ago, he remarried, and ever since then, I've had to work, pay my bills, and trust, going from spoiled little daddy's girl to working girl cut me deep," she joked and then offered K.P. something to drink, and he accepted.

She returned with a beer, and K.P. removed his jacket and rolled up his sleeves to get started. She excused herself and came out in tight leggings and a fitted T-shirt that she pulled over her ass, showing off her curvy figure, but K.P. had no interest. She put her hair up in a loose ponytail, and she looked cute, but K.P. planned to help her out and head home.

By the time they were done, she had offered him his third beer, and he looked at his watch, and it was close to eight. "Nah, I'm gonna head home."

"Come on, man, have another one while I set some things on my new unit. I don't have company too often," she said, and K.P. agreed to stay a little longer. She got him another beer and continued talking and getting to know more about him. "So how did you meet your wife?"

"We met at a housewarming party. At the time, I was married and should have never gotten involved, but I was so taken by her the very first moment we met."

"So you left your wife for Janiece?" she asked, shocked. She thought surely she could take him from that fat-ass bitch. She looked like she just had a baby yesterday, not a few months ago.

"Yes, I did, and I'm not proud of my actions or how I handled things back then, but it went down like that. It is a very long story, but Janiece and I are at our happiest right now, and our marriage is perfect. Broken hearts and tears are behind us," he added, taking a swig of his beer.

"Well, sometimes you must go through the bad to get to the good."

"That is very true, and I couldn't agree with you more."

She placed the last item she had on her new stand and then stepped back to admire it. "Thanks again, Mr. Paxton, for putting the unit together for me. It's more beautiful than I thought it would be. I wanna get a couple more things to go on it, but I love it."

"It was nothing. That boyfriend of yours needs to get himself together. You're too young and beautiful to be waiting around on him," K.P. said, and she blushed.

"I know, Mr. Paxton. He is about to get his walking papers if he doesn't get it together, trust me," she said, and he opened the door to leave.

"Well, just always do what makes you happy. Don't waste your time with someone who makes you unhappy. Take it from me. It's better to move on than to stay where you're miserable."

She nodded with a smile.

"Good night, Robin. I will see you at the office tomorrow."

"Good night, Mr. Paxton, and thanks again," she said and shut the door behind him. She smiled because she thought she had Kerry figured out. She figured he left one wife. Why wouldn't he leave another? She had to work this one differently because, apparently, he was happy with his wife, unlike the other sex-deprived, overworked, horny bastards. K.P. was dapper, fine as hell, and she knew Janiece was on the job to keep him satisfied, so she had to figure out a subtle way to make him interested because each day she spent with him, the more attracted she was becoming to him.

She spent more time in the morning making sure her hair, makeup, and clothing were perfect, but he barely paid her efforts any mind. She'd make sure everything at the office was done superbly to impress him, but all he would do was tell her what a great job she was doing and keep moving. She'd linger in his office after their morning meeting, trying to make small talk, but K.P. always had a ton of work on his desk to get to, so she'd have to cut the small talk short and let him get to his work. She admired his work ethic and family values and wanted him for herself. She wanted him to love her even more than he loved Janiece and give her the lifestyle he gave Janiece and their children.

The next morning, she got to work bright and early and made sure she was looking good. She looked over K.P.'s schedule and decided she'd pull the "wrong file" move. That meant giving him the wrong file and showing up at the restaurant with the right one. Since she came all that way by cab, she'd be invited to join them and get a ride back to the office with him. Juvenile, yes. But it got her a nice meal, and she got to sit across the table from him, secretly imagining that they were there, as a couple, on business.

She had done that a few times, which always worked like a charm. She'd smile, impress the client, and maybe even flirt a little, and on the way back to the office, her former bosses would thank her for sealing the deal. Even though K.P. probably didn't need any help, she would attend the meeting anyway, just to watch her future husband at work.

When Robin got to the restaurant, the hostess pointed her in the right direction, and K.P. was alone.

"Robin, what are you doing here?" He looked shocked when she approached.

"I'm so sorry, Mr. Paxton, but I got here as fast as possible. I tried to catch you after you left because I realized I had given you the wrong file. I ran out so fast to get in the Uber, and I called but kept getting your voicemail. I was hoping to get here on time," she said as if she were in a panic.

"It's okay, Robin. Charles called and said he'll be a couple of minutes late. No harm done," he assured her.

"Thank God," she said and sighed. "I thought I'd lose my job," she said, handing him the right file, and he gave her the other one. He invited her to sit, and she did not refuse. The client walked in, did introductions, and got down to business. Before leaving, Robin excused herself to go to the ladies' room.

"Kerry, man, tell me you're tapping that," Charles said as if he didn't know Kerry better.

"What? Charles, man, we've done business for a while now, and you know I don't fuck around on my wife."

"I know what your mouth's saying, but she would have to be an exception to the rule, man. Baby's body is right. No way could she be my assistant because I'd hit that," he said and took a sip of his drink.

"Yes, she is a dime, but I'm good. My wife is all the woman I need," he said and opened the black case to pay the bill.

"Yes, your wife is a beauty, so is mine, but damn! If Monique still had a body like that, I'd be stuck to her like glue. Mo' is still a gorgeous woman, don't get me wrong, but my kids have damaged her figure."

"Well, Charles, women's bodies change after having kids, and Robin is still young with no kids. When she gets married and pops out a few kids, her husband may be singing the same tune you're singing in a few years," he said, and they laughed until Robin approached.

"What did I miss?" she asked, curious to hear the joke.

"Not much," K.P. said, and he was set to leave.

Chapter Twenty-three

"C.J.!" Cherae yelled when she saw her son. It had been two weeks since the incident, and her face was almost completely back to normal under her makeup, and she was happy to see her little boy.

"Momma, you're finally back. How was your trip?" C.J. asked because Kennedy and Julian told him that she had to go out of town for a little while, but Cher called him a couple of times a day.

"It was awful without you," she said and hugged him tighter.

"I had fun, but I missed you a lot," he said.

She smiled. "Momma missed you too, so much," she said.

"Can we go home now?"

"Well, we are going to go to Auntie Katrina's for a couple of days, and then we will go home," she said because she was still scared to be at home alone. She spent the first few nights at Kennedy's parents' house, but she didn't want to be alone, so she finally called Katrina and told her what was happening. Katrina rushed to pick her up, went by her house, got her a few items, and told Cherae that if she ran into Cortez, he would catch a bullet. She stayed with Cordell and Katrina until her face was better, and now she thought it would be best to stay a little longer since Cortez made bail. She got a new phone and uploaded her contacts from her Gmail account, but Cortez left tons of messages on the house phone, telling

her he wanted to work it out and to call him, but she
didn't.

She had access to her clients on her tablet, so she called
them all to tell them she had a family emergency and
was taking a leave of absence. She still had plans to buy
Cortez out and take her house. She earned everything she
had and wasn't going to hand it all over to him. She just
prayed he'd stay away from her.

"How are you doing, babe?" Kennedy asked. She and
Cher took a seat.

"Better," she said with a faint smile.

"You know you're not in this alone. Whatever you
and C.J. need, don't hesitate to ask," she said, and Cher
nodded.

"I know, Kay. I just can't believe this is happening to
me. I mean, Cortez just turned into this monster, Kay,
but I still love him. He beats the shit outta me, but I still
love him, and I miss the man I married," she cried, and
Kennedy put her arm around her and squeezed her.

"I know, Cher, but it will get easier in time. There is no
excuse for his behavior. You are not a punching bag. I'd
never tell you to leave your husband, even if he had an
affair, but this . . . You can't stay with a man who beats
you, Cher, because that is putting your life in danger, and
with that, I say don't go back. Next time you may need
more than a couple of stitches, and I'm not ready to bury
my best friend," Kennedy said.

Cher knew she was right. "I know, Kay, but what do I
tell my son?"

"You tell him that you love him and will always protect
him. When he gets older, you can tell him the truth or not.
Just focus on keeping you and C.J. safe and worry about
the questions later," she said.

Cher nodded. "This is so hard. I mean, I never thought
this would happen to me," she said.

"I know, baby, but we must take the good and the bad and make the best of it. I never thought in a million years that I'd have a sister, but I have one," she said, and Cher forgot all about that.

"Oh, Kennedy, I'm so sorry. I mean, how is it going with Kenya? I mean, how are you dealing with that?"

"We are fine, just spending a lot of time getting to know each other. I have a niece. She's seven. And she met the twins, and so far things are going well. We agreed to sell the house, and so far everything is okay," she said, and Cher smiled.

"Well, I can't wait to get to know her too."

"I can't wait for you two to get acquainted. I mean, Kenya is so much like Mom in many ways, her mannerisms and the way she sings. Man, she can sing."

"So can you," Cher said.

"No, I mean, she is really good."

"And so are you," Cher defended her.

"Yeah, I guess. Maybe it's because she is much more like my momma than I am. I mean, she looks more like Momma to me, and I can see Momma in her, just the way she carries herself and her demeanor. It's weird, but she has more of my momma in her than I do, I think, and in a way, it makes me happy, but at the same time, I am a little jealous."

"Well, you have a lot of Mom in you, but you're on the inside looking out, so you can't see it," Cher said.

Kennedy smiled. "Yeah, maybe I do," she said.

Julian walked in. "Hey, Cher, how are you doing?"

"I'm doing better, Julian, much better, and thank you and Kennedy so much for taking care of C.J., and you, Julian, for having my back," she expressed sincerely.

"Hey, Cher, it's cool. We are family. I just wish you had told us earlier. Even when I asked you, you said everything was fine."

"I know, Jay, but I hoped things would get better, you know? And I was embarrassed," she said. Her eyes welled.

"Hey, Cher, it's us, and absolutely nothing should embarrass you. We have been through way more than enough drama to be embarrassed," Kennedy said, reaching for her hands.

"Yes, and if Cortez ever puts his hands on you again, I'm gonna visit him again, and next time I won't be so nice," Julian said.

"Well, I hope he has sense enough to honor the restraining order. Kat and Cordell went over and had all the locks changed for me, and my alarm system has a brand-new code." Cher was glad that her family and friends were there for her and her son. She would not have made it without them.

"So when are you going home?" Julian asked.

"In a few days," Cher replied. "I'll be at Kat's for a little while longer. I found a new location for my office, and Kat and Cordell have been with me every step of the way, packing up my stuff from the other office and getting the boxes moved in for me. I already got the ball rolling to make a legal part from our company. Terry has been helping me with that, and I finally filed for divorce. Cortez was served two days ago at the office, so soon this nightmare will be over."

"Are you sure you will be able to manage on your own, Cher?" Kennedy asked, and Cher was finally open and honest.

"I'm more than fine, Kay. I was so busy trying to make my husband look good that I gave him way more credit than he deserved for our business to be as successful as it is. I turned over more than seventy percent of the profit in the last four years so that I will be buying him out," Cher announced. "Plus, I got my 'in case a nigga act up' fund," she said, because that was her new motto: never let a man leave you penniless.

"Wow, Cher, that is a relief. As horrible as the entire situation is with Cortez, doesn't it feel good to have that financial freedom?" Kennedy commented.

Cher remembered a time when she relied on everybody but herself. "It feels damn good," she said and smiled brightly for the first time since the brutal incident.

"So are you ladies hungry?" Julian asked.

"Starving," Kennedy said.

"Well, I'll grab you two a glass of pinot, and I'll whip us up some dinner," Julian said and exited.

"Girl, it has to feel good to have a husband who can cook," Cher said and dabbed the corners of her eyes. She no longer felt like crying.

"Yes, girl, I would cook more, but Julian is just so much better at it than I am," she said, smiling at Cher. "Are you sure you're all right, my friend?" Kennedy asked.

"No, but I am going to be," she said, giving Kennedy a hopeful smile. They sat in silence, and Julian walked back in a few moments later with two glasses of wine and a tray with cheese, crackers, and fruit.

"You know my weakness," Cher joked.

"Mine, too," Kennedy said, reaching in quickly for a cube of cheese.

"Yes, I do. Dinner will be ready soon," Julian said and headed back to the kitchen.

Chapter Twenty-four

"Come on out, Deja, so we can see," Alicia said, and Deja finally stepped out of the dressing room.

"Wow," Devon said, looking at his baby girl in her dress. She was shopping for a dress for her party, and since Leila had her hands full with party planning, Devon agreed to take her.

"Daddy, what do you think?" Deja asked, and the way her face was glowing, he knew she loved it.

"It's beautiful, baby, but I don't know, maybe it is a little too grown up for you," he said because it was a bit sexier on her body than it was on the hanger. Deja was slim, but her frame was a perfect hourglass. She was a cheerleader, a track star, and on the dance team, but she had her mom's curves. Her body was toned, and even though she was turning 15, her body looked like she was 19 or 20 in that dress.

"No, it isn't, Daddy," she insisted, turning to the side.

"D.J., it is. Your mother would kill me if I approved something so sexy, and I would kill every boy who thought you looked sexy in it."

"Dad, you're being old-fashioned. Miss Alicia, what do you think?" Deja asked.

"I'm afraid I'd have to agree with your father, Deja. I mean, it is a nice dress, no doubt, but I could see Angel wearing it for her twentieth," she said.

Deja clicked her tongue. "You are always taking his side," she pouted, stormed into the dressing room, and slammed the door.

"Deja!" Devon yelled. "Open this damn door right now and apologize," he demanded, and she hesitated at first, but her daddy called her name one more time with a little more bass in his voice.

"Devon, it's okay," Alicia said, holding up her hands.

"No, it is not okay," he said, and she opened the door.

"I'm sorry," she said with attitude.

"Drop the attitude and apologize like you mean it, or else you can put your jeans and sweater back on, and we can head back to your mom's."

"I'm sorry, Ms. Alicia," Deja said and stood and waited for Devon to give her the okay to try on the next dress. Devon went over and sat next to Alicia.

"Baby, it's okay," Alicia whispered.

"It's not. That is not the daughter we raised, and she will not disrespect you or any other adult, as a matter of fact," he declared. He gave her a gentle kiss. She smiled. They waited for Deja to come out in the next dress, and it was another beautiful one that met with Devon's approval.

"Wow, Deja, that dress looks gorgeous on you," Alicia complimented her. "It's the perfect color, the right size, and positively beautiful on you."

"What do you think about this one, sweetheart?" Devon asked, and Deja fidgeted with it a little before she answered.

"I like the other way more, but I like it, Daddy. I think we will have to have it altered here a little," she said, pinching the underarm part of the dress. Her breasts weren't big enough to fill the top, so it gapped under her arms.

Alicia got up and told her to drop her arms, and she pulled the sections under her arms tight so she could get a good look. "Yes, right in here, and that will make it a perfect fit," Alicia added.

"Yes, that makes it better," Deja said, and her attitude disappeared. "Dad, I think this is the one," she said, smiling and admiring herself.

"Yes, that will make it perfect, D.J. Now this dress is perfect," Devon said, smiling at his baby girl. "Are you sure this is the one?" he asked, hoping it was because they had been to four stores.

"Yep, this is the one."

"Oh, thank God," Devon said, relieved.

"It ain't over. We still have to find shoes and accessories."

"Today? You have to get all of that today, baby girl?" he asked.

"My party is this weekend. It's already last minute as it is," Deja said, turning to the side.

"Well, I guess, if it has to be," he said, not happy.

"Baby, how about you go to the food court and take my iPad, and Deja and I can hit up a few more stores to get the rest of her things?" Alicia volunteered.

"But you can't use my card, baby," he said.

"I got it," she said.

"No, I can't ask you to do that," he disputed.

"I don't mind, Devon."

"No, Alicia, I don't want you buying things for D.J. I got it," he said.

"Okay, well, I will give you all the receipts, and you can pay me back if that makes you feel better," she suggested.

"Now that is a plan," he said.

Deja went to change back into her clothes, and after they paid, Devon headed for the food court, and the girls continued to shop. After Deja got all she needed, he took them to dinner and then dropped Deja off at Leila's.

The next day, Alicia promised Devon she'd bring Deja home from dance practice, so she sat on the bleachers and waited for Deja to come out. She looked and noticed Deja had left her bag on the bleachers next to her, so she grabbed it and headed to the locker room. When she walked in, she overheard a conversation she wished she had not.

"So you're really going to go through with it, Deja?" asked Jasmine, one of her girlfriends. Ms. Gray knew all the teens and their voices.

"Yes, the night of my party. My mom said I could spend the night with Kimberly, and you know Kimberly's mom works the night shift, so when she leaves, West is going to come over," she said, trying to keep her voice low, but Alicia could hear her.

"Okay, where are you guys gonna do it at, and did you get condoms?" another girlfriend of Deja's asked.

"Kimberly's brother is gone away to school, so we are going to use his old room, and of course I got condoms. I know better," she said, and her girlfriend Destiny spoke up.

"Deja, I think that is a very, very bad idea. What if you get caught, pregnant, or catch an STD? Your first time is supposed to be special with the man you love and want to marry," she said, and everyone laughed, but Deja didn't.

"This is special, Des. I do love West, and we will be married one day. What is the difference if we have sex now or later? We are going to be together forever," Deja said.

"How can you say that for sure, Deja? I mean, it's like, we are freshmen, and by the time we graduate and go to college, things could be different, and you can't take back your virginity," Destiny argued.

"Yeah, Deja, she is right. I mean, I know you and West are in love, but are you sure you want him to take your body first? Destiny is right. Once you do it, it's done," her teammate, Asia, said.

"Well, Asia and Des, I'm doing it Saturday night. I love West, and we are going to be together forever," she said.

Ms. Gray guessed she realized she didn't have her bag at that moment because she said, "Oh, snap, my bag." Alicia hurried out the door and, when Deja snatched the door open, pretended like she had just approached to bring her the bag. "Wow, thanks, Ms. Gray. I didn't realize I had forgotten my bag. I won't be long," she said.

Alicia gave her a faint smile and wondered if she should tell Devon what she overheard or stay out of it.

Chapter Twenty-five

"Baby, how are you feeling?" Isaiah asked because Christa was sick all the time. Everything made her nauseated, and she couldn't wait until it passed. She was seventeen weeks and knew she was having a girl.

She was so excited that she began buying every pink, yellow, and purple outfit she could get her hands on. She put her place on the market willingly, and that day was the day the designer was coming out to meet her to talk about converting their guest room into the new baby's nursery because the other room was Jaiden's.

"I'm not all right. I don't know why everything makes me nauseated. That is why I can't gain weight, and these supplements are a waste of time because I throw them up before they can dissolve," she cried.

"Awww, baby, I'm sorry. Listen, I will make you some buttered toast, and I will talk with the designer so that you can rest," he offered.

"No, this is my moment, and I want Ivy's room to be perfect," she said. After they got the news it was a girl, they decided to name her Ivory, with Ivy as a nickname, because she would not be an Iyeshia like Iyeshia wanted. Isaiah's sister had a boy a few days earlier, even though she'd prayed for a girl. Both times she had her ultrasound, the baby wasn't positioned for the doctor to give her a positive confirmation of the sex, and she was bugging Isaiah by text, begging him to name his next daughter after her, even though she didn't name her son after him.

"Listen, Chris, the baby's room will be perfect. I have your notes, and I'm positive I can do it. He won't be here for another hour or so anyway, so you may feel better by then," he said, and she sat up.

"Yes, you're right," she said and smiled.

"I know I'm right, and your color is coming back to normal, too, babe," he added. "I'll run down to make you some toast," he said and got up.

"Ivy wants apple jelly." She smiled.

"I know she loves apple," Isaiah teased and headed down to make her toast.

She ate four slices of toast. Christa got up and went into the bathroom, and when she walked out of the bathroom with a tank and a pair of thongs on, Isaiah looked at her.

"What is it, babe?"

"I can finally see your little bump. I can finally tell that you are actually pregnant," Isaiah said, pulling her close.

She looked up at him, and his eyes were watery. "Awww, babe, don't make me cry. I kept telling you that eventually I'd look pregnant, too."

"I know, Chris, but your belly was so flat. I was like, is my kid okay in there?"

"She is fine in here," she said.

He dropped down to the floor, lifted her tank, and kissed her stomach. "I missed this with Janiece, and I'm just so overjoyed right now," he expressed and laid his face against her stomach. "I'm so happy to be here for my new baby, and I am so excited."

The baby kicked, and Christa felt a strong kick at that time. She'd feel a little something every now and again, but that was the first kick with some power.

"Did you feel that?" she asked.

"Yes, I felt that. Wow," he said, touching that spot, and the baby moved again. "You can hear me," Isaiah said to her stomach, and the baby continued to entertain her parents for a few moments with her movements. "Babe, I think she recognizes my voice," Isaiah said, moving his hand around her belly. Christa figured he was trying to catch her kicks.

"Yes, it feels like she does," she agreed. "Oh, Isaiah, I'm so anxious for next week, and I can't wait to meet li'l Ivy. I will be the best mother on the planet, and she will be on every billboard in Chicago."

"Whoa, babe, we are not turning Ivy into a model."

"Ummm, what would be so bad about that? I've modeled for over twenty years, Isaiah," she said, lifting his head to look at him because he was too busy rubbing his nose on her stomach.

"Nothing, I just want our daughter to choose what she would like to be, not for us to make her into what we want her to be," he said.

She agreed. "You're right, baby, and I'm sorry, but please don't tell me that I can't have her pictures displayed at my agency, because I won't hear of that. I know, like, six photographers who will be on it every month. I don't want to miss a moment," she said, being her quirky self.

"That's fine, babe, but no modeling, got it? When Ivory gets older, I want her to decide what she wants to do. If that is modeling, great, but we will not be like those parents on TLC torturing our baby to live out some adult fantasy," he said, and she knew by his tone that he meant it.

"Agreed. However, I won't lie, there will be a lot of picture taking, and that, my love, you can't deny me of," she said.

"And I won't," he said, putting his attention back on her bump.

Christa suggested they go back to bed, and he followed. When they were comfortable, she closed her eyes and pulled Isaiah's head closer to her body. "I can't wait until next week. I'm looking forward to the wedding."

"Me too." He planted another soft kiss on her stomach.

"I can't believe I will be eighteen weeks pregnant on my wedding day, and more than that, I can't believe my sister canceled on me at the last minute. I know the wedding was supposed to be at a later date, but I was sure she'd leave her man's side for my wedding," Christa whined again. Her sister Charley was on the road with her man, who was a musician, and she called Christa earlier that morning and told her she couldn't make the new date.

"I know, babe, but if she can't, she just can't. Don't hold it against her. We changed our plans."

"I know, but I wanted her to be my maid of honor, and I miss her. Last time, Leila was my matron of honor, so I wanted my sister this time."

"So ask Leila again," he said.

"I did, and she can't. Now that she is my official wedding planner, she has too much going on to stand up with me. Hell, she told me she may not even be inside the church for our exchange of vows because you know our reception is immediately after."

"Why don't you ask Cher? You and Cher seem to have gotten pretty tight. You told me that you and she go way back," he said.

"Yeah, we hated each other way back, but I guess we are good now. I know it's last-minute, but I will ask her. Because of the countless roommates and anorexic model socalled friends over the years, I've become close to Leila, Cher, and Kennedy. That is my circle now, and of course, your ex and I are cool now, but no way would I ask her, so I'll ask Cher," she said.

Isaiah didn't want to let her go, but he allowed her to get some things done since she was up and feeling better.

The designer arrived on time, and Isaiah left the room when they started talking numbers. Christa knew they had been spending a lot for the wedding, and the new furnishings they had purchased to transform the house from Janiece's old house to her new house was a lot, but she had the nursery under control. She was far from broke, so she'd tell Isaiah later that this was all her.

Her groom did well and took care of everything, so this dream nursery was her bill, and she'd be sure to put his mind at ease.

Chapter Twenty-six

"Please put a box of flowers between each table so we don't have to keep walking back and forth across the room just to get the centerpieces done," Leila directed her staff. "Remember, people, this is my daughter's big day, and I still have to head home and change, so work with me, not against me!" she ordered because no matter how early she started, it seemed like time was passing by too quickly.

"Mrs. Johnson, the DJ is here to set up his equipment," one of her staff members said.

"Already?" she asked and wondered why he was so early.

"Yes, ma'am, he says he wants to set up and come back later."

"Oh, that's fine. He is thinking ahead. I like that. Show him where he's going to be," she said, and she was off to assist the DJ. Leila spent another two hours giving orders and ensuring the place was perfect. She waited for Kennedy, Cher, and Katrina to show up before she headed home to change and get Deja. They were in charge of checking invites and making sure Deja's guests were okay until she arrived.

It was six thirty, and the party was scheduled for eight, so Leila was relieved she was making good time. When she got home, she was pissed that the house was a mess and the kids were running around like crazy.

"D.J.!" she yelled, and Deja ran down the steps in her robe. "What in the hell is going on here?"

"I don't know. As soon as Daddy dropped me off from getting my hair and nails done, Daddy Ray rushed out. He said he had something important to do."

"So you didn't think to keep an eye on your brothers and your little sister?"

"I was, but tonight is the biggest night of my life. Auntie Christa's makeup girl just finished my face, and I have to practice my birthday speech," she said.

Leila couldn't help but smile. The young lady before her eyes was growing up, and she thanked God she still had Rayven to baby because she could no longer baby Deja.

"You know what? G'on. Let me see where your daddy Ray is and why he didn't call Tab to come early," she said, going for her phone. "And D.J.," she called out before she ran back up the steps and she turned her attention back to Leila, "you look beautiful, baby girl, just like a princess."

"Thank you, Ma." She smiled and then jetted back to her room to finish getting ready.

"Rayshon, where in the hell are you? You left these kids here running amok and tearing up my damn house?" Leila blasted into the phone.

"No, I left them with D.J.," he returned.

"Well, Deja is in party mode, and she ain't thinking about her siblings. Where are you, and why didn't you call Tab to ask her to come early?"

"Well, I had to make the final arrangements for Deja's gift, and I didn't have a lot of time to get it done and get back home and get dressed, so I had to rush out," he said.

"And what did you get D.J.? All this secret mess is driving me insane," she said, going up the stairs so she could shower.

"I'm not telling. You will see when she sees," he said.

Leila had to shower and get dressed, so she didn't argue. "Fine, just get your ass here now because Deja will die if she is late for her party," Leila said, stepping out of her jeans.

"I'll be there soon," Rayshon said.

Leila ended the call and headed to the shower. After she was fresh and a few seconds from putting on her clothes, she called and ordered her children pizza and was so happy to see Tabitha walk through the door.

They managed to leave the house in time for Deja to make a grand entrance. The hall was full of teens, and Leila was pleased with the turnout. She figured since Deja was involved in so many activities, she was popular to have so many show up.

Leila went to the stage and introduced Deja so they could sing "Happy Birthday to You," and afterward, Deja gave her speech and thanked everyone for coming out to celebrate her fifteenth birthday with her. Leila and Devon couldn't stop her from dancing with West the entire evening because they knew Deja had it bad for that boy.

"It's time for gifts," Leila announced, and the crowd applauded. "We thank all who came out and for getting Deja all these wonderful gifts, but her dads—yes, I said 'dads'—got her some gifts that they felt needed a grand announcement. Devon and Ray, please come up and present your daughter with her gifts," Leila said.

Devon and Rayshon, both looking fine as hell, walked onto the stage, and Leila blushed because they were both studs, and one was once hers.

"Well, this is certainly a party," Devon joked. The kids laughed. "I won't be long because I don't want to ruin my one and only daughter's fifteenth celebration with an embarrassing speech and childhood stories about how adorable she was." The teens laughed again. "D.J., you are my pride and joy, and fifteen years ago, when you were born, I had no idea you would knock me off my feet. You've grown into a beautiful, smart, and talented person, and, West," he said, looking directly at him, "if you break my baby's heart, I will shoot you," he joked. That time even Deja laughed. "All right, all right, I'm joking, but don't get any ideas, West," Devon said. West gave a little boyish smirk.

"D.J., I know you probably think I didn't hear you the million and one times you asked for the Microsoft Surface, but I did, so from me to you, this is one of the many gifts that Alicia and I got for you," he said, handing her the bag. She took it out and held it up with a smile wider than the sea. "Happy Birthday, baby, and your other stack of gift requests are with all the others," Devon said, and she hugged his neck tight.

"Thank you, Daddy, and thank you, Ms. Alicia," she said.

Devon gave her a final hug, handed the mic to Rayshon, and exited the stage. "Wow, I was like, please don't let his gift be better than my gift," Rayshon joked. Everyone laughed again. "Deja, I met your mom when you were a baby, and I've also watched you grow from an adorable, chubby baby into a teenage work of art. You are beautiful, just like your mother, and again, I pay attention, and I watch when you think I'm not watching, and your daddy Ray's gift to you is . . ." he said and paused, and the lights dimmed, and Deja was confused.

Then she heard his voice sing "Happy Birthday to You," but he was nowhere to be found. Once he finished the song, Ray continued, "Your mom and I give you Phoenix Keys," he said, and the teens went wild as he took the stage, and Ray got off quickly. He sang the first song to Deja, and then she got off the stage and went to the center of the front row to enjoy one of her favorites.

"Rayshon Johnson, how in the hell did you get Phoenix Keys to perform at this party, and secondly, how much did this set us back? Because I like name-brand wine, and boxed wine ain't my thing."

"Well, we can thank Christa. Her sister's boyfriend has worked with all of the best artists in the industry. Let's just say that she knew somebody who knew somebody who got me in touch with the right somebody to get him here. One hour is all we got. And you don't have to drink boxed wine, but the kids will be eating generic cereal for the next year," he joked.

Leila let him hold her on the side and watched her eldest enjoy the party of the century. By the third song, Leila got a tap on her shoulder, and she and Ray followed Devon and Alicia out and got the news about their daughter's plans to give up her goods.

"So you heard this with your own ears?" Leila yelled furiously at Alicia.

"Yes, I did the other day," she said.

"So why are you just now saying something, Alicia? You should have said something right away!" Leila barked.

"I'm sorry, Leila, I didn't know if I should say something," she said nervously.

"Do you have children, Ms. Gray?" Leila shot at her. She was angry more at Deja but took it out on Alicia.

"Lei, calm down. The fact is, we know what D.J. is planning to do, so we have to stop her and then talk to her," Devon said.

"Yes, after the party, we take her home and talk to her together," Ray said.

"No, that is not how things are going to go down. I know my daughter, and as much as she thinks she is ready to do this, she isn't, so I say we say nothing," Leila said, and Devon thought she was crazy.

"Lei, are you crazy? Do you think I'm going to let my fifteen-year-old daughter go and lie up with some boy for one second? She has no idea what she is getting herself into," he yelled.

"Devon, she won't do it. I promise you, D.J. won't do it," Leila insisted.

"What if you're wrong?" Ray said.

"If I am, our baby will no longer be our baby," she said and returned to the party.

Devon and Ray stood by and didn't want to go with Leila's plan, but they didn't challenge her.

Ray and Leila dropped Deja off after the party and told her to call if she needed them. Leila watched her baby walk in with her friend, and she just told herself she had to trust that her child would make the right decision.

"What if you're wrong, Lei? I am trying to back you, but I want so bad to sit out here and watch for this little motherfucker and beat his ass."

"Let's go home, Ray. We have to trust D.J. and let her make decisions. I hope my daughter returns a virgin, but if she doesn't, there is nothing we can do. We can't lock her up, and if it's not tonight, it will be another night, or another time, Ray. If she wants to have sex with this boy, it's not gon' change if we take her home tonight. I have talked to her and did all I could as a mother to show her her value, and now I have to let her implement what we taught her," she said, and they drove off.

Chapter Twenty-seven

When Ray and Leila got home, Devon's car was out front, and Leila knew Devon was ready to go off. "What's this kid's address?" Devon demanded. "I'm going to get my child," he barked.

"Devon, calm down and stop yelling," Leila said, trying not to yell.

"Lei, this is some bullshit, and I have a right to go and get my daughter," he said, and his eyes welled. "She is still my baby girl, and I will not leave it up to her to make the right decision. She is not ready for sex," he said sadly.

"Ray, take Alicia inside, please, and let me have a moment with Devon," Leila said, and Ray nodded and invited Alicia inside. "Come on, Devon, let's take a walk."

"Leila, I don't want to take a walk. I want to go and get Deja right now!"

"Pick her up and do what, Devon? Send her to her room? Slide her food under her door, go to every class she has or walk through the mall with her and her little chatty-ass girlfriends to make sure she is not talking about sex and so-called love and West? Deja is smart, Devon. We have talked to her, educated her, and equipped her with all the instructions for moments like this. Devon, like I told Ray, if not tonight, she'll do it tomorrow, or next week or whenever, so if you want to go and scoop her up, I'll tell you where she is, but if she does go through with it tonight, and she wants to, she will. Please, Devon, give our baby the benefit of the doubt and a little space. She is a good kid," she said.

Devon's phone rang. He pulled it out, and it was Deja. Devon answered quickly. "D.J., where are you?" he answered, putting her on speaker.

"Daddy, can you pick me up? I don't want to be here. Kimberly's mom isn't here, and it's not as cool as I thought it would be," she said, and Leila could hear her voice shaking.

"Of course," he said, and he and Leila went inside and let Ray and Alicia know they were going to pick up Deja.

When they pulled up, Deja was out in a flash. "Mom, I didn't know you'd be coming," she said and shut the door.

"Well, we were all at the house recapping your party," she said and winked at Devon.

"Well, since you're both here, I can talk to you both," she said and put her head down.

"What is it, baby? You know you can talk to us about anything," Devon said.

"I know," she said and paused, sniffling.

"What's wrong, sweetheart?" Leila asked, turning around in her seat, and Devon pulled over.

"He dumped me," she said and cried. "He called me a little girl and told me to call him when I was ready to be a woman," she cried.

Devon's jaws flared. "Where does he live? Devon yelled.

"Devon, that's not important," Leila said, looking at him like he was crazy. Their daughter was heartbroken. "Deja, tell us what happened, baby," Leila said gently.

"Well, when you and Daddy Ray dropped us off, West was in the backyard waiting for me. I let him in, and he started touching me as soon as he came inside. And I told him that I wanted to talk a little bit first, and he said we did enough talking, and he pulled me close and started to kiss me. That was cool because I did kiss him before, Mom. I know you told me not to, but I did. After that, he kept touching me, and I didn't like it as much as I thought I would. I told him that I wasn't ready. I told him I needed more time. Then he called me a tease," she cried. "And he told me that he could have any girl he wanted, and since I promised him to give him sex when I turned fifteen, he wanted it, and when I told him that I didn't want to anymore, he called me a baby and left. I thought he loved me," she cried, and Leila undid her seat belt and opened her door.

She climbed into the back seat with her, and Devon followed. "Shhhh, baby, it is okay. He is a jerk, and if I get my hands on him . . ." Devon said.

Leila shot him a look and shook her head.

"Baby, don't cry. It's okay," Devon said, consoling her.

"I thought I was ready, Ma, but I'm not. I got condoms and heard everything that you said about safe sex when the time is right, and this wasn't the right time, and I'm sorry I didn't talk to you first like I promised," Deja cried to Leila, and deep down she was happy that her baby was still a virgin but pissed that that little West kid broke her heart. They sat in the back for a while before returning to the house.

They gave Alicia and Ray the quiet signal because they didn't want Deja to know they knew. All four said good night to Deja, and Leila made them some coffee. They chatted for a while, and Leila was happy for Devon and Alicia. They seemed so happy together.

"Well, we are going to head out," Devon said, standing.

"Okay, we'll walk you guys out," Leila said.

Alicia asked Leila for the restroom, and she pointed the way. Ray began to clear the table, and Leila and Devon made their way to the door.

"Alicia is the one, Devon," Leila said because she had a great feeling about her, and she made it a point to apologize for snapping at her earlier.

"I know, and it is taking everything in my bones to keep from asking her to marry me."

"Why won't you?"

"Because it's like my third marriage, and Christa and me—" he said, starting with excuses.

Leila cut him off. "That's all in your past. Don't hold on to your past. Make moves for the future, Devon. I know that look in your eyes, and I see what she is like, taken by your words. I was her years ago, so don't hold back. Ask her. Engagement doesn't mean a wedding tomorrow. It just says, 'Hey, I think you're fucking great, and I want you forever,'" she said, and Alicia approached.

"Are you ready, Devon?" Alicia asked. Ray stepped up behind Leila and put his arms around her waist.

"Yes, let's hit the road, and, Lei, we should get together for dinner one night this week," he said and winked.

"Just let me know," Leila said, knowing that meant ring shopping. "Remember, Kennedy is the woman to see for that special gift," she said and winked back.

"I remember," he said, and they made their exit.

Ray instantly had questions, and Leila filled him in after they got in bed. Leila was exhausted but not too tired to spread her legs for her husband. What he did to her helped her get the deep sleep she needed, because Christa's wedding on the first weekend in June was next on her list.

Chapter Twenty-eight

"Oh, my goodness, you look gorgeous," Janiece complimented Christa when she walked in and saw her. She wasn't too fond of her after the whole "sell the house" crusade, but she had to admit she was a gorgeous bride. Even after almost five months, she didn't look fat in her dress.

"You think so?" Christa said nervously. "I'm ready to get it over with because it feels like I'm going to blow chunks any second. I can't tell if my nerves or the pregnancy has my stomach doing somersaults."

"Yes, you are looking beautiful, and with that baby, it could be a bit of both," Janiece said and smoothed Christa's bangs. "Isaiah's eyes are going to dance when he sees you," she said.

"I hope so. I just want to exchange vows quickly because I feel nauseated, and the crackers are not working. This baby has me feeling so weird."

"Don't worry, Christa, it will be over so fast. You'll wonder why it took so long to plan the eight- or nine-minute ceremony," she said, joking, but Christa didn't laugh.

"Garbage, garbage, garbage," she said, pointing with one hand and fanning her face with the other. "I am going to blow," she said, fanning herself with both hands. Janiece raced for the trash and rushed over to Christa. She hurled, and Janiece ensured she didn't get anything on her gown.

She held on to her veil and tried not to get sick herself. She looked around, snatched the box of Kleenex off the table, handed several to Christa, and Christa wiped her mouth. Janiece snatched a few more, dabbed Christa's forehead, and grabbed something to fan her.

"Thank you, Janiece, thank you. I know you don't like me much, so thank you," she said.

"I do like you, Christa. I didn't like ya much at first," she said and smirked. "I just had to accept that you were the new woman in Isaiah's life, and people do change when they have someone to change for. The changes that he's made were for the good of your relationship, and I was wrong to put my nose in. I was wrong to voice my opinions," she said, dabbing Christa's forehead and giving her a little smile.

"So you don't hate me anymore?" Christa asked.

"No, and I am so happy you came along to give Isaiah that love that I was never capable of giving him, because he deserves it, Christa, and I hope you two are even happier together than me and K.P."

"Thanks, Janiece," she said with a smile, and Janiece knew she needed a stick of gum immediately.

"No offense, but if you are going to kiss Isaiah after the exchange of vows, you will need about four sticks of this," she said, giving her a few sticks of gum from her purse. Christa ripped them open quickly.

"Christa, it's time," Leila said, coming through the door.

"Are you ready?" Janiece asked, and Christa nodded. Janiece suggested that she touch up her lipstick, and she did. After her last mirror check, they walked out, and Janiece hurried to her spot in line, wondering how she became a bridesmaid in her ex-husband's wedding.

Although Janiece thought Jaiden was too young to be a flower girl, Isaiah insisted. She took almost four minutes to walk all the way down the aisles, with Janiece pleading for her to come to her because she was too busy looking at all the people. When she finally made it, she went to stand by her daddy and not by Cher like she was supposed to, and Isaiah just gave his cool nod.

Christa waited for her cue to walk down the aisle with her dad. She smiled when she saw Isaiah, and she tried to keep her eyes locked on him, but her eyes scanned the room. When she saw Devon with Alicia, she wondered who she was, but she put her attention right back on Isaiah—the love of her life, the man she wished she had met before all the others who came before him. She held her bouquet with one hand and her stomach with the other one that was in her father's arm and said to herself that this was so far the best day of her life.

She handed Cher her bouquet, and instead of Isaiah taking her hands, he placed his hands on her belly, and she rested her hands on top of his. At that scene, every eye watered, including Janiece's.

She was so happy that Isaiah had found someone whose heart belonged solely to him. She smiled and winked at him after he said, "I do," and he smiled a beautiful smile at her, reminding her how happy he was on the day of their wedding, but she didn't feel sad at all. She looked over at K.P., smiled at him, and let the air out of her lungs with a happy release.

After the vows and presentation of Mr. and Mrs. Isaiah Lawton, everyone applauded as they walked hand and hand out of the church. Leila informed the wedding party to go back inside for pictures, and Christa and Isaiah proceeded to their receiving line.

After all the photos were taken, they headed to the reception hall, which was full of Isaiah's and Christa's friends and family. Christa cried as she watched a video of her sister giving her congratulations. The Lawtons gave speeches of praise to Isaiah's new bride, and Janiece knew they were happy that her heartbreaking ass was out of the picture. She was out of their son's pathway to happiness. Iyeshia praised Christa at all times to purposely get under Janiece's skin, Janiece thought, so she made sure she kept her distance. Even though she and Isaiah were great friends, she knew one day she and Iyeshia might end up in a fistfight.

Devon was on his way to the restroom when he ran into Janelle, and she paused. He knew she was there because she was a bridesmaid, but he didn't want one-on-one time with her. When he saw her, he looked around to see if Alicia was anywhere close before he spoke.

"Janelle," he said.

"Hi, Devon," she said nervously and looked around. He figured she didn't want Greg to see them talking.

"You look beautiful," he said. That was the first impression he got the night he met her, and she was still just as beautiful. Her curly hair was shorter, but she still looked good, he thought, admiring her.

"Thank you, and you're looking great yourself," she said, looking around again. "How have you been?" she asked, and before Devon replied, Greg approached.

"There you are," he said and looked at Devon, and Devon looked him dead in the eyes.

Feeling uneasy, Devon extended his hand toward Greg and introduced himself.

"Hello, I'm Gregory," he said and shook his hand. "Wait, did you say Devon?" he asked and raised his brow.

"Yeah, ummm, Christa and I were married, and now she and I are friends," he said, trying to make the encounter less weird, and then Greg punched him, knocking him to the floor.

"Oh, my God, Gregory, what is wrong with you?" Janelle yelled, rushing over to Devon, trying to help him up.

"How dare you come within two feet of my fucking wife!" Greg yelled, and everyone started to race out to see what was happening.

"Gregory!" Janelle yelled in shock, and Devon managed to stand to his feet.

"Janelle, let's go!" Greg yelled, and Janelle stood frozen. "Now!" Greg yelled, and everyone was watching.

"Baby," Janelle said, grabbing his arm and bringing him back to reality.

He blinked a couple of times and came back to that moment. Punching Devon had felt real, but it was only he, Janelle, and Devon in the hallway, not a circle of spectators.

"I'm sorry," he replied, turning his attention to Janelle. "The kids are fine," he said, telling Janelle what he came to find her for, wanting to get the hell away from his wife's ex-lover.

"Well, I have to hit the men's room. Take care, Janelle," Devon said and headed into the restroom.

"So that was him?" Greg asked, and Janelle didn't want to answer, but she did.

"I'm afraid so. If you want to go, baby, I completely understand," she said, looking teary-eyed at him.

"No, baby, that is in the past, and you are mine, and that doesn't hurt anymore," he said and kissed her. She smiled at him. He thanked God things were finally okay. She and Gregory were close, and their marriage was stronger than before the affair, and now that they were trying to have another baby, they spent every free moment making love. They found their way back to their table.

Janiece was seated next to Kerry, not at the wedding table with the wedding party because all the speeches and toasts were made. They danced and drank, and Janiece was shocked to see Robin, K.P.'s assistant, walk in.

"What is she doing here?" Janiece asked. Robin waved when she saw them.

"I invited her," K.P. said and waved her over.

"Why?" Janiece asked with attitude, but she was over to their table in a flash.

"Hey, guys, I know I'm late, but I got lost," she said and took a seat by Janiece. "Janiece, you look great," she said, and Janiece wanted to say the same because she looked like a superstar fresh out of a magazine, but she just thanked her with a faint smile and wondered why her husband thought it would be okay to invite her to their friend's wedding.

"Thanks, Robin. K.P., a word please," she said and stood and K.P. rushed out behind her. "Why in the fuck did you invite her to our friend's wedding?" she spat angrily. She already didn't like this girl, and seeing her pissed Janiece off.

"Well, she was going on and on about not having any plans for the weekend, and I asked if she wanted to come to a wedding, and she said yes. I called Isaiah, and he cleared it with Christa, so she took the spot Rose would have had. That's it."

"That's it?" Janiece said, looking at him like she wanted a different answer.

"Yes, Jai, what else would it be?"

"K.P., I don't trust her. There's something about her that I don't like, and I don't know what it is, but she is not like Rose, and if I catch you fucking around on me with her, I will kill you!" she yelled.

"What! Janiece, come on, be real. You know I'm not that guy. That is absurd," he said with his brows bunched together.

"No, Kerry, you are that guy. I was your damn mistress for five damn years, and you are that guy!" she barked.

K.P.'s expression went from confused to angry. "Really, Jai, fucking really?" he said and walked away. When Janiece returned to the table, K.P. got up and vacated his seat, and Janiece didn't chase him.

"Is everything okay?" Robin asked.

Janiece wanted to tell her that it was none of her damn business. "Yes, everything is fine. Why wouldn't it be?" Janiece said and slammed her glass on the table. She got up to find Janelle to talk to her.

"Hey, boss man," Robin said, coming out on the balcony where K.P. was. It was the first weekend in June, but it was still a little chilly, so not many people were out there.

"Hey, Robin," K.P. said and took a sip of his drink.

"Is your wife mad because I came?" she asked.

"Yeah, pretty much. I mean, it's comical, but in a way, I can see where she is coming from."

"What do you mean?"

"Let's just say that the past sometimes can be your worst enemy. I mean, after all the years Janiece and I have had together, good and bad, she thinks I'd do to her what I did to Kimberly," he said. They talked a lot at the office, and Robin could tell that K.P. was comfortable with being honest with her about things.

"Well, I can see her point, but if you treated me like you treat her and took care of me like you take care of her, I'd trust you," she said, touching his arm. At that moment, Janiece walked out but paused. She didn't approach them, but Robin did see her walking away.

"Well, Robin, it's a lot more complicated than that," he said and pulled away. "I'm going to head back inside and find my wife. Enjoy yourself and don't worry about my wife and me. Janiece and I are good," K.P. said. He went back inside and tried to find Janiece, but he couldn't.

The night ended, and he finally found her in the hotel lounge at the bar. He'd texted and called her phone a million times. "Jai," he called out, and when she turned to him, it was clear she'd had too many. "I've been looking all over for you," he expressed.

"I thought you were bussssssy entertaining your . . . your damn new hoooot-asssssss secretary," she slurred.

"Okay, Jai, that's enough. Let's go home," he said, trying to get her off the stool.

"Get your hands off me!" she yelled, and K.P. was shocked. He had never witnessed Janiece acting so erratic.

"Jai, get your ass up so we can go home and discuss this," he demanded.

She looked at him with watery eyes and slid off the stool. She followed him to the car with no words, and after he helped her into the passenger seat, he stood outside the door and wondered how she went from trusting and believing in him to this. He got in, and she turned to look out the window.

The next morning he let her sleep in because he knew she had a lot to drink the night before, but he couldn't wait until she was up and coherent so they could talk.

Chapter Twenty-nine

K.P. sat at his desk and hoped he and Janiece could talk that evening about her insecurities. He sent her flowers and ensured the card said that she was the only woman for him. He tried to talk to her the day before, but she kept putting him off and using the kids as an excuse, and after his shower, she pretended to be sleeping when he got into bed. He called her name a few times, but she didn't respond, so he slept.

That morning she was up before he was, and when he came down, she focused her attention on the kids and Phyllis. She gave K.P. a weak kiss before he departed. He called her a few times that morning, but she didn't answer. He called Phyllis, made plans for her and the kids to be out for the evening, and told her not to let Janiece know. When K.P. walked in, he nodded, and Phyllis began to gather the kids so she could get them out of the house.

"Where are you taking the kids?" Janiece asked, and Phyllis looked at K.P.

"They are going out for a couple of hours so you and I can talk, Mrs. Paxton," he said, and Phyllis didn't move, until K.P. gave her an approving nod.

Once they were gone, Janiece had no excuses or distractions to keep her from the conversation she tried to avoid. "So are you going to talk to me and tell me what is going on? And why all of a sudden do you think I'm going to do to you what I did to Kimberly?" he asked and stood and waited for her to respond, but she didn't right away. She just lowered her head.

"Janiece, baby, come on, tell me what's going on in your head. Why are you so insecure suddenly, and why would you think I'd mess around on you with Robin, of all people?" he asked.

She sat quietly, and he was getting more frustrated with trying to make her talk. He blew out a deep breath and then went to the wet bar to pour himself a drink. He came back to the sofa and sat and just waited for her to talk, but the minutes were going by, and still no words came from Janiece's lips. "I can't fix it if you don't tell me what's wrong," he said, attempting to get her to talk to him.

"I don't know why I'm insecure. I don't know why I feel that you would cheat on me, Kerry. I don't want to feel like this, but I don't feel as confident as I used to about myself and this relationship and marriage."

"Janiece, what have I done to make you feel this way? I mean, my routine is the same. I hold you, and I touch you. I kiss you, still send you flowers, and tell you how beautiful you are to me at least five times a day to show you that you still have my interest. I haven't stopped showing you love and affection, Jai, so why are you putting me in this cheating box? I know I did Kimberly wrong and had an affair with you for years while I was married to her, but you know it was because of my love for you, and that hasn't changed. It's not fair for you to keep accusing me and giving me the cold shoulder."

"You're right, K.P., and I'm sorry, okay? I see her and how young and gorgeous and flawless she is. I have gained at least fifty pounds since we've been back together. I'm always busy with the kids, and I feel like you may step out to have someone more beautiful and interesting. Someone who matches who you are. You're successful and handsome, and Robin is like the ideal match for you," she said and dropped her head.

He lifted it by her chin. "Baby, you're my match. You've always been my match. I'm not attracted to Robin. I don't look at her in that way. I would be a liar if I said that I didn't think she was beautiful because she is, but I am in love with you, Jai, and you can't hold me responsible for how you're feeling about yourself because I don't make you feel that way. I think you are just as beautiful, Janiece, and I love how you look. You are the mother of my children, and I knew a few pounds might come with that territory. For me, please trust me. I'm with who I want to be with, and I'm where I want to be. I've loved you since day one, and that hasn't changed.

"If you want to make some changes, baby, I'll support you. Hell, call Rayshon. He's a personal trainer. I'm sure he'll take you on as a client. And if Phyllis isn't enough to help with the kids, enroll them in daycare so you don't have to deal with them every day if you need a break. I'm willing to do whatever it takes, Janiece, to make you happy," he said and got up and sat closer to her.

"Anything?" she asked.

"Yes, baby, anything. I want you to be happy," he said.

"Then fire Robin," she said.

He couldn't believe his ears." Janiece, what? Are you serious? You want me to fire my assistant?" he asked because that wasn't an option. Robin was great at her job, and he did like her working there.

"Dead serious," she said, looking him square in the eyes.

"Jai, you're being unreasonable. I can't fire her without cause. She's a great employee," he said.

"So find someone else who can be just as great."

"Janiece, I love you, and you know when it comes to this house, I will bend over backward to make you happy, but when it comes to my business, that has nothing to do with this house, and you are overstepping," he said, being honest.

"Kerry, are you fucking serious? All I'm asking you to do is to fire your damn assistant," she yelled and stood.

"And the answer to that is no. I will not fire a great employee because you think she is too pretty to work at my company," he said.

"It's not just that she works at your company, K.P. This chick sits right outside your damn office door every day. She spends more hours in a day with you, and she must be a little more than just an assistant. You invited her to our friend's wedding."

"Janiece, this is petty and childish, and I'm not going to continue this conversation with you if it means you are telling me what to do with my business. I am not going to fire her," he declared.

"Well, this conversation is over!" she yelled, stood, and stormed out.

K.P. began to pace, wondering how Janiece could demand that he terminate an employee because she was jealous of her. Janiece slammed the bedroom door, and then K.P. slammed his office door.

"Momma Jai, here is your scarf," K.J. said and handed her a scarf that wasn't hers in Kerry's car. Janiece hadn't talked to him in almost two days, and her chest tightened when she saw the scarf.

"Where did you get this, K.J.?" she asked, examining it.

"It was on the floor back here," he said, and Janiece couldn't wait to get inside. K.P. had been working from home the last couple of days to keep the peace, Janiece thought, because the days he would come home from the office, she'd be in a terrible mood.

Janiece got inside, Phyllis was in the kitchen cooking with Jordan in her high chair, and Jaiden was sitting at the table having a snack. She kissed them both, told K.J. to clean his room, and then asked Phyllis where K.P. was.

"He's in his office, ma'am," she said.

Janiece headed to his office, scarf in hand. "What was she doing in your car?" she barked as soon as she barged in, and K.P. was on the phone with a client.

"Hold on, Allan," he said, taking the phone away from his ear and covering the mouthpiece. "What?" he asked, confused.

"You had that tramp in your car!" she yelled.

"Allan, let me give you a call back," K.P. said and hung up so fast that Janiece knew he hadn't given the person he was talking to a chance to agree or say bye. "What are you talking about? Who are you talking about?" he asked with a look of misunderstanding.

"Your bitch left her scarf in your car," Janiece yelled and threw it at him.

"Robin is not my bitch, and she may have left it. I don't know. I'll have to see if it's hers."

"Why was she in the car?"

"Jai, really? We go to lunch meetings and dinner meetings all the time. Robin has ridden in the car before, a few times. You never said anything to me when Rose worked for me. You know we ride together to meetings, so you're being ridiculous."

"How many times?" she asked.

"Janiece, this is crazy. Stop this bullshit. You've got to stop it. This thing you got going on has to stop. I'm not having an affair with Robin or with anyone. Robin is just my assistant, and I'm not interested in her, and I am not going to fire her, and that is that. I love you, woman, and you are going to stop this insecure bullshit and let me love you the way I've loved you, and that is with everything in me, so stop this," he said and walked over to her. He lifted her head and kissed her. Janiece loved K.P., and she knew her husband was sincere, but she definitely didn't trust Robin, and since she couldn't convince her husband to see things her way, she knew she'd have to deal with Robin herself.

She closed her eyes and enjoyed the soft kisses her husband planted on her neck, and her body wasn't as angry with him as she was before. Her body wanted him, and her anger wasn't strong enough to shut her body down. Within a few moments, they were naked on the leather sofa in K.P.'s office. They hadn't made love in several days, and she couldn't deny that was exactly what she needed. They both lay there out of breath, pleased with the orgasms that they shared.

"Janiece, I love you. Please trust me," K.P. whispered in her ear because he could still see the sadness behind her sexually satisfied eyes.

"I do, K.P. I do. I just don't trust Robin," she said.

He pulled the throw on the back of the sofa over them and then wrapped his body around hers. There were no more words, and they both took a much-needed nap together in the same spot they climaxed.

Chapter Thirty

Devon sat in his car and tried calling Alicia several times before going in, but he still couldn't reach her. He wondered if he was doing the right thing or if it was too soon to ask Alicia to be his wife. Leila's words about not getting married right away made him comfortable, but he still feared Alicia would say no, and he didn't want to be shot down in front of his friends, especially Deja. When he finally went inside, he told the hostess who he was, and she led him to the back of the restaurant, where he reserved four tables for himself and his close friends.

He spotted Leila, Ray, and Deja and hurried over because he needed to ask Leila again, was she sure it wasn't too soon to ask her?

"Devon, relax. it is going to be fine, and yes, it is a little early, but you don't need to date someone forever to know if they are the one. You can date someone for ten years and then marry them and still not make it. You can date a person for a month, marry them, and stay together forever. Just listen to your heart," she said, giving him a warm smile.

"I know. Asking Christa to marry me was easy because I knew that is what she wanted. You, I mean, you and I were meant to get married back then. Our love was too deep not to. I love Alicia, and I know she is the one, but I'm terrified," he said, being honest. "I mean, we never even discussed marriage, and if she says no . . ." he said.

Leila signaled for the server, and he rushed over. "Listen, my friend here is a little tense. Can you bring him a shot of Johnnie Walker right away?" she said, knowing Devon's drink.

"Yes, ma'am," the server said, and he was off.

"Devon, you have nothing to worry about. She loves you, I know it," she assured him, and their friends started to arrive, so they went to join everyone. All were seated, even Christa and Isaiah. They waited for Alicia to arrive, and Devon wondered what kept her. They had eaten appetizers and had had a few drinks and were ready to order, but Alicia wasn't there. Finally, she returned Devon's call, and he got up and stepped away from the table to talk to her.

"Baby, where are you? We have been waiting for an hour. My friends are ready to order dinner," he said, hoping everything was okay.

"Devon, I am so sorry, but I can't make it."

"You can't make it? Why?" he asked, disappointed.

"Because something has come up, and I can't get into it right now," she said, and Devon wondered what was so important that she canceled. He had been waiting all week for this day. "Listen, I will call you later," she said and ended the call, and Devon was confused.

He returned to the table, which was hard, but he broke the news to everyone. "I'm sorry, you guys, but Alicia isn't coming," he said, and everyone began to ask a million questions.

They all knew he wanted to propose, so they knew he was disappointed. Although he wanted to break down and cry, he held a straight face and smiled despite how he felt. They all ordered dinner, but Devon had lost his appetite. After he poked around his plate with his fork for a while, he finally asked for his food to be wrapped, and the server took it and bagged it to go. As they left, they all had comforting words for him, and Leila, Ray, and Deja were the last to leave.

"Daddy, I can go home with you. We can pop some popcorn and watch our favorite movies," Deja offered because she knew her dad was sad.

"Nah, go on home with your mom, baby. Your dad will be fine," he said.

Leila insisted, "D.J., remember you promised to help me with those centerpieces I need to finish before tomorrow morning."

"Okay," she said. They all headed to the cars. Ray gave Devon a few positive words, and then Leila walked with Devon.

"Devon, it must have been super important for her not to come," she said with a smile.

"Yeah, well, I know now this may not have been the right time," he said, giving her a faint smile.

"No, it just means something came up. See what happened first, Devon, before you change your mind," she insisted, and Devon was a little too irritated to hear it.

"If you say so," he said. Leila hugged him, and Rayshon pulled up with the car.

"Good night, Daddy," Deja said after she let her window down.

"Good night, pumpkin. I will see you this weekend," Devon said, giving a final wave to Ray and Lei, and they drove off.

He got in his car and decided he'd go by Alicia's house to see what happened, and when he got there, he saw a white Suburban with North Carolina plates in her driveway, and immediately he knew it was her ex-husband, and that pained his stomach. He tried calling her, but he got no answer, and he texted her but got no reply, so he pulled off after waiting twenty minutes in front of her house.

When he got home, he tried her again several times, and after he got nothing, he showered and fixed himself a drink. The weather was nice, so he sat on his balcony and stared at the city lights. "Love has whipped my ass again," Devon said out loud. "Karma is a bitch. Leaving Leila was the worst mistake of my life," he said and polished off the rest of the bottle of scotch.

The next morning, he called the office and told his assistant that he'd be working from home because he was in no shape to go into the office.

Chapter Thirty-one

The next day when Deja got to Alicia's class, she walked in with a serious attitude, and Alicia knew why. She didn't say much to Deja, and she turned her head every time she looked at Deja. Alicia called on Deja, and she gave the right answer dryly.

"Deja, a word, please," Alicia said when class was over.

Deja clicked her tongue and rolled her eyes. "Yes, Ms. Gray," Deja said, not calling her Miss Alicia like she did when the other students were not around.

"I know you're upset with me, and I don't blame you, but some things happened yesterday that I had no control over," she tried to explain.

"Like what, Ms. Gray? Did someone die? Did you have an accident? I mean, what was so urgent that you didn't show up? My dad invited all his friends to meet you, and you stood him up. Do you know how you made my father look? So no, you have no idea how upset I am, and I don't appreciate how you treated my dad and why you left him hanging like that," Deja said, not holding back what she felt. The late bell rang, and Deja had to hurry. "I gotta get to class," she said and hurried out of Alicia's class.

Alicia hated that she didn't show, but her ex and son showed up unannounced as she was getting ready to leave. She was so happy to see her son that she couldn't just rush out, and she definitely couldn't take him to dinner and meet Devon like that. She was so caught up in her reunion with her son that she didn't rush over to her phone when she heard it sounding off. Plus, his father was there, and she didn't want to talk to Devon in front of him. The first thing he asked after she gave her son a ton of kisses and hugs was where she was going looking so good.

"To dinner with some friends. I have plans," she had answered.

"Well, I guess you better call and cancel them," he'd said. She didn't want to, but she also didn't want to walk out when her son had just arrived.

"Excuse me," she'd said, taking her phone into the other room to call Devon. She'd wanted to explain the situation, but her ex walked in on her, so she ended the call before saying bye. She wanted to call Devon back, but her ex didn't have a room reserved, and her son begged her to allow his daddy to stay there. Unwillingly, she gave in and let him sleep in her guest room. She was too afraid to tell him she was in a relationship because all the times they talked, she would allow him to believe they still had a chance because she wanted her son back.

The next morning she tried Devon on her way to work, but he didn't answer. She texted him, and he didn't respond. She knew he was pissed because he had been planning that dinner for a week so that she could meet everyone close and personal to him. She met everyone briefly at Christa's wedding, but it was too much for her to talk to them.

Finally, after the day was done, she tried Devon again, but he didn't answer. When she got home, she was unpleasantly surprised that her ex had made dinner, and she rolled her eyes at her ex during the entire dinner.

"Feels like old times," Anthony said.

"What old times? You were never home for dinner. You were always 'working late,'" she said with air quotes.

"Not all the time, Alley. We had our moments."

"They were few and far between," she replied.

"Dad, you said you and Momma weren't going to fight again, ever," their son said.

"And I meant that, son. Trust, we are not fighting. We are just talking," he said.

"Then why is Mom so angry? Are you mad because I'm home?"

"Of course not, baby. I am so happy you're here, and I want you to stay with me forever," she said and touched his cheek.

"We are going to be together. Daddy said we are taking you back to North Carolina with us," he said, and Alicia shot Anthony Sr. a look.

"Did you tell him that?" she asked, trying to maintain a steady tone.

"I said maybe, okay? I figured we'd spend some time together and rekindle our marriage, and we could be a family again. I've changed, Alley," he said, looking at her sincerely and looking fine as hell.

She loved Devon, but there was something about her ex-husband that still could make her heart skip a beat. She looked down at her plate and decided to wait until later to talk to Anthony. She didn't want to upset her son and tell him that his father was a lying, cheating, whore-ass dog.

"I doubt it, but we will talk later," she said and finished eating dinner. She cleared the table and cleaned her kitchen. She checked her phone and wondered how Devon could be so angry not to return her calls or text. She knew she didn't show up for dinner and didn't answer or reply to him the night before, but she thought she'd hear back from him by nightfall.

She entered the living room, and Anthony brought their game system with them and connected it to her television because they were playing some boxing game. She sat and watched her ex-husband and son interact, and she could tell Anthony was doing a great job as a father. She just wished he had done a good job being a husband. After a couple of hours of texting Devon, she finally decided to let it go and wait. After they said good night to their son and ensured he was sleeping, she returned to the conversation.

"So when are you leaving?" she asked Anthony because he was lying on the sofa with the remote, making himself at home.

"I don't know. I am on leave for thirty days, and I was hoping you and I could work on our thing while I'm in town."

She laughed. "Anthony, that's not going to happen, okay? I know I may have said some promising things over the phone before, but things are different. I don't think you and I can start over or rekindle our thing. I don't want to fight with you over A.J., okay? I want my son back here with me, and I think you should reconsider."

"I told you that you can't have custody of him, and he won't be back in your life permanently unless you want us both," he said, sitting up and looking her in the eyes. "I miss you, baby, and I want another chance. You can move to North Carolina with me and A.J., and we can be a family again. Angel will be okay, and we can visit her."

"Anthony, we were never a family. You cheated on me our entire marriage, and I can't return to that," she cried. "I don't want to go back to that."

"I wouldn't do that. I'm over that, Alley, and I am ready to be right with you and do right by you," he said, getting up and moving close to her, and there is just something about an ex that gives you a dumb moment because she let him kiss her.

"No, no, no, Anthony, stop, okay? Don't. I can't do this with you because I'm involved with someone else," she confessed and broke away.

"Involved? With who?"

"Does it matter? You and I are not going to happen, and I want my son back," she demanded.

"I want you back," he said, pulling her close again, and she pulled away.

"Anthony, you and I are over, and tomorrow, you need to get a room because you can't stay here," she said and stormed off. She went into her room. She slammed the door and tried to calm down. She was angry with herself for letting him kiss her and for feeling weird, believing it might work this time, because she knew she had fallen in love with Devon.

She went for her phone and tried Devon repeatedly, and that time she left him a voice message asking him to please call her back. She said she was sorry for not showing up the night before and missed him. She paused and got in, "I love you," before the voicemail cut her off.

Chapter Thirty-two

Kerry sat at his desk looking over last month's Vegas office reports, which weren't making any sense. The numbers were way low, and he was baffled because they had their ups and downs in the industry, but the numbers were so low that they caused a visit, not a conference call. He decided he wouldn't let the manager of that branch know he was going to visit. A surprise visit was necessary to see what was going on and not give him time to make excuses or alter any documents.

"Robin, can you come in here for a moment?" K.P. said after he buzzed her phone.

"Sure, I'll be right there," she said and hurried in to see what he needed. She tapped and then entered and took a seat quickly.

"Have you gotten a look at May's numbers?"

"Yes, I did," she said.

"Did you notice the drastic drop?" he asked, looking through them again, making sure he wasn't reading them wrong.

"I did, but I haven't been here that long to know what each quarter should or should not look like, so I thought maybe last month was just a slow month."

"Well, I am going to have to go out there to see what is really going on," he said.

"So when shall I book our flight?" she asked, but he didn't mean her too.

"Oh, I'll be going alone, Robin. I don't want to drag you out there."

"Drag me, ha. This is Vegas. I'd gladly go. I know that there is going to be a lot of paperwork and files to go through to get to the bottom of this, and if the secretary there is seeing these same numbers and not doing anything to fix it, you are going to need me to help you with some of the workload," she said.

K.P. knew she was right. He didn't know if he would have to fire everyone on the spot and bring on new staff, and he had no idea how long it would take to get it back to normal. He could be there for a few weeks, and he was curious why Madison didn't email or call him.

"Well, I guess you're right. Who knows what's going on there? Book us something for a week from today, and my travel agent's number should be on the phone roster that Rose left. Tell him we will need a spacious living space with four bedrooms," K.P. said, and Robin was on it.

When K.P. got home and told Janiece that he had to go to Vegas and Robin was going with him, she hit the ceiling. No matter how many times K.P. stressed to her that it was business, she disputed it and accused him of sleeping with her. K.P. grew furious with her for accusing him when Robin was the last thing on his mind. He told her to think what she wanted to think. Whether she wanted him to or not, he was taking Robin, which was final. Janiece was so angry with his decision she opened her mouth and said the last thing he thought he'd ever hear her say.

"If you go and take her, this marriage is over," she cried with a face full of tears.

"Are you serious? You are going to give me an ultimatum, Janiece? You will stand here looking me in my face after everything we have been through and tell me that you don't trust me when I say that my relationship with

Robin is strictly professional? You are going to seriously keep accusing me of cheating on you with my fucking assistant!" he yelled and wanted to shake the shit out of her. He hadn't done anything to deserve how she was treating him, and he felt at that moment that he didn't want to be with her if she thought so little of him.

"That woman is after you, Kerry. Why can't you see that?" Janiece yelled.

"But I'm not after her, Jai. That is the fucking difference. Do you think I'm stupid enough to have an affair with Robin and flaunt it in your damn face? If I was interested or wanted this woman, do you think I'd be this resistant for one second or take her on a business trip that you know about? Use your head, Janiece. I'm not an idiot, and if you can't trust me, maybe this marriage is over," he said.

"Just like that! You will choose that bitch, your funky-ass assistant, over me?" Janiece cried.

"Nope, Jai, that ain't it. I'm choosing me. I should not have to deal with this shit when I know I'm a good man. I am a good goddamn husband. I've never cheated, thought about cheating, or wanted to cheat on you, and just because I won't yield to your insecurities. you want to be done with me? If that's your decree, Janiece, you do what you must do because next week, my assistant and I will be going to Las Vegas to handle my business. If you can't deal with that, you do what you gotta do," he said and walked out. He grabbed his keys and headed to Marcus's place.

Janiece sobbed until she fell asleep. The next day, they didn't speak, and before Janiece knew it, a week had passed, and it was time for K.P. to go. They barely spoke those days, and she watched him kiss their kids goodbye.

He stood and looked at her and waited for her to say something, but she didn't, so he headed for the door. She stood there frozen and then ran out behind him to stop him.

"K.P.!" she yelled, and he stopped and turned to her, and she ran into his arms, almost knocking him over. "I'm sorry, baby. I'm so, so, so, sorry. I love you so much, and I'm so sorry," she cried.

He kissed the top of her head. "It's okay, Jai. I love you, and it's okay, baby, it's okay. I'd never—" he tried to say.

"I know, I know, baby, I know, and I'm sorry. I trust you, I trust you, baby, and I'm sorry," she cried.

"I gotta go, sweetheart. I will call you as soon as I make it to my gate," he said, and she held on to him tight.

"Okay, okay, K.P. I love you. I love you," she said and finally released her grip.

"I love you, too, Janiece," he said, giving her a final kiss. "If I'm not back in three days, you can come to Vegas with me, okay? No matter what, in three days, you come," he said, and she nodded up and down. His shirt was wet from her tears, but he had no time to change. She let him get into the car's back seat after giving him one last kiss.

She waved bye, standing in the driveway and watching her husband leave. She told herself that K.P. was the man she married, the man who was madly and deeply in love with her. She told herself that Robin was not a threat, and her husband wasn't the same man to her as he was to Kimberly. She also said in three days she'd be on a plane if her man wasn't back at home with her and their kids.

Chapter Thirty-three

Cher drove to her new office feeling better than she had felt in days, trying to be positive despite her home situation. She had plans to go back home that evening after work because she told herself she wouldn't live in fear anymore. She just hoped Cortez would stay away and honor the court order because she wanted to sleep in her own bed, cook in her own kitchen, and not live out of a suitcase. Plus, C.J. was sleeping with her at Katrina's, which definitely had to stop because he slept wildly and snored like a grown-ass man.

As Cher parked, her cell phone rang, and it was Terry. "Hello," she answered.

"Hey, Cherae, is this a bad time?"

"No, not at all. I just got to my new office."

"Your new office, that's great. I'm happy to see you are moving on and not letting your situation get you down," he commented.

"And you know it. I have to keep busy, or I'll go insane," she said, getting out. "So what's up?" she asked, bringing him back to why he called.

"Oh, I'm sorry," he said and laughed a little. "I came across two documents you didn't sign, and I can't submit them without your signature. Are you free for lunch?"

"Sure, just name the place," she said and unlocked the door. She went to the security keypad, keyed in her code, and then locked the door to wait until her new receptionist arrived. She had plans to hire more agents, but she hadn't gotten around to that just yet.

Going out on her own was a courageous move, but she knew she couldn't go back to the agency with Cortez. She was a bit nervous at first, but after she checked their joint account and saw Cortez didn't clean it out, she took what was hers, leaving him way more than he deserved because she wanted him to stay away. Even if he had gotten stupid with their money, she wasn't worried because she had put away some money on the side, so she would be fine until the courts settled her and Cortez's business and assets.

She confirmed that she knew where the restaurant was located, and then she unpacked the boxes her sister and Cordell packed for her when they went by the office to clean it. At first, Cortez tried to stop them, but after Cordell flexed a little and Katrina showed her claws ready to attack his ass, he let them get Cher's things. Thirty minutes had passed, and she was surprised to hear a knock because her assistant wasn't due to come until ten, and it was only eight forty-five.

She slowly made her way to the door, and her face turned pale when she saw him. "No, no, no. Go away. You're not supposed to be here!" she yelled, trembling. It was Cortez, and the sight of him scared her to death.

"I'm not going to hurt you, Cher. I just want to talk," he yelled through the glass.

"No, I am going to call the police if you don't leave this instant!" she yelled, wondering why she walked out of her office without her cell phone, and she was too afraid to move over to the receptionist's desk to get to the phone. She imagined him breaking the glass and going for the lock.

"Cher, come on, I swear I didn't come here to hurt you, and I'm sorry for hurting you. I just want to work this out. I miss you, and I'm going crazy without you and my son. I wanna come home. We can work this out, Cher, and if you let me come back, I will go to counseling, therapy, anger management, or whatever. Just tell me what you want, and I'll do it," he expressed sincerely, but Cher wasn't falling for it.

"Cortez, please go. I don't wanna call the cops on you, but I will," she threatened, finding the strength to make it to the receptionist's desk. She had to get to the phone if he had plans to break the glass.

"Cher, why are you doing this to us? You know I love you, and I am sorry for putting my hands on you. I swear that will never happen again. Just open the door so we can talk," he said, shaking the door like a maniac, trying to pull it open.

Her heart was racing, but she picked up the phone, and Cortez held up his hands in mock surrender. "Okay, okay, Cher. I'll go," he said and backed away.

She held the phone tight until he got into his car and pulled out of the parking lot. She was trembling and breathing heavily. She couldn't believe how afraid he had made her, and she decided at that moment that she needed a gun.

Cortez was tall and built, and she knew she couldn't match him if she wanted to, and she declared he would never hit her again. She finally put the phone down after a few moments. She ran into her office, and she called Terry.

"Cher, what's up? We are still on for lunch, right?"

"Yes, and I have to ask you another favor," she said, peering out of her office. She was scared even to leave.

"Sure," he said.

"Can you please come by my office right now? Cortez just showed up, and he scared the shit out of me, and I'm not sure if he is really gone," she said, still shaken up.

"Sure, I can be there as soon as possible," he said, and Cher could tell he was ruffling papers. She heard what sounded like latches closing on a briefcase, so she knew he'd hurry.

"Thank you so much, Terry. I don't know what I'm going to do. I don't know how he found out about my new location," she said, hoping he wouldn't return.

"Who knows, Cher? Just hang tight. I'll be there shortly."

"Can you stay on with me until then? I know I shouldn't be this scared, but I am," she confessed.

"It's okay, Cher. Whatever you need," he said.

They talked until he pulled into the parking space next to her car. She unlocked the door and locked it again quickly.

"Thank you, Terry," she said and put a faint smile on her face. She blinked, but she couldn't blink back the tears.

He walked up and held her. "Shhhh, it's okay. I won't let him hurt you," he said, and Cher felt safe.

"I wish that were true. You can't be with me twenty-four seven," she sobbed.

"Yes, I can," he said and lifted Cher's chin. There was an attraction between them since the first night they met, and even though Cher tried to deny it, it was there. He kissed her deeply, and another knock on the door made Cher jump, but it was only her new receptionist. She wiped her face with her hands and let her in. Terry took a seat in her office while she got acquainted with her new receptionist and showed her around. Cher didn't want to leave her alone while she went to lunch with Terry, so she told her just to come back the next day.

Cher and Terry headed to lunch, and after the papers were signed and the business was out of the way, they began to talk about their attraction to one another. Cher smiled and enjoyed Terry's company, but she was hesitant because she thought maybe it was too soon to start seeing someone.

"So when will you let me take you on a real date?" he asked.

"What do you call this?" she joked.

"I thought this was a business lunch."

"Well, I feel like it's a business-lunch-slash-date. I mean, I signed the papers two glasses of wine ago," she said and smiled.

"True," he confirmed, gazing at her. Cher was in her early forties, but it looked like she was still in her early thirties. "You are truly gorgeous," he said, and she put her head down. "Did I say something wrong?"

"No, I just don't care to hear that compliment anymore. I've heard it so many times that I think it's the only thing men like about me, and 'gorgeous' went to my head for a long time. I want to be recognized for what's in here," she said, pointing to her heart, "not what's out here," she said, moving her hand in a circular motion around her face.

"Well, I hear you, and I understand, but I can't help but admire your beauty because that is all I can see, but if you give me a chance to get to know what's in there," he said to her chest, "I'll be able to tell you that you have a beautiful inside to match your beautiful outside," he said.

She smiled again, felt attracted to Terry, and wanted to get to know him.

"So tell me a bit about you. I mean, the real stuff, not the first-date stuff, because you don't have to impress me with words. Skip to the real you," she said, and he decided to be honest.

"Well, I am from Chicago, born and raised. The eldest of four, I have three younger sisters. As you know, my mom is no longer here, and my dad is still serving a life sentence for what he did to her," he said and continued after a deep breath.

"I went to Harvard, been practicing law for fourteen years, and I made partner quite some time ago. Let's see, I'm divorced, one daughter is thirteen, well, she is my ex's daughter, but she only knows me as her dad, and I just ended a two-year relationship with someone about four months ago. Now I'm single, have been dating a little, nothing serious, and that's that. You know where I live because you sold me my house.

"I have no fetishes or addictions, and when I can make the time, I love to cook, and I'm actually good at it," he said and Cher hoped everything he said was legit and that those were not just impressive words.

"So why did you and your ex break up?" she asked and sipped.

"You want me to be honest?" he joked.

"Yes, I want you to be honest."

"She had intimacy issues," he said softly.

"I'm sorry, come again?"

"She had issues with sex," he said, and Cher held in her laugh and wanted to know more.

"Explain," she said.

"Well, I'm not sure what happened to her, but she never wanted to have sex, and when she did allow it, it had to be completely dark, and I couldn't touch her in certain places, and she didn't want to touch me, and it was just an unhealthy sexual disorder. I tried to understand because I cared about her, but she wasn't getting any better, and she refused to get help. I tried to make it work, but when you love someone, you want to be intimate with them, and it would be weeks, and she wouldn't allow me to touch her. I begged her to see someone, but she told me I was the one with the problem, so I told her that I couldn't handle it and wasn't happy. I came home from work one evening, and she was gone and left me a note.

"It hurt so bad at first, you know, and I tried to convince her to come back, but we both knew it was better that she didn't," he said, took a sip of his drink, and looked around the room. His eyes landed back on her. She was quiet, so he said, "Tell me about you."

"Well, you know I am married to an abuser, I have a son, and right now I'm going through a divorce," she said and laughed. "My horrible life in a nutshell," she said and polished off her drink.

"Your life is not horrible. You are still here, standing strong and moving on, so there is a brighter side," he said, sounding positive.

"Yeah, I guess," she said sadly.

"What are you doing tonight? There is this spot called Roberson's, and the food is delicious."

"I know. My best friend and husband own the place," she said.

"What? Get out! That is my favorite spot. I go so often. They know me by name," he said, and Cher wondered why she never ran into him before.

"Oh, yeah, well, they know me by name too," she joked. He laughed, and Cher looked at her watch. It was after three, and she had to get her son. "Listen, I have to get my son. I will get a sitter, and you can pick me up around eight," she said, and he waved for the bill. He paid and they left.

Cher got C.J. and her things from Katrina's, and she felt funny walking into her house. It was quiet and spotless, but it didn't feel like home, she thought as she went from room to room, making sure the place was okay.

She set her alarm and called her local sitter, and she agreed to sit with C.J. that night. She dressed, and Terry picked her up on time. She had a ball with him, and Kennedy and Julian thought it was hilarious that Cher walked in with one of their regular customers. Kennedy and Julian ended up sitting with them, and they ate and drank. Cher was happy to see Kennedy smiling because she hadn't smiled much since the funeral. Cher and her new friend helped get her mind off her dad for a little while, Cher figured, and she was glad.

When Cher got home, she felt better and wanted to see Terry again, and she hoped he'd ask her out again.

"Thank you for tonight. I had a great time," Cher said.

"No, thank you. I've thought about you a lot lately, and I am so glad you agreed to have dinner with me. I was hoping we could get together again and laugh over another meal," he said.

"I'd like that," she said with a smile.

"How about Saturday night?" he asked.

"I will have to confirm with my sitter, but I'm sure that won't be a problem," she said, reaching for the handle to get out.

"Let me walk you to your door," he offered, and they both got out.

"Again, thanks, Terry," Cher said, pausing at the door. She wanted him to kiss her like he kissed her earlier that morning before they were interrupted by Pat, her new receptionist.

"You're welcome, Cher. I had a great time," he said, and they stared for a couple of moments, and he leaned in and gave her what she wanted. It was soft and nice, and Cher hated that the night had to end. They broke away from each other with bright smiles. "So Saturday, right? Let's say around seven," he said.

"That sounds good," Cher said, and he headed for his car. "Good night, Terry," she said.

"Good night, Cher," he replied and waited until she was inside before he got in.

Cher was on cloud nine until she looked at the caller ID on her ringing cell phone. It was Cortez, and her thought was, *who the hell gave him my new cell number?*

Chapter Thirty-four

"What about this?" Kenya asked Kennedy, and she looked up.

"I guess Goodwill," Kennedy said to another one of her dad's suits. Most of them were new and had never been worn, and Kennedy was surprised her daddy had so many tailor-made suits that she had never seen him in. They were too big for Julian because Kennedy's dad was close to six five, and alterations were out of the question. "This is going to take forever," Kennedy said because they had been there for hours, and it seemed they weren't making any progress.

"I know, so how about we take a break and go and grab a bite and a glass of wine or two and come back and get a little more done today?" Kenya suggested.

"Yes, that sounds good," Kennedy said, and they headed down the steps. They went out, and Kennedy decided she'd drive. "So how is the job search going?" Kennedy asked because Kenya had just recently gotten laid off from her job.

"Not so good. I have been on several interviews, but no one has called me back yet."

"What exactly do you do?"

"Well, pretty much anything. I don't have a degree, but I've worked clerical and sales mostly," she said. "I'll admit I'm a little embarrassed because you are a college graduate and have a much better lifestyle than I do. This inheritance from your father is a blessing. It was enough to handle a lot of back debt. I got a newer car now, so lack of transportation isn't an issue. I am just trying to reserve as much money as possible until I can get real income. My husband is a police officer, but he doesn't make much, and even though we own our home, we have a mortgage. Before the inheritance, we were on the verge of losing it. Our marriage is going sour, and things are not good now," she shared, and Kennedy reached over and grabbed her hand.

"Why didn't you tell me before?"

"Because I was a little embarrassed. You have a beautiful home, a great husband, and you're educated. And I sometimes wonder if I'd had Mom whether I would have turned out like you. Your life is so great. I just want better for myself, like a do-over or something."

"Well, it's never too late to start over, Kenya. Plus, you have me now, which means you have a family. I'll support you and help you. You don't have to stay with him if you don't want to, and I'm not saying we are rich, but we're okay. I know a few people, and a few of my friends have businesses. I'll check and see if they are hiring for any positions," Kennedy offered.

"Thanks, Kennedy, that would be great. Thank you for everything," she said humbly, and Kennedy was glad to help.

"As a matter of fact, hold on," she said, digging for her phone. She called her store, and the Bluetooth connected to her car.

"KBanks Jewelers, this is Tiffany," she sang.

"Hey, Tif, this is Kennedy. Is Teresa around?"

"Sure, hang on," she said.

"Kennedy," Teresa said when she picked up. "Hey, hon, how are things?"

"Better. Taking it one day at a time," she said and got back to why she was calling. "Listen, I told you about my sister, and she is currently looking for a job. You think you could mold her into a jeweler? She has sales experience, and I'm sure she'd be a good fit," Kennedy said, knowing Teresa wouldn't say no. How could she? Kennedy was still the owner.

"Of course. She is your sister. How can I say no?" Teresa teased.

"You're right about that," Kennedy said and laughed a little.

"When can she start?" Teresa asked.

She looked at Kenya and smiled.

"Tomorrow," Kenya said with a bright smile, looking like Kennedy's momma, Kennedy thought, but she didn't comment on it.

"Okay, tell her to be here at nine, so we can get her paperwork done, and I can show her around."

"Okay, cool," Kennedy said, about to hang up, but Teresa called her name.

"Kay, are you sure you want to hire family? I mean, you've only known her for five minutes," Teresa said, and Kennedy knew she meant well.

"Well, Ree, she can hear you because you're on speaker, and don't worry," she said.

"Okay, and, Kenya, nothing personal."

"It's cool. I understand your concerns. You're not the only one with the same apprehensions."

"Thanks for understanding. Kennedy, call me later," she said, and they hung up.

"Wow, Kennedy, thank you so much. You and your family have been more than generous to me," she said.

"Kenya, you are my sister, and I know Momma had her reasons for not telling me about you, and I am sure my daddy wanted to tell me but kept his word to my momma even to his grave. The life I had with Momma you should have had also. I am glad I know now that I have a sister, so you don't have to say thank you. It is my pleasure," she said, pulling into the parking lot of Julian's restaurant.

"I heard this place is nice," Kenya said.

"I hope so. It's one of ours," Kennedy said, reaching behind the seat for her purse.

"How many restaurants do you guys own?"

"We own four restaurants and six nightclubs. We spend most of our time at Jay's and Roberson's, though, because those are my husband's babies."

"Wow, that is great. How do you have the time?"

"Well, it's a lot of work, but it has its benefits. So far, we've been blessed, and business has been truly good. If you're looking to start a business, I will help you, but it takes dedication," Kennedy said and opened her door. When they went inside, the staff recognized Kennedy immediately, and she introduced everyone to her sister. They ordered drinks and appetizers to start and were quiet for a few short moments.

"How did you and Julian meet?"

"Wow, I haven't told that story in a long time," Kennedy said and laughed.

"Well, I'm dying to hear it. I mean, he is like this knight in shining armor, the way Rob used to be," she sighed.

"Used to be, huh? It's okay to talk about it," Kennedy said, hoping she wasn't prying.

"To be honest, before your dad died, we were splitting up. He moved out, and then word got to him through some mutual friends about the inheritance, and boom, he comes home singing a new tune. I love my husband, Kennedy, and I want to be with him, but I believe he only came back because of the money and not me. I am so serious when I tell you I had to change the limit of how much could be charged to the account daily because he was spending money like we became millionaires," she said, sharing.

"Did you confront him about it?"

"Yes and no. I guess I was afraid he'd leave again, and that is something I don't want. We have our daughter, and she needs both of us. I just told him that he has to slow down with his spending. I haven't seen a dime of his paycheck since we got the money. He just does whatever he wants with his entire paycheck."

"Do you want my advice?"

"Sure," she said, and the server placed their drinks on the table.

"Well, you can do it one of two ways. What I would have done years ago is talk to him and hear what he had to say and probably end up never knowing if it was for me or the money, and that is the option you use if you want to be naive because you truly want him to stay even if it is for the money. Option two: the new and improved Kennedy would withdraw every dime and put it into another account, tell him that there was a mistake in the inheritance, and you have to return what's left and see how he reacts. See if he sings the same 'I wanna work it out' tune or if he heads for the hills again," Kennedy said because she hated the idea of her little sister being played by a man who knew he had her heart in his hands.

"But we have spent a lot of it. I mean, I have a good amount left, but not enough to not go to work," Kenya said.

"So tell him the lawyer has agreed to work out a reasonable repayment plan to see if his attitude shifts. If he starts singing the same song as before the money, let him go, Kenya. I know you love him, but you are beautiful and don't have to waste your time on a man who doesn't love you back. The ultimate decision is yours, little sister."

"I don't know, Kennedy."

"Well, I know now that you truly are my sister," Kennedy said, and Kenya tilted her head with a curious look.

"Listen, I've been on the played end a time or two, maybe even three times in my life. Believe it or not, Cher and I wouldn't be speaking this day if it weren't for me wising up and doing what was best for me. Cher and I went through a horrible episode that put us apart for a long time, but if I hadn't taken a stand when I did and did what I did to cut off the relationship, I'd probably be single, with no kids, because I almost let Julian slip through my fingers. After all, I didn't want to face the truth. Cher and I are good now, Kenya, and who is to say you and Rob won't make it and live happily ever after? Make sure he is there for you and your daughter, not the money. Trust me. You will feel better when it is all done with or without him."

"What if he leaves? I'm not the young and hot chick I used to be. And I'm far from being skinny," she said, and her eyes watered.

"Then you can cry over ice cream or wine on my shoulder until you get over him. And you are beautiful, Kenya. So what you are not young and thin? Neither am I, but I found someone to love me as I am, and so can you. You shouldn't be with him if you have doubts, Kenya. You are too good and too gorgeous for that. Whether you believe me or not, it isn't going to stop eating at you. If by chance you choose option A and talk to him, he convinces you that it's not about the money and that money runs out, and he leaves you, you are going to feel worse," she said.

Kenya agreed. "Wow, it's going to be hard, but it has to be done," she agreed and paused when the server came back with their appetizer. "I mean, before I was contacted about the inheritance, my house was close to being foreclosed on, and he moved out even though I lost my job, and I was terrified, Kennedy. I was thinking, 'God, what am I going to do? I have this little girl, and I have friends, but you can't depend on them for everything.' I got tired of borrowing money, you know. I have a few friends who began to avoid me because I owed them so much.

"Rob came home the day we were originally supposed to go to the reading of the will, acting like a husband, apologizing for walking out and promising me that he wanted to work it out. He started making plans for the money before I knew how much it would be or when I would get it. I tried to avoid the truth, Kennedy, but I honestly don't think he would have come back if your daddy hadn't left me anything, so I do wanna know," she said, and Kennedy reached for her hand.

"It will be okay, Kenya, and you are not alone. You have me. We are sisters, and we have much more catching up to do. I know we barely know each other, but I don't want to see you sad and hurt, especially over a man," she said, trying to make her little sister smile. She reminded her so much of their mother that Kennedy felt close to her even though they hardly knew each other.

"Thanks, Kennedy. You are way more than I expected a sister could be. Just wish me luck, and," she said, holding up a finger, "if Rob is full of shit and leaves me after I put him to this test, I'm going to need all the chardonnay and ice cream that you can afford because, despite it all, I love him," she said. Kennedy squeezed her hand again.

"I know, Kenya. Trust me, I know," she said, and Kennedy waved for the server to order more wine. They ate and decided to pick up their kids before heading back to the house to pack up more of Kennedy's father's things. They ordered the kids pizza, and Kenya promised Kennedy that she would be strong and do what was necessary to learn the truth.

The next morning, Kenya met with Teresa at the jewelry store, and on her lunch, she withdrew all the money from her account but $700—the amount in the account the day they got the check from the firm. She opened a new account and put every dime into it. When she got home, she broke the news to Rob, and he was furious. He cussed and fussed and told her he needed to go out for some air, and the next morning when Kenya got up to get ready for work, he still hadn't come home.

Chapter Thirty-five

Leila pulled up to her agency and was surprised to see Devon's car. She got out of her Armada and headed for the door, and Devon approached with coffee and muffins. She opened the door and went to turn on the lights, and Devon set the bag and coffee on the counter. She came out and looked at him, and she laughed.

"Why are you laughing?" he asked.

"Because I bet you I can tell you what flavor muffins are in that bag," she teased.

"What? What are you talking about?"

"When you are in a great mood, you get strawberry cream cheese. When you are excited about something, you normally get cranberry, and if I remember accurately, when something is heavy on your mind, you get the apple," she said, and he laughed with her.

"Wow, I didn't even know that about myself, and you are right," he said.

"So which is it this morning? I'm guessing apple because it's ten a.m. and you're not in your office," she said and reached for the bag, and it was apple. "Okay, spill it. What's going on?"

"First of all, I hate that you've become my best friend."

"Well, I think I've been in your life the longest, so I earned that spot by default. Now tell me, what brings you here?"

"I think Alicia is back with her ex-husband," he said.

Leila looked at him strangely, wondering why he would think that. "So are you going to tell me why you think she is or what happened?"

"Because the other night, I went by her place after leaving the restaurant, and there was an SUV in her driveway with North Carolina plates. I sat outside her house, called and texted her for about fifteen minutes, and she didn't answer or reply to my texts."

"Well, Devon, you won't know for sure unless you ask," she advised and took a bite of the muffin.

"I know, but I don't want her to think I was stalking. Yes, I went by, but I didn't expect to get there and see his vehicle in her driveway."

"Have you called her?"

"No, but she's been blowing up my phone and texting me. I haven't replied, and she left me a message last night."

"What did she say?"

"I didn't listen to it."

"Devon, come on, man, are you kidding me? You are a grown-ass man. Listen to the message, call her, and get to the bottom of what's happening. Don't be playing this game of not answering phone calls and texts. See what she has to say."

"I know, Lei, I know. I'm just afraid she is going to confirm what I think, and I'm not ready to feel that pain right now."

"Or maybe she can confirm that she is not, and maybe there were other issues that prevented her from answering your calls and texts the other night, and you can proceed with your proposal," Leila suggested.

"I don't know, Leila. I think I should just let this one go."

"Okay, I guess you don't love her then," Leila said and grabbed one of the cups of coffee.

"Excuse me. Lei, you know that I love her. Where did that come from?"

"From the coward standing in front of me afraid to put himself out there. Listen to me, Devon. You have to face the truth, whatever that truth may be. If she and the ex are back together, you move on. If they are not and you want to be with her, ask her. If she says no, then you deal with that, Devon. If you don't go to her and handle this, you will be more miserable, so stop being a bitch about it and man up. I've never seen you run away from love with your damn tail between your legs, so go and get your woman," Leila encouraged him.

He thanked Leila again for her advice, and when he got into the car, he listened to the message she had left the night before, and he let out a sigh of relief when her last words were, "I love you."

He headed to the school instead of his office. He went to the office and asked if she was available, and the secretary called her room and said a parent was there to speak with her, and she told them she'd be available ten minutes after the next bell. It would be her lunch break, so they gave Devon a visitor's pass after he showed his ID. When the bell rang, he headed to her classroom and tapped on the door. When she saw that it was him, she rushed to the door.

"Devon, I'm so happy to see you," she said and wrapped her arms around his neck. "I called you a thousand times yesterday," she said, and he pulled away, and she looked confused.

"I have something to ask you, Alicia, and I want the truth," he said seriously.

"Okay, what is it?"

"Are you and your ex-husband back together?"

"No. He came into town the other night, but we are not back together, Devon."

"Did you sleep with your ex-husband?"

"No, hell no. Where did you get that from?"

"Why didn't you make it to dinner and then turn around and ignore my calls for the rest of the night?"

"Devon, listen, baby, okay. I'm sorry I missed dinner. I didn't know Anthony and A.J. were coming into town. Before I headed out the other night, the bell rang. I thought you decided to pick me up instead, and when I opened the door, it was my ex and my son. I was shocked, but I was so happy to see my son. I couldn't just leave when my baby had just arrived. When I called you, nosy-ass Anthony walked in, and I hadn't told him that I was involved with anyone, so I ended the call."

"Why didn't you tell him?"

"At first I didn't, but last night he started talking about us getting back together," she tried to say.

"Is that what you want?"

"Baby, no, wait, let me finish. He told my son that we were going to work it out, and I was surprised, but after I put my son to bed, I made it clear to Anthony that there would be no getting back together and told him that I was involved with someone. Devon, I told him the truth, and I also told him that he needed to find another place to stay while he's in town," she said genuinely.

"Alicia, are you sure you don't want to work things out with him?"

"Devon, I'm positive. I love you, and I wanna be right here with you. And I know that may mean I don't get sole custody of my son, but I will not be forced into a relationship with Anthony. I will only get to see my son for breaks and the holidays, but that is the effect of the foolish choice I made years ago when I gave Anthony custody. I have to live with my decision, and I want to do that with you, not go back to him because I don't want him, I want you," she said, and Devon pulled her close.

"I love you, Alicia, and I am glad I was wrong. I thought the worst and am so glad I was wrong."

"All you had to do was talk to me, Devon."

"I know, and I'm sorry for ignoring you yesterday. I was just angry."

"I'm sorry, too, for not answering the other night. I just panicked that night, and I'm sorry I missed the dinner and missed meeting your friends. I was looking forward to it," she said.

"That's not all you missed," he said and had the ring in his pocket.

"What else did I miss? Did something spectacular happen?"

"No, but something spectacular was supposed to happen," he said.

She looked confused. "Like?" she asked, and Devon reached into his pocket.

"I wanted to ask you something important," he said and opened the box, and her mouth opened wide as the sea.

"Ask me what, baby?" she said excitedly. He knew that she knew what that diamond meant.

"To spend the rest of your life with me?" he said, taking the ring from the box and sliding it on.

"Oh, my. This is real. You're not joking," she said, blinking a thousand times.

"Yes, this is real and not a joke," Devon said, hoping her answer would part her lips quickly.

"Yes, Mr. Vanpelt. It would be an honor to spend the rest of my life with you," she said, and Devon was able to breathe. He took her into his arms and squeezed her tight. "I can't believe this. I didn't see this coming," she said.

"Well, I was terrified you'd say no," he said, being honest.

"Are you crazy? No way would I have turned you down. You are the man of my dreams," she said and gave him another kiss.

"I love you," he said.

"I love you too, Devon."

"So when do I get to meet your son?" he asked.

"How about tonight? We can go to dinner, just in case my ex is still lurking around my house."

"That's fine, but know that I will be picking you up," he said.

"Fine, but understand that Anthony can be an asshole at times, and when he sees this ring and knows the truth, he will probably turn into a major asshole," she said.

"Well, I know how to deal with assholes, Alicia, so I'm good," he said and smiled.

She kissed him and admired her ring, and they chatted until her lunch break was done. Devon kissed her good-bye and said that he and Deja would be there around seven thirty, and he left. As soon as he got into the car, he called Leila to tell her the good news.

Chapter Thirty-six

When K.P. and Robin made it to the villa, he called Janiece immediately, and Robin rolled her eyes. She knew his wife was insecure and was giving Kerry the blues, and she wanted to relax his mind. Kerry had her on speaker, and she could hear Janiece expressing how much she already missed and loved him. He assured her he'd call her after dinner, and Janiece got off the phone satisfied.

"This place is beautiful. I feel like I'm in a dream," Robin said, walking into the great room.

"Yes, this is nice. I've stayed with my wife before a couple of times, but we'd always get the honeymoon villa, nothing this large. I just wanted something large enough in case the family had to fly out here. The romantic theme we had didn't come with four bedrooms and four baths," he said and chuckled a little.

"Wow, I can imagine that this would not have been the honeymoon choice. However, this place is the bomb, and if the family has to come, I will stay out of the way," Robin said and went over to the bar to fix a drink. "Do you mind if I have a drink before we go to dinner? I feel a little edgy from the flight," she expressed.

"No, I don't mind at all," he said and approached her. "I'll have a scotch myself. And if the family does join us, I want you to be a part of everything. I need Janiece to get to know you. This space is large enough for us all. I just want my wife to see that you are an amazing assistant," he said, and they went to the patio and sat.

"Wow, boss, this is spectacular. The pool and hot tub are like so inviting. And I hear you. I want Mrs. Paxton to know that we are strictly business. If we are here long enough for her to come out, I'll do my best to kill any ill thoughts. You are a good boss," she said with a smile. They sipped, and then she yelled, "Hell, I wanna take a swim. I'll order food," she said, went to the pool, and dipped a toe in. The water was nice and warm. The sun was going down, and it was a beautiful view.

"We can order in, and if you brought a swimsuit, go change and take a dip," he said, looking out at the sunset.

She hurried inside and came back ten minutes later in a two-piece. K.P. ordered dinner for them, and it arrived an hour after she played around in the pool.

"Man, I could live out here on this patio. All I need is food and water," she joked and sat across from K.P. She looked over at him, and he looked sexy as hell. They had dinner, and Robin was so happy to be alone with him.

After a while, she convinced him to take her to the strip because she had never been to Vegas. She kept pulling K.P. in different directions and felt like she was with her man. K.P. gave her a couple hundred to play the slots with while he played the tables. She tried to refuse, but he was always a generous host, so she just went with it. Back-to-back drinks had her nice and horny, but she knew it was too soon to make her moves.

When she went to his table, he was $7,000 up, so she stood as he played. After he was done, she convinced him to go into a club, and since she knew he was tipsy too, it didn't take a lot of convincing. They stepped into one of the clubs, and she got him on the dance floor. They danced a couple of songs, and then he tapped Robin on the shoulder and told her he was ready to head back. K.P.'s car took them back, and K.P. went straight to the shower and did not return for a long time.

Robin tapped on his door and begged him to come out to the pool with her. He came out in a tank and pajama pants. He sat, and she walked by him slowly with her plump ass and round hips, giving K.P. an eyeful, and she noticed that he didn't turn away.

"Robin, it's late. I'm exhausted, and we have a full day tomorrow."

"I know," she said and dived in. She swam to the other side and came up in front of K.P. She smiled, lay back, and then did a few backstrokes. Her breasts were sitting on top of the water, and she knew K.P. had to admire her body.

"Interesting," he said and stood. "I'm going to turn in," he announced, and Robin paused.

"Already?"

"Yes, it is late, and we have an early morning. Good night."

He went inside, and she swam to the steps. She wanted the night to end differently, but she reminded herself that she had three days to seduce him, so she got out and headed to her room. She had to bed him before Janiece and the kids landed in Las Vegas. As an assistant, that would give her a couple more nights alone with him. She thought she'd be able to arouse him the first night. Still, she knew now that K.P. wasn't like the rest of the old horny-ass dogs she used to work for, because a sexy two-piece was always the weapon that had her bent over in front of a pussy-hungry CEO, groaning. Still, K.P. had a healthy marriage and acted as if she were invisible.

"Oh, well, I'll get him tomorrow," she said aloud and went to shower. When she got out, she admired herself while tossing seductive ideas around her head. She knew she would have him fucking her in the pool before they got on a plane to go back to Chicago, so she figured she'd wear the wavy look until the trip was over.

***

The next morning, K.P. was up early and ready to get to the office to see what was going on and if he had to fire everyone. Robin walked out dressed to impress, looking flawless and smelling good as usual, and when K.P. looked up, she hit him with her beautiful smile.

"Good morning, boss man. You're looking sharp. Is that a new suit?"

"No, this is a suit I left behind when I was here before that they kept for me," he replied and sipped his tea.

"Well, that is a nice color, and it looks good on you," she said and took a seat.

"I ordered breakfast. I got a little bit of everything. I didn't know what you'd like," Kerry said.

"Thanks, Kerry, this is nice," she said, and he arched a brow and let the fact that she called him Kerry and not Mr. Paxton go since they were not in the office.

"Well, a car will be here in about fifteen minutes," he said and looked at his watch. "I'm going to run and call Janiece," he said.

"Okay, I'll hurry," she said and started to load up her plate. She ate quickly when he headed to the office space on that floor.

After her delicious breakfast, she went to the restroom to touch up her makeup. The car arrived, and her stomach was doing somersaults because she didn't know what to expect when she walked in with K.P. She hoped the matter took longer to resolve than that day since Collin was out of town.

She knew she scrambled up the numbers and hoped no one else was there to reveal her secret that morning. She knew she'd break K.P. by the time Collin was back, and there was no way he'd be mad or terminate her after she put the good-good on him.

They walked in unannounced, and when Madison saw K.P., she hurried over to greet him. "Mr. Paxton, how nice to see you," she said, and K.P. greeted her with a hug. Madison started way back when he opened that location, and she was still there and doing an outstanding job, according to her evaluations.

"Hey, Mattie, how are you? It is great to see you too. Why didn't you tell me that you were expecting? Janiece is going to flip."

"I'm sorry, sir. This was a surprise, and I didn't get happy about it until a couple of weeks ago, so I'm having a baby," she said, and K.P. smiled. "What brings you out to Vegas, sir? It's been ages since you've graced us with your presence."

"I am here to see Collin and go over some numbers," K.P. said, and Madison looked at him strangely.

"Well, Collin won't be back for another couple of days. He is on vacation. I thought you knew, sir."

"No, I didn't know. I didn't get that info. The last thing I got from him was the month's numbers, which prompted me to come out here."

"Wow, well, Collin revoked our access to that info maybe like a year ago, and I have no idea how to see those reports anymore. I mean, I can call him for you. I'm sure he'll give you his passcodes, but his office is locked."

"No, Mattie, no worries. I'll be in town for a couple more days, so I'll just come back on Thursday. Just do me a favor and let me surprise him. I don't want him to know I'm in town," he said, and Mattie nodded in agreement. "Restricted access makes no sense and makes me a bit more suspicious because you are the executive assistant of this office."

"I agreed that was a bit much, but I didn't want to make waves. I love my job, and I just do what he asks and go home, so no problem, sir, I won't say a word," she assured him.

"Thanks, Mattie, and today lunch is on me. Just order whatever the office wants and charge it to the company card," K.P said, and he and Robin left. The car was still out front, so he took them back to the villa.

"So what now?" Robin said, relieved. She was so happy she'd have a couple more days with him, and she planned to take advantage.

"Nothing, chill time. You can catch some shows, gamble, and see the sights," he suggested.

"That's cool. We should go to the wax museum. I heard it's nice."

"No, I meant you," he said.

"Come on, Mr. Paxton, this is Las Vegas. I can't sightsee by myself. You gotta hang with me. It would be boring to go alone," she whined.

"Okay, let's go back and change, and I'll show you Vegas," he said, and she wanted to do flips.

"Ohhhh, goodie, I'm so excited," she said, bursting.

When they got back, K.P. went to change and came out in something casual. Robin came out in a long, sexy sundress and flats, looking like a superstar as usual. She expected K.P. to compliment how gorgeous she looked, but he didn't compliment her. His phone rang, and he held up a finger and walked away. She knew that was his bugging-ass wife, Janiece, as he went outside to take the call while Robin impatiently waited.

He spent the first five minutes getting updates on the kids and the next twenty assuring Janiece that he loved her and would be home by Thursday night or Friday, so she didn't need to come. He told her that Collin was out of town, and as soon as he was done meeting with him, he'd be on the first plane home, and Janiece disputed this. He tried to explain that it would be pointless for her to come for a day, but she pouted that he was going back on his word.

"Jai, I said three days, meaning if after three days I'd have to stay longer, and that is not the case. Yes, it will be three days of me being here before I finish up, but that is it. I'll be home the next day if all goes well. If not, then we can talk about you coming here."

"Okay, Kerry, whatever. Have fun," she snapped and hung up.

K.P. wasn't in the mood, so he didn't call her back. He went inside to see Robin sitting on the sofa waiting, so he told her, "Let's go see Vegas!"

Chapter Thirty-seven

Christa stood in her baby's nursery and held her little belly. She was excited and couldn't wait to meet her baby. She hoped she looked like Isaiah because he was beautiful in so many ways to her. She went over to her baby's ultrasound picture and rubbed her finger across it, and Isaiah walked in.

"Hey, Mrs. Lawton, can you believe this is our life?" Isaiah asked.

"No, honestly, I can't. I mean, if you had asked me a couple of years ago where I saw my life going, I never would have imagined it being this good. Being madly in love, married, and pregnant, nope, never saw this good thing coming," she said, beaming. She hadn't felt that happy in her entire life.

"I agree. When Janiece moved back in and tried to make our thing work, I felt every time I touched her that she didn't belong to me, but I pretended that I couldn't see it. I ignored it because I wanted it to work badly, but it's the opposite with you. I feel it in your touch, your kiss, and how you look at me. I didn't have that with Janiece after I came home," he said, walking up close to her, and he wrapped his arms around her.

"I know it was like that with Devon. I know I may have been a pain in his ass with the Leila comments and my insecurities, but that look he used to give her when they were in the same room, I never got that look from him, and I just thank God I get that look from you. When you look at me, it's like your eyes can touch my insides, and I know that this is the real deal," she said. He kissed her neck. He moved down to her breast. "Baby, are you trying to get some?"

"Is it that obvious?" he joked.

"Yes," she said and closed her eyes. She put her hand over his hands and helped him to massage her breast, and then the doorbell rang. "Who the hell can that be?" she asked, surprised at the chime.

"I don't know," Isaiah said and adjusted his jeans. They both headed for the door, and it was his ex-wife. "Jai, is everything okay? Is my daughter okay?" Isaiah asked in a panic.

"Jaiden is fine, Isaiah, but I need to talk to you. Janelle is out of town with Gregory on this couple thingy, and I need someone to talk to," she cried.

"Okay. Christa, babe, can you give us a minute?" he asked, and Christa nodded and then headed up the steps. "Have a seat," Isaiah offered, and she did.

"I think my husband is having an affair," Janiece blurted.

"K.P.? Ha, he is the husband of the century," he said, making fun of her.

"It's not a joke, Isaiah. I think he is sleeping with his assistant."

"Okay, Jai, what makes you think that, and have you confronted him?"

"Yes, I confronted him, and he denies it. Now he is off in Vegas on 'business,'" she said, doing air quotes, and Isaiah still wondered why she came to him.

"What has he done to make you feel insecure?"

"Nothing, Isaiah, he hasn't done anything, but she is gorgeous, young, pretty, and flawless. She is single and has no kids, and I know she is trying to seduce my husband."

"Okay, Jai, listen. It sounds like you are having a problem with him having a hot assistant. K.P. loves you, Janiece, and I can't see him throwing away everything over some hot assistant."

"How can you be so sure, Isaiah? I mean, I was K.P.'s mistress for five fucking years," she said, holding up five fingers.

"Yes, he didn't love Kimberly, but he loves you. That man suffered ninety days with you being here with me and still took your ass back, Janiece. K.P. loves you too much," he said, trying to make her feel better.

"What if you're wrong?"

"I don't know, Jai. If you feel so strongly, go out there and see what's happening. Just pop up. I'm sure if something is going on, somebody will get caught with their pants down," he said, and Janiece thanked him for listening and for his advice.

She left, and as soon as she got into her car, she called to get an airline ticket.

Chapter Thirty-eight

Devon arrived on time with Deja, and they got out. He walked up to Alicia's door and was greeted by her ex. Devon and Deja came in, and he prepared himself for whatever.

"Hi, I'm Anthony, Alley's husband," he said, and Devon laughed a little.

"I'm Devon, Alicia's fiancé," he said, and Anthony's jaws flared.

"Have a seat. Alley will be out in a minute," he said.

Devon and Deja sat on the sofa, and then a little boy came out, and Devon assumed it was her son. He looked like the photo but a little older.

"Dad, are you coming with us to dinner?" he asked.

"No, son, it will be your mom and her friend Devon here, and . . . I'm sorry, sweetheart, what is your name?" he asked Deja.

"My name is Deja," she said and smiled at Alicia's son.

"Why can't you come too?"

"Because your mom doesn't want me to come, but we will have dinner together as a family tomorrow," he said, and Devon smirked. He knew Anthony was a sarcastic asshole.

"Okay," A.J. said sadly and put his head down.

"Hey, Devon," Alicia said when she entered the room, and Devon stood.

"Hey, baby, you look beautiful," he complimented her and kissed her. He could feel Anthony's eyes on him, so he thought it would be best to get going.

"Thank you, so do you," she said and turned to Deja. "Hi, Deja," she added.

"Hi," Deja said.

"Well, this is my son, Anthony Jr. A.J., this is Devon and Deja," she introduced them.

"Nice to meet you," Devon said and shook his hand. "Are we all set?"

"Yes, let me grab my keys," Alicia said and went into her bedroom. They were leaving when Anthony called Devon's name.

"Can I have a word?" he asked, and Alicia looked at Anthony with a look, but Devon gave her a nod to go and get into the car.

"Okay, Anthony, what is it?" Devon asked once Alicia and the kids were in the car.

"So tell me, how long have you and Alley been seeing each other?"

"Why do you need to know that information?" Devon asked, looking him in the eyes.

"Because that is my son's mother, and she is my concern," he snapped.

"Your son is your concern, and my relationship with Alicia is not any of your business, and I don't have to tell you how long we've been together. If you want info about us, ask Alicia. You will know if she cares to disclose that to you."

"Listen, Devon, I'm only trying to talk to you man to man, but I see how it is. I'll just holla at Alley. It's not hard to get what I want from her," he said, and Devon didn't even flex. He shook his head and decided to end this conversation.

"Good night, Anthony," he said and turned to walk away.

When he got into the car, Alicia wanted to know what was said. "What did he want?"

"Nothing important," he said and pulled out of the driveway.

They went to dinner and had a great evening. When they returned, Devon asked Alicia to go home with him, but she insisted he wait until school was out. They only had two more days before school was over.

"Okay, I'll wait, but I will be honest, I don't want Anthony here," he said, and Alicia agreed.

"Baby, I know, but I don't want to make waves with Anthony or upset my son. Anthony is harmless," she said and gave him a sweet kiss. He wanted her and didn't want their night to end, but he had to get Deja home.

"Okay, but I'll see you tomorrow, right?" he asked.

"Yes, I'll come home and grab A.J., and we will be over," she said, and he gave her one last kiss. She went inside, and then he went and got back into the car.

"Dad, how are you okay with her ex staying there?" Deja asked.

"I'm not, D.J., but I have no control over that. Alicia is my fiancée, not my daughter. I can't make her make him leave."

"But if she loves you, she'd tell him to leave."

"Listen, Deja, people can be friends with their ex and not have anything going on."

"Seriously, Dad?"

"Yes. Your mom and I are like best friends, so it's possible, D.J.," he said.

"I guess you're right," she said and looked out the window.

Devon grabbed her hand. "Your daddy's got this, baby, so don't worry about your old man. I trust Alicia, and I'm not worried, so you shouldn't worry."

"Okay, Dad, if you say so," she said, and they chatted for the rest of the ride. He dropped her off and headed home.

Chapter Thirty-nine

Janiece tried to get a flight out that day, but everything was sold out. She would have to be on standby, so she decided to take a flight the next day. She talked to K.P. several times and didn't mention once that she'd be coming. She just wondered what she would find once she arrived. That was the kids' last day of school, so Kimberly picked them up, and the next day she would drop Jaiden off to Isaiah, and Phyllis would have Jordan.

She packed but had to try on everything to see what fit because she had put on so many pounds since she had Jordan, and none of her cute clothes fit, so she grabbed her keys and told Phyllis she was going out for a while.

She headed toward the mall and was grateful that the stores stayed open until nine. She went straight to Ashley Stewart and Lane Bryant because she was a solid eighteen. Her stomach was still smaller than her ass, so she thanked God for that, but her hips, ass, and thighs were out of control, she thought when she stood in the three-way mirror.

She made it out of the mall and called LaGenia's to see if she could get in in the morning because her flight didn't leave until six thirty p.m., and she was due to land at four p.m. She decided she'd get there, hit a few slots, and pop up later that night when it was close to bedtime.

She wondered how she would get a key because she didn't accompany her husband at check-in, so getting into the villa may be difficult. No matter what, she had to find out if K.P. was lying or being loyal. She got an appointment the next morning at nine and couldn't wait to get on the plane. She couldn't sleep that night because she was so anxious, so she went downstairs for a glass of wine. She looked at the clock. It was after eleven, so it was only after nine in Vegas, so she called K.P., and he didn't answer. She texted and said she was still up and to give her a call back, but she hadn't heard back from him by one. She climbed into bed and finally fell asleep, anxious for the next day.

When they got in from the long day of sightseeing and gambling, K.P. went to shower, and then he looked around for his phone. After they made it to the strip, he realized he didn't have it and decided not to go back for it. He called it from Robin's phone, and it must have somehow fallen out of his pocket and into the cushions after he spoke with Janiece earlier. He and Robin sat talking for a few before they headed out, so it had to have fallen then.

He had several missed calls and text messages from Janiece, but he said he'd call her in the morning. After he showered, he grabbed a drink and went out to the pool because that was where Robin was. He could see her body underwater swimming, so he just took a seat.

"What a surprise. I thought you went to bed," she said, holding on to the side of the pool.

"I was about to, but since there is no work tomorrow, I can stay up for a while," he said, and she got out and had on a different bikini. She went for her towel and wrapped it around herself and sat on the other lounge chair near him.

"The water feels nice, and you should take a swim."

"I didn't bring any trunks," he said and took a sip.

"You don't need trunks. You have boxers, and they look the same, believe it or not," she said and smiled.

"Well, they are not the same," he said and laughed.

"I've seen boxers before," she teased.

"I'm sure you have, but I'm your boss."

"Okay, and? I will still respect you in the morning. You've seen me in my PJ's and a bikini. Kerry, you don't have to be shy," she said and winked.

"Robin . . ." He'd started to correct her about calling him Kerry, but he was not an anal boss, so he stopped. "I don't know. Maybe I will. I thought about the hot tub earlier."

"Well, you should try it. I know you are my boss and all, but you can relax. I won't be offended, nor will I lose respect for you," she said, and K.P. relaxed a little. He and Rose had some alone moments, but the feeling differed. Rose wasn't a flirt, for one, and Rose would have never walked out in a two-piece, that was for sure.

"Maybe," he said and took another sip.

"You are like the coolest boss I've ever had. I've had some mean, old bosses before who were angry for no reason, but I honestly enjoy working for you."

"Thank you. I can say that I worked for a long time for a man I didn't want to work for because I wanted to keep the peace with my ex-wife. Mr. Grayson wasn't a horrible boss, but I was always on edge around him, and I never wanted to make an employee feel that way."

"Well, you're doing a great job," she said.

He got up to refill his glass. When he came back, she was no longer covered with her towel. She was lying back in her two-piece, sipping her drink. He took his seat and lay back, watching the pool water dance.

"Can I ask you a question?" she said.

"Sure," he said, but she was quiet. He waited for the question, and when she didn't say anything, he looked at her. "Robin?" he said, and she looked at him.

"Have you ever wanted to be with someone off-limits?" she asked, hoping he didn't decline to answer.

"No, I can't say I have."

"Well, you are lucky," she said and set her drink down.

She got up, jumped back in, swam over to the hot tub, pulled herself out of the pool, and got in. K.P. wanted to resist. He got up, took off his tank, and stepped out of his pajama pants, revealing his black boxer briefs. He eased down, and it did feel good. He took a sip and put his drink on the side of the hot tub. He looked at Robin and wanted to get the conversation over with.

"So who do you have the hots for who's off-limits?" he asked.

"Well, he is a little older, very good-looking, funny, and smart, but he has a lady, and I know I shouldn't fantasize about him or want him like I do, but I can't seem to get him out of my mind," she expressed and K.P. decided to make sure if it was him she was talking about so she would understand not even to try him.

"Well, Robin, I would advise trying to get over those feelings. If he is married, that automatically makes him off-limits. My wife was my mistress, and trust, I put her through hell with having her on the side," he explained, and then he reached for his drink and took a sip.

"No, he's not married, just has a woman in his life. Plus, I have already fallen in love with him. It worked out for you and Janiece, right?" she asked.

"Yes, but I got married for the wrong reasons to begin with, and when I met Janiece, I was in a bad place with my ex-wife, and I should have done the right thing and ended the marriage, but I made some horrible choices that caused us all a lot of pain, so you may not want to go there with this guy if he is not available."

"I understand what you mean, but I just want this man so bad, and every time I see him, I imagine what it would be like to just share one night with him," she said, and K.P.'s dick reacted to those words, so he took another sip.

"Okay, let me ask you this—how do you think he feels about you?" he asked to see if she thought he had any interest.

"I honestly can't tell. I think he knows or has a feeling that I'm feeling him, but he hasn't done anything to show me that he is interested. I'm constantly looking for a sign from him to know that he is interested," she said.

"So you mean to tell me that you'd be intimate with this man if he gave you a chance, even though he has a woman?" he asked.

"That's the hard part because I want him just that bad that I would. I hope you don't think I'm a horrible person," she said and put her head down.

"No, I don't, because I kept a mistress for years, as wrong as it was, and I couldn't help that I wanted to be with Janiece. I just say it's not worth it, Robin. You shouldn't want to be any man's chick on the side, and you shouldn't allow him that opportunity to make you his sidepiece. You are too gorgeous and too smart, and I can't see it being difficult finding a man."

"It's not," she replied. "I just want who I want, and I just might go for it and see what happens," she said. "I hope my personal opinions won't be held against me," she said.

"No, this is all off the record, and as long as you continue to do a great job, you have your position. Your personal life, outside the office, is yours," he said.

"Thanks, boss," she said and smiled. "Can I refill your drink?" she asked, coming out of the water.

"Sure," he said, and she bent over to get his glass, giving him a view of her tits.

He watched her ass sway as she walked over to her towel and wrapped it around her body. She grabbed her glass, stepped into her flip-flops, went inside to refill their drinks, and K.P. adjusted his dick. He knew he could hit it if he wanted to, but that was out of the question, even though his dick wanted to so badly. He knew Robin meant him, but he figured if she outright said it, he'd tell her he wasn't interested. He knew then where Janiece was coming from, but Janiece had absolutely nothing to fear because he knew better, and he wasn't going to go out like that, no matter how sexy Robin was.

She returned with their drinks and slid back into the hot tub. They didn't talk much, and K.P. just sipped his drink and looked up at the stars. They made small talk, and once K.P.'s glass was empty, he decided to go to bed. She asked him to wait for her to finish her drink, and when he got out, he extended her hand and helped her out.

"Thanks," she said, looking him in the eyes, and she gave him her sexy smile again. K.P. thought she was hot, but love whipped lust's ass, because he ignored the wood in his boxer briefs.

"You're welcome. Good night, Robin," he said and went for his tank and pajama pants. He went inside and took another quick shower before turning in.

Robin did the same and lay there wondering what to do next. She figured she had opened the door. He just needed to come in. She told herself that she wasn't getting back on that plane going back to Chicago without knowing how Kerry's dick felt inside of her body.

She tossed the covers to the side, closed her eyes, and thought about his body dripping water from the hot tub. She began to massage her breast as she thought of the bulge in his shorts that he couldn't hide before he got out of the hot tub. She got a good look at it when he helped her out of the hot tub, and that sent her right hand down to her spot, and she began to rub her clit.

She imagined K.P. coming into her bedroom, spreading her legs wide, filling her pussy with his steel pipe, and beating her cervix with his steady pumps. She began to get wetter, imagining his tongue pleasing her nipples, and she pinched her nipple harder, wishing it were him pleasing it with his wet mouth. She pressed and rubbed her clit harder and whispered his name as if he were there with her.

"Yes, Kerry, baby, that's it, do it, baby," she said softly and moaned as she played her imaginary love scene in her mind. She was now on top in her fantasy, riding him, while he squeezed her ass firmly and called out her name. Her mind shifted, and she was taking him inside her mouth, and then she climaxed. She didn't mean to, but she moaned loudly as her body jerked and released its natural orgasmic fluids. She breathed heavily, smiling because it felt so good to release the orgasm she was waiting to have with K.P. She pulled the covers back over her body, turned over, and told herself she would just go for it. The next night she'd have to make her move, and she wasn't going to back down from her quest.

Chapter Forty

Cher was at her son's school to pick him up, and she was livid when she learned that Cortez had already done so. She forgot to alert the school not to allow him to pick up her son, and now she knew she had to see him. She got in her car and wondered what she should do. Cortez had been blowing up her phone, and she never answered. She still had no idea how he got the number, but that wasn't important. She had to figure out how to get this nut to give her son back without violence. How she felt at that moment, she wanted to punch him in the throat. She dialed his number, and he picked up on the second ring.

"I knew I'd get your attention," he said into the phone.

"Cortez, what the hell? Why did you pick up C.J.?" she asked nervously.

"I had to find a way for you to talk to me, Cher," he said.

"About what, Cortez. Huh? What do you have to say different from what you've said before?" she yelled because she was furious.

"Cherae, I'm so sorry, and I don't want to lose you, baby. I'm getting help, and I'll do whatever you want, just please—"

"Where is my son?"

"C.J. is fine, Cher. Just listen to me, baby. I can change. I love you, and I will never put my hands on you again. I stopped drinking, Cher, and I'm getting myself together," he cried, and she didn't believe him.

"Cortez, I can't. You treated me like a punching bag and then said, 'I'm sorry, Cher, I'll never do it again' too many times, and now you wanna come back, now you wanna get help, and now you wanna change after you have destroyed what we had. Cortez, I loved you and wanted this to work out, but the last time you put your hands on me will truly be the last. Now I want my son, dammit!" she barked, and Cortez was vexed with her for not giving in to his request.

He never thought Cher would leave him, and now that she had, he knew he had to change because he wanted her back. "Okay, listen, Cher, I know you're angry right now, and I'm willing to give you time," he tried to say.

"Cortez, I don't need time. I am not going to change my mind. I am done with you!" she yelled.

It took every muscle in Cortez's body to keep him from going off. He had issues and decided to take C.J. back to her and give her a little space.

"Okay, Cher, I will drop C.J. off," he said.

"No, take him to my sister's house, and she can bring him to me. I don't want to see you, Cortez. I don't want you to come anywhere near me, and until the courts decide on custody and visitation, you can't see C.J."

"Cher, you know I'd never hurt my son," he said.

"You know what, Cortez, I don't know that. I thought you'd never hurt me, but you did, and I don't trust you with my son," she said and hoped he'd bring C.J. to her. "And if you don't have my son at Katrina's in an hour, I will call the cops," she said and hung up. She called Kat as soon as she hung up and told her the situation. Kat told her she would call her once C.J. was there.

About forty-five minutes later, Katrina had her son, but she was scared to go by Katrina's. Katrina assured her that Cordell was there and he'd come out when she got there, but she was still nervous that Cortez would be somewhere close by waiting for her. When she got on their block, Cordell came out and walked her in, her hands shaking.

"Calm down, Cher. It's okay, you're safe," Katrina said. Cordell came in and handed her a glass of merlot.

"Kat, I can't live this way. I'm scared to walk out of my house every morning, and at night I can't sleep, and I'm constantly looking over my shoulders," she said and took two back-to-back swallows.

"I'm sorry that you are going through this. I can come and stay with you for a little while. My husband won't mind," she offered.

"I can't ask you to do that, Kat."

"Listen, it will be no problem."

"No, I just have to find a way to get over this fear, and I'm thinking about getting a gun," she said, and Katrina was shocked

"A gun, Cher? Are you sure you want to do that?"

"Kat, I don't feel safe in my own home, and I want to feel safe and not feel defenseless. I can't fight him, Kat, and I have to defend myself and protect my son," she said, and Katrina agreed, but C.J. was young, and she knew guns were dangerous. She and Cordell owned a gun, but they didn't have children.

"How about a dog?" she suggested.

"Hell, I need one of those, too," she said, polished off her drink, and asked for a refill. Katrina got up to refill her glass, and her phone rang. She was relieved when she saw it was Terry. "Hi," she said and smiled. She was happy to hear from him.

"How was your day?" he asked.

"Eventful. Cortez is driving me crazy. He took my son from school today."

"What? He has your son?"

"No, he's with me now." Katrina handed her the glass, and she mouthed the words "thank you." She continued to fill Terry in on what happened and told him again about wanting to get a gun, and he agreed to go with her to get one. She didn't want to be alone, so she asked him if he could come over, and of course, he agreed. She called Kennedy to take C.J. because Kat and Cordell both worked during the day, and even though Kennedy worked also, she had a sitter who watched C.J. too when he was there. Kennedy told her she could bring him and headed home after she dropped him off.

When she got home, that nervous feeling returned, and she prayed that Cortez would stay away. She got out with her fingers on her phone, telling herself she would call the cops immediately if she spotted him. When she made it inside, she keyed in her alarm code and turned her alarm back on quickly. She showered quickly and couldn't wait for Terry to arrive because she was always on edge. When the security guard at the gate alerted her he was there, she felt so much better.

"Finally," she said. When she opened the door, he had two grocery bags.

"I'm sorry it took me a little longer. I wanted to cook for you, so I stopped by the store to get something to prepare for you."

"Wow, come on in," she said, taking one of the bags. They headed toward the kitchen, and Cher put the bag on the counter. "This is so nice of you, Terry. I am starving," she said, and they began to remove the items from the bags.

He rolled up his sleeves, went to the sink, and washed his hands, and Cher volunteered to help, but he asked her to take a seat. She pointed out where her pots and pans were and helped him to navigate around her kitchen. He made a garlic angel hair pasta dish with chicken breasts, which was delicious.

"I've always dreamed of having a man who could cook," she said before taking the last bite of her food.

"Well, if you and I become an item, you will have one," he said, and they began to clear the table and clean the kitchen together.

They settled on the sofa with a couple of glasses of chardonnay and shared endless conversation. It was getting late, but Cher didn't want him to leave because she didn't want to be there alone.

"Well, I should go," he said and stood.

"Please, stay," she said quickly. He paused. "I mean, I would like it if you stayed with me."

"I can stay if you want me to," he said.

"Yes, I want you to," she said and stood. "I just feel safe with you being here, Terry, and I want to get a good night's sleep for a change. I'm not trying to get you in my bed or anything like that. I just don't want to be alone," she explained.

"Cher, it's cool. I'll stay, and I am not thinking anything sexual unless that's what you want," he joked, and they laughed. "No, for real, I'll stay." Cher was relieved.

She ensured everything was locked up, her alarm was set, and they went upstairs. He took off his shoes and shirt, and Cher put on pajamas. She pulled the covers back and told him that he could remove his pants if he wanted to, and he did. They climbed into bed, and Cher turned out her lamp. She scooted close to him, and he held her, and for the first time since the brutal encounter with Cortez, she got a good night's sleep in her bed.

Chapter Forty-one

Leila was closing up for the night, and she realized she was supposed to call Rayshon back hours ago. She had gotten so busy that she didn't do what she said she would again. Looking at the clock, she knew he would be upset because she had worked past dinner and the kids' bedtime.

She hit the Bluetooth button and tried calling him, but she didn't get an answer. She drove home feeling horrible because she hadn't been paying her husband enough attention lately. She seemed always to be working or helping someone else with their situation these days. The business was picking up quickly, and now Christa was planning the baby shower of the century. Leila's only focus was party planning, and she knew Rayshon would be angry, but what could she do?

When she walked in through the garage door, the house was quiet. She put all the work she had brought home onto the island and headed straight for the wine cooler because she was exhausted. She opened a bottle and poured it quickly, and he entered the kitchen.

"Another late night, I see," he said, startling her.

"Ray, you scared me," she said, taken by surprise. She didn't hear him come down the stairs.

"I didn't mean to scare you," he said, coming into the kitchen, and then he leaned on the counter.

"I know I'm late again, baby, and I'm sorry. I have a ton of deadlines approaching fast, and I have a lot on my plate."

"Lei, I know a new business takes a lot of time and work, but I haven't touched you since you opened this business because you come home late with more work. I not only share my bed with you, but I'm also sharing my bed with invitations, fabric samples, and colored swatches. The kids are like doing almost everything for themselves, and I know I was the one who suggested that you start this party-planning business, Lei, but I am starting to regret it. I miss you being a wife and a mother to our children," he said.

"Baby, I know what you mean, but work is demanding right now, and I don't mean to neglect you and the kids, but what am I supposed to do, Rayshon? I have a lot on my plate right now," she expressed.

"I know, Lei, I know that. I just wish you could scale back and remember your family. I know it feels great to be back in the workforce, and Parties by Leila will be a huge success. I know you can do it, babe, but we must find a medium where we are all happy."

"The only other option right now, Ray, is for me to hire someone, and I can't afford that just yet," she said sadly.

"I'll tell you what. You hire someone and let me take care of that part."

"Rayshon, this is my business, and I don't want you to worry about my business expenses."

"But you are my wife, and we are in this together. I understand you want to do everything alone, but let me help you, babe. If you have an issue, consider it a loan." He smiled.

"No, baby, I will figure out a way," she insisted.

"It's already figured out, and it's done. I will write you a check in the morning, and you don't have to pay back the entire loan in cash, you know," he said, coming close to her.

"Oh, is there another form of repayment option on the table? Let's hear it before I agree to take this loan from you," she said, moving closer to him. She knew Rayshon was her safety net, but she wanted him to hold off putting money into her business until she gave it a fair chance. She figured she'd go to him only if it were dire, not for her to hire someone to work.

"Well, there are a few sexual favors I wouldn't mind having for repayment. And you will be repaying me by making it home for dinner on time, and coming home to take care of our kids will be all the repayment I need. Honestly, Lei, it's not about the money. It's about you not being here at all. Everything is the shop this, the shop that, and I remember way back when I was doing the same thing. When I opened gym number three, you were pregnant with Rave, going through the motions of losing your store, and it caused major problems in our marriage. I don't want to have to go through that again. Money isn't an object to this family, our happiness, and our time together. We are in this together, Leila, and as much as you want to do this on your own, you can't because I'm not happy.

"The kids have been eating crap from the microwave for weeks, and we can't be so consumed with our businesses that we don't have time for this family. I've changed my routine and schedule, remember, for the sake of this family. I stopped working seven days a week because you guys needed me home, so before this gets out of hand, let me help you. You need an assistant, you need help, and we have the money, so don't take it as a loan. It's an investment in our family business, and I am not going to let you let work come first," he said.

Leila listened carefully. "I hear you, baby, and I'm sorry that I didn't hear you before. I do need help, baby, and I was too cowardly to admit it, but I'm overwhelmed.

I've been so busy trying to prove to you and everyone that I will be a success. I bit off way more than I can chew, and I'm exhausted. I just didn't want to fail. I didn't want to lose another business like the first one, and I went in with an 'S' on my chest. Now I want to take it off. Baby, I'm tired, and I miss you, and I miss the kids, and I need you," she said and walked into his arms.

"Leila, it's okay. I got you, and you are not a failure, my love. I had no idea you felt this way. This is why you are killing yourself. Baby, you've been in business less than six months, and you know this takes time. Taking on all these clients by yourself is insane," he said.

"I know, Ray, I know," she said and took a deep breath.

"Well, don't worry. We will hire an experienced party planner or even two, and you will run your business like an owner and stop killing yourself trying to do everything by yourself, you hear me?" he said, lifting her head.

"Okay." She nodded. "Thank you, Rayshon. You are my hero, knight, and everything."

"Yeah, I am," he said and kissed her.

"Yes, you are," she said, letting him hold her tight.

"Now with that said, can I please take you upstairs without a swatch, a glue gun, or a tablet? I want to make love to you, and I hope you are not too tired because yo' man is ready to put in some work."

"I was tired when I walked through that door, but I feel a burst of energy, so let's go," she said and followed Rayshon up the steps.

They looked in on their kids, and Leila kissed her babies gently because they were sleeping. They tapped and looked in on Deja. She was still up on her laptop.

"Hey, D.J., you're still up?"

"Hey, Momma, I'm just looking at different dance routines. I won't be up long," she said, and Leila kissed her forehead.

"All right, you better not be. We are going to turn in," Leila said and tried to walk away.

"Ma," D.J. called out.

"Yes, baby," Leila said, turning back to her.

"Can I talk to you?"

"Sure, D.J., what's going on?" Leila said and sat on her desk chair.

"I'm a little afraid to ask," she said and put her head down.

"Deja, you can ask me anything."

"Well, I wanted to ask Daddy Ray, but I was afraid he'd get mad."

"What is it, Deja? Do you want me to get your daddy Ray?"

"Yes," she said and nodded her head up and down. Leila got up and went and got Rayshon.

"What do you think this is about?" Rayshon asked.

"I have no idea," Leila said, and they went to Deja's room. Leila sat on her bed, and Rayshon sat in her chair.

"What's going on, baby girl?" Rayshon asked.

"Well, I wanted to ask you and mom about Shon," she said, and Ray and Leila looked at each other. They knew one day she may ask since she was older.

"What do you want to know?" Leila asked.

"Is it true that you had an affair and his mother tried to kill my mom?" she asked and put her head down. "There are rumors around school that my father cheated with a crazy lady who is in jail, and she tried to kill my mother."

"Who told you that, Deja?"

"Mom, everyone knows, and I've wanted to ask for a long time, but I thought if something like that were true, you would have told me, and I went online and looked up Karen Morgan and found out she was committed for her attempt on Mom's life," she said.

Rayshon and Leila told her the entire story. They told her the truth, and when they were done, Deja handled it well.

"So you never cheated on Mom?"

"No, but if I had made different choices, I would not have been accused. I'm not proud of my actions, Deja."

"It's fine, Daddy Ray. I just wanted to know the truth. Are you guys afraid she will get out one day and maybe come for Shon?"

"We have felt that way, Deja, but we don't dwell on that. We just pray that she stays locked away forever," Rayshon said.

"But what if she doesn't?" Deja asked, concerned and seemingly fearful.

"Deja, baby, don't worry, okay? Karen will never hurt this family again, and Shon is legally our son now, and she can't just come and take him back," Leila said and pulled her close.

"Okay. I'm okay. I'm just glad I finally asked. I was afraid you guys wouldn't tell me."

"Listen, Deja, you're fifteen now, and you are not a baby anymore. If you ever want to talk to us about anything, I mean anything, you come to Devon or us, understood?" Ray said, and Deja nodded.

"Now is there anything else you want to know?" Leila asked.

"No, that's it," she said.

Leila and Rayshon stood to leave but kissed her good night first. They went down the hall to their room, and neither felt like making love anymore. Karen was a sore topic, and they prayed that she stayed locked away. The judges promised them that they would be notified if ever she was up for parole or release, and so far, they had not been, but Ray made a note to make some phone calls the next day just to make sure.

Chapter Forty-two

"So he's gone?" Kennedy asked, and Kenya nodded with a face full of tears.

It had been three days since she arrived to find that all of his belongings were gone. She tried calling him over and over, and he never answered. She went by the station and was informed he had a new shift. She called around and found out that he had gotten back with the woman he had been caught with a couple of years ago. She went by there, and to her surprise, she was no longer there.

When she got home that evening, not only were his things gone, but his house key was on the table. She'd called Kennedy immediately, crying on the phone. She told Kennedy where she lived.

"I'm so sorry, Kenya," she said and held her.

"I can't believe that bastard left. He said he loved me. He looked me in my fucking eyes, Kennedy, and lied to me again!" she yelled angrily. "I paid his muthafuckin' bills off. I took my money, my damn inheritance, and paid his debt. All the debt that his ass put us in, and I let him play me," she cried.

"Kenya, it is okay. You will be fine, and trust me when I tell you that you are better off. You don't see it now, but you are. You and Ryan will be okay, and you don't need his lying, cheating, low-down ass!" Kennedy spat with tight lips.

"I know, Kennedy, but it hurts. I feel like the ones who are supposed to love me the most keep throwing me away. My mother was supposed to be my first love, but she left me, and now my husband, the man I exchanged vows with. The only man I've ever loved left me too. Why did our mother do that to me? Why didn't she want me?" she sobbed.

"Kenya, it sounds like you may want to see someone about how you feel, li'l sis. It sounds like abandonment issues, and I'm no doctor, so I can't help you with the whys, but I will be here for you until you feel better," she said tenderly and squeezed her hand. "I can't speak for Mom or why she did what she did, and I can't make excuses for her, but you have me now, and I will never leave you or turn my back on you," Kennedy said.

Kenya sobbed harder, and Kennedy reached over to pull her into her arms. She continued to hold her until she calmed down. They sat silently for what felt like forever, and Kenya finally spoke up.

"I've tried to forgive her, you know. I want to forgive her, Kennedy. I do, but sometimes it just hurts me so bad. Sometimes I cry for days because she wasn't here for me. My father did his best, and we were close, but I wanted her to call me. Write me a letter. I wanted to hear her voice. Even if it was to scold me, I wanted her. All my friends had a mother, and all I had were the few flings in and out of my dad's life."

"Okay, and now you have me, your niece and nephew, and Julian. You have a family now."

"I know I do, but there are moments when I look at how beautiful and smart and accomplished you are, and I get so jealous and angry with her all over again. I felt if I'd had her like you had her, I would not have turned out to be such a mess," she cried.

"Kenya, you are not a mess, and I'm so sorry that Momma wasn't there for you, but you will have to forgive her. We are not children anymore, Kenya. We are grown women and can't go back or change our past, but we have control over our future. I can't make up for what Mom did to you, but I will be here for you now. I will be here for you and help you to get through this, and whatever you want to do with the rest of your life, I will help you. I will do whatever I can within my power," Kennedy said, and Kenya noticed her eyes shift to look around the room.

Kenya knew her place wasn't as lavish as Kennedy's, but she kept it clean. She knew the sofa they sat on was worn, but she was doing her best. To get her attention again, she said, "Thank you, Kennedy. I am grateful for you, and I'm glad that God has blessed me with a sister like you," she said. "I know my place doesn't measure up to yours, but I try," she added.

"I know you do, Kenya, and I am not looking down on you. That's the furthest thing from my mind, but I want to make a suggestion that I hope won't offend you."

Kenya looked at her with sad eyes. "Offend, Kennedy. I know better. What's on your mind?"

"Why don't we keep the main house, and you and Ryan move there? The house is paid in full, and as you know, it had a major overhaul done about two years ago. You can go to school without a mortgage, and it would be less of a burden."

"Your parents' house? No, Kennedy, I couldn't do that. I mean, that house is beautiful, but I couldn't," she expressed, not wanting to cause any issues with her sister. That house was gorgeous with hardwoods and a new white kitchen with granite and stainless steel. The bathrooms had been redone, and the original claw-foot tub still lived there, but it didn't look as old as the 60-year-old house due to being refurbished. The house had all the original arches and character from that era, but the renovations made it modern and beautiful. Kenya feared that if she changed the drapes, it might cause conflict.

"Kenya, my daddy left the house to us both, and since I have a house that I love, it's only fair that you take the house. Cher can help you get this place where it needs to be and sell it, so please, don't say no. You own it too."

She hesitated at first. "Kennedy, I don't know what to say," she said, and her eyes welled again. "I mean, I don't know how to thank you," she expressed because that house was beautiful, and she admired it the first time she saw it, but when Kennedy said to sell it, she didn't speak up. She didn't feel she had the right.

"You don't have to do anything except pack. We can keep all the furniture you choose. That way, we'll have less to move out, and if you want to get rid of everything and do your own thing, that's up to you."

"The house is perfect how it is," she said, smiling. She and Kennedy discussed plans, and then her cell phone rang. Her daughter said she needed to be picked up from her friend's house. Kennedy offered to call Boomer to transfer the deed into Kenya's name only, but Kenya insisted that she didn't. She told her that that house was still their house, and she wanted Kennedy to have her half of the ownership still.

They called Cher, and Cher agreed to check out Kenya's house. She came by, did a walk-through, made notes, and reminded Kennedy in front of Kenya that she was only taking it on because they were family. "I don't sell less than million-dollar homes, so you owe me, bestie," she added before she left.

Within a couple of days, all the items that Kenya wanted to keep were at the main house. Everything else went to the dumpster, and Kennedy shelled out the six grand Cher needed to do some repairs on Kenya's house.

It only took the crew Cher hired a week to get it done. Cher had a decorator she said owed her a favor who staged the place for them at no cost. At the first open house, she had multiple offers, and it took less than a month for Kenya to be free of that house and to serve Rob with divorce papers.

She was starting to feel confident about her life, and she and Kennedy got closer each day. After meeting Leila, she landed a singing job on the side with Leila's company. Kenya sang at weddings, anniversary parties, banquets, private parties, or wherever a vocalist was needed, and she was finally happy. She owed it all to her big sister Kennedy. She never knew her mother, but she thanked God for blessing her with a sister, and Kennedy made sure Kenya knew how much she loved her every day.

Chapter Forty-three

Janiece landed in Las Vegas a little later than she thought she would due to bad weather. When she finally got her bag, she went out to grab a cab and had second thoughts on the ride to the villa. She hoped she wouldn't find out the worst, and she prayed her husband wasn't cheating on her. After being dropped off in front of the office, she went inside, and the agent at the desk smiled brightly when she greeted her.

"Hi, and good evening. Are you checking in?" she asked.

Janiece, at that moment, felt foolish. "Actually, no, my husband is here. His name is Kerry Paxton, and I was hoping I could get a key. I wanted to surprise him. I just flew in from Chicago, and I wanted to, you know . . ." she said with a smile, but it faded when the clerk replied.

"I'm so sorry, ma'am, but if your name isn't on the room, I can't give you a key," she said pleasantly.

"I have ID, and I've stayed here with him before," she said, and that didn't mean a thing.

"I understand that, but I'm so sorry. I can call him if you'd like," she said, reaching for the phone, and Janiece stopped her.

"No, no, don't call him. I wanted my visit to be a surprise. Are you sure I can't get a key? Like, is there a manager here I can speak to? I've stayed here with him before," she said, wondering if she should go into her purse and pull out a couple of Benjamins. Money talked, and some people would do anything for it.

"I can get him. Hold on," the young lady said.

Janiece stood patiently waiting. She looked around and wondered what she was going to do. She didn't want to alert Kerry, but it was looking as if she was going to have to.

"Yes, ma'am, how can I help you?" the manager said when he came from the back.

"Listen, I just flew in from Chicago, and I had plans to come down and surprise my husband. I have an ID, but your clerk tells me I can't have a key. My husband and I have stayed here twice, and normally my name would be on the room, but since he arrived a couple of days ago . . ." she tried to explain while he clicked a few keys.

"What's your husband's name?"

"Kerry, Kerry Paxton," she recited.

The manager looked in the system. "And are you Janice?" he asked.

Janiece corrected him. "Janiece. J-a-n-i-e-c-e," she said, spelling it out.

"Well, your name is on the reservation because your name is on the profile. We copy all information from the previous visit when it's a repeat guest. If you have a valid ID, I'd be happy to give you a key."

She quickly pulled out her ID again and handed it over to him, and he made her a key and gave her a few instructions on how to get there after she declined the bellhop. She headed to the villa, but the closer she got, the more nervous she became. She stood a few feet away from the door and had second thoughts. She took a few deep breaths and then proceeded to the door. When she opened it, she was surprised that no one was there. It was spacious, way larger than what they'd normally get, but K.P did mention he wanted four bedrooms for her and the kids to visit.

She entered the first room with two twin beds, and it looked like the room hadn't been touched. She went into the next bedroom, which was cute, with a queen-sized bed and sitting area. She went into the third one, which resembled a main suite, with sliding doors that gave access to the pool, but with such a small living space, she knew it wasn't the largest.

She noticed women's clothing and accessories, so she figured that was where Robin was staying and was relieved that she was set up in the spare room, not the main room.

She entered the last room, which was indeed the main suite. It was enormous with a sitting area, fireplace, French doors that accessed the pool, and an en suite bathroom suitable for her and her man. After seeing his suits in the closet and all of his toiletries on the vanity, she felt foolish.

She put her suitcase in the closet and said she'd unpack later. She waited for them to come in, but after two hours, she was starving. She grabbed her purse and phone, went to the front desk, and they got her a cab.

She went to dinner and was tempted to call K.P. and tell him she was in town, but she didn't. Her phone rang, and when she saw it was K.P., she answered quickly.

"Hey," she said.

"Hey, where have you been all day? I tried calling a few times, and your phone went straight to voicemail. I called the house, and Phyllis said you were out."

"I went shopping and to the salon. Now I'm having dinner."

"Alone?"

"Yes. How was your day?"

"It was cool. Robin convinced me to see the Motown review, and we went by the wax museum. We just got in."

"So you guys are in?" she asked, wanting to hurry back.

"Yeah," he said.

"So what are you going to do tonight?"

"Nothing. You know, tomorrow Collin will be back, so I am going to shower, have a drink, and call it a night."

"Where is your assistant?"

"Come on, Jai, don't start that nonsense, babe. I can't deal with that," he huffed.

"It's cool, just call me before you go to sleep," she said, waving for her server.

"I will," he said, and they hung up.

Janiece paid and hurried back. Her heart was racing, and she was sure she'd walk in on them doing things they shouldn't be doing.

"I'm going to shower," K.P. told Robin after he had made his calls to check on his family.

"Are you turning in or coming out to the pool?" she asked.

"It's still a little early, so I'll sit out with you, but tonight I'm just going to chill. No hot tub for me."

"That's cool. Go shower, and I'll fix you a drink," she offered, and he nodded.

He had a good time with Robin that day, and hanging with her was cool. He was happy she wasn't talking about her crush in their office building, but she did a lot of flirting and took every opportunity to touch him. He couldn't wait until the next day to handle business and head back home. He was flattered, but he had no intentions of crossing any lines with her.

Robin rushed into her room and stripped out of her clothes. She grabbed her robe and decided it was time to go for it. She wasn't going to back down, and she was going to get what she wanted. She walked out of her room in her robe and crept into his room. She heard the shower, so she eased into the bathroom. The steam filled the room and clouded the mirror. She let her robe drop to the floor and stepped into the shower behind him, and K.P. jumped.

"Robin, what in the hell!" he yelled. "Get the hell out of here. What in the hell is wrong with you?" he yelled.

She was stunned by his reaction. She rushed out, not stopping for her robe. She heard the water turn off, so she ran into her room and grabbed a towel. When he banged on her room door, she knew she had to go out and face him.

"I'm sorry, Kerry. I thought you wanted this too!" she cried, shaking when she opened the door. She wished she hadn't gone for the gusto because she didn't expect him to be angry.

"What made you think that?" he continued to yell as he tightened the towel around his waist before walking away.

"I'm sorry," she cried, following him into the living room.

"No, wait, Robin. Why would you do something like that?" he asked. He was dripping wet, and so was she.

"Because we were having such a good time, and I just thought that . . ." she said sadly.

"Well, you thought wrong, Robin!" he retorted. "You have to leave. You shouldn't have crossed that line. I'm your damn boss, and I don't do bullshit like this with my assistant or other women. I have a wife!" he yelled.

She began to cry. "Kerry, I'm so sorry. Please, please, I'm begging you," she said, and then Janiece walked in.

"What in the hell is going on, K.P.?" she shouted when she saw both of them half naked and dripping wet.

"Jai," he said in shock.

"What the fuck is going on? Why are you two naked and dripping wet?" Janiece asked.

"I'm so sorry, Janiece. I told him that I wasn't inter-ested. I was in the shower, and he came in on me," she announced.

Kerry's mouth widened in disbelief, and he took two or three steps back.

Janiece charged at K.P. "You motherfucker! You lied to me!" she raved, and K.P. tried to restrain her.

"Robin, how could you? What in the hell is wrong with you? Get your shit and get the fuck out of here now!" he blasted, holding on to Janiece tight, and she couldn't break free.

"Kerry, let me go now. Take your damn hands off me!" she continued to yell.

"Janiece, calm down. Robin is lying. She came in on me," he tried to say.

Janiece didn't believe him.

"And, Robin, why in the fuck are you still standing there? Get the fuck up outta here," K.P. blared again.

"Janiece, I'm so sorry. I . . . I . . ." Robin stuttered.

"Get out! Get the fuck out of here. You home-wrecking bitch!" Janiece barked and wanted K.P. to let her go so she could get her ass. No way did she believe that she was innocent. Robin rushed to the other room, and K.P. let Janiece go, and she slapped his face so hard she was scared he'd slap her ass back. "How could you?"

"Janiece, you need to calm the fuck down and cool your heels! Robin is the one who came into my shower. I got off the phone with you, talked to Kimberly and the kids, and then headed into my room to shower. Five minutes later, she walked in naked, into my shower, and I threw her ass out. Right before you walked in, I told her to get her things and leave," he explained, and Janiece just looked at him.

"You are a liar, and she doesn't have to leave because I'm going," she said, and K.P. snatched her by the arm and dragged her into his room and forced her into the bathroom, and it was still steamy, and the shower was still wet as hell, and you could tell the shower was just on.

"That is her fucking robe, on the goddamn floor," he barked, pointing it out. He snatched her arm again, forcing her to the other side of the villa. He kicked in the door, and Robin quickly gathered her belongings. He took Janiece into the bathroom and shoved her into the shower.

"Now if I came in on her as she said, her shower would be wet, not mine. I chased her out and told her to get the hell out right before you walked in. Now who are you going to believe, your damn husband or that lying bitch?" K.P. snapped, infuriated.

She had never seen that look on her husband's face before. Janiece quickly processed what her husband had just said. She ran out and jumped on Robin. She had her down on the floor, and K.P. had to pull her off.

"Get out, bitch, get the fuck out now!" Janiece screamed, struggling to escape, but K.P. wouldn't let her go. Robin got up and started packing, moving faster as she shook to gather her things. K.P. pulled Janiece out of that room into the living room.

"Baby, calm down and just let her leave. I have to put on something," K.P. said, holding the towel that barely covered his ass and dick hairs. Janiece followed him into the other room. He grabbed a tank and stepped into the pajama pants on the chair.

"She got three minutes to get the hell up outta here, K.P., or I am going to jail tonight."

"Jai, calm down before you catch a damn case. You were right, okay? Once she is gone, it's done, okay?" he said, and Janiece was pacing because she was fuming.

"I told you to fire that bitch, K.P.," she hissed.

"Jai, I know, okay, I know, baby, just please. This has been enough drama for me for one day, okay, and I just want her gone," he said, and then they heard the door slam loud enough to wake the dead. They went out to see if she was gone, and she was. K.P. breathed relief, then called the front desk and asked them if they could deactivate her key. They told him he'd have to come down for new keys, and he agreed to go down immediately.

When he returned, Janiece was a bit calmer, and she was sorry that she hit K.P. across the face. "K.P., I'm sorry for hitting you," she said when he sat across from her.

"I'm sorry for not listening to you. I can honestly say I saw it once we got here, but I never thought Robin would pull something like that. I've been nothing more than professional with her. Yes, Janiece, we hung out the last couple of nights by the pool, and last night I did get in the hot tub with her," he said, and Janiece's eyes bulged. "Hold on, don't go there. She was on one side, and I stayed on my side, Janiece. We've been talking, hanging out, having drinks outside of work, so she took that as an invitation, Jai, but I promise you I didn't encourage or flirt with her. I realized that I could have gotten with Robin, but I didn't because I didn't want to. I liked her as a person, and she was honestly a great employee, Janiece. I didn't think it would come to this," he expressed, and she got up and sat beside her husband. She reached for his hands.

"Thank you, K.P., for telling me everything. I want to be able to trust you, and I know that girl wanted you and I am relieved that you didn't go there because I honestly thought you would. She is gorgeous, and in a way, I wouldn't have blamed you for the way I treated you," she said and smirked.

"Why do women always say that shit and know they don't mean it? If you had walked in on me screwing that woman, Janiece, I know I wouldn't have made it out of here alive."

"You damn right," she said and got up and kissed him. "Now that your assistant is gone, can we undress and take this out to the hot tub? This time you don't have to stay on your side," she teased, and he smiled.

They went to change, and her swimsuit and his boxers were off once they were settled in the hot tub. After a round in the hot tub, they went another round in the bedroom before a night of deep sleep.

The next morning, when Kerry walked into the Vegas office, Madison greeted him before calling Collin to alert him that K.P. was there. After only ten minutes of him showing K.P. the true numbers and the original email he sent, K.P. realized that Robin had set the entire ordeal up. He couldn't believe she had gone that far to get him out of town.

He just hoped when he got back to Chicago, she had sense enough to vacate his office, and he called security to make sure they knew to confiscate her badge and parking pass. He met Janiece back at the villa, and they decided to stay a couple more days so they could be alone and put the Robin episode behind them.

Chapter Forty-four

Cher hadn't heard anything from Cortez, and she was finally starting to feel relaxed. She got a dog, purchased a gun about a month ago, and thanked God every day that Cortez didn't call, text, or come by her house or office. She was counting down the days until they were divorced. She and Terry had been dating and seeing a lot of each other, and she decided she would officially announce him as her new man and finally allow him to do the things he wanted to do to her body. They decided to take things slow because Cher wanted to make sure she was ready to be involved with someone new, and after their six-week courtship, she knew she was ready.

Terry spent his days ensuring Cher kept a smile on her face and feeding her his home-cooked dishes. He spent so much time at Cher's place she had to introduce him to C.J. because she was always dropping her baby off and picking him up from Kennedy. That night she decided she'd cook and introduce him to C.J. Kennedy tried to drop him off and keep going because she and Kenya were headed to the movies, but Cher insisted they come in first.

"Girl, come in and have a glass of wine with me," Cher said nervously, and Kennedy could detect it.

"Cher, what's going on with you? What's wrong?" she asked as Cher poured wine into three glasses.

"Have a seat. How are you, Kenya? It's good to see you again. We need to get together more often," she said.

"I'm fine, Cher," Kenya said and took a seat, and Cher handed her a glass.

"Cher," Kennedy said and grabbed her hand. "Cherae Monique, what is wrong with you?"

"It's Terry. Tonight is our night, and I am so nervous, Kennedy. I mean, I feel like I'm out of practice. It's been a while since I've been with a man. Cortez and I were barely getting it in the last couple of years, and before that, our sex life had become boring," she said, and Kennedy laughed.

"Cher, are you serious? Sex is like riding a bike or swimming. You never forget once you've learned, and when you get started, it will all come back to you." She continued to laugh, and Cher didn't think it was funny.

"Kennedy, I'm serious. I think I'm a bit rusty," she said and took a gulp.

"Well, after you polish off a couple more glasses of that, I'm sure you will feel more confident," she said and sipped.

"I don't know, Kay. I mean, I'm so ready, but I'm so nervous," she expressed.

"Cher, Kenya and I have a movie to catch, and your ass is too old to be having sex jitters. When Terry gets here, you have dinner, a couple more glasses of chardonnay, and make sure C.J. is sleeping before you serve him up," Kennedy teased and stood. She polished off her glass and set it down.

"Fine, Kay, go and see your movie," she said, taking their glasses.

"I will call you tomorrow, and I'm sure you will have a good report," she said, and Cher walked them to the door. She went back to finish cooking dinner before heading up to shower and get ready.

Her son knocked on her door while she was applying her makeup.

"Come in," she said, and he entered the bathroom.

"Hey, Momma, are you going on a date?"

"A date? What do you know about dates?" she asked.

He hunched his shoulders. "Nothing. I just thought that is what grown-ups called going to dinner with someone."

"Well, that is what it is called, but I'm not going on a date. I cooked dinner tonight because I've invited a special friend to have dinner with us. He is a guy I like, and I think it's time for you to meet him," she announced.

"So my daddy isn't coming back, is he?" he asked sadly.

"No, baby, he's not, and I'm sorry," she said.

"Well, I miss him a lot, but I don't miss him making you cry," he said.

Cher paused and turned to him. "I know, baby, and Momma didn't want it to be this way, but Daddy and I weren't getting along like adults are supposed to, and we had to part. I hope you understand that I love your daddy, but I forgave him a lot of times, and finally, God told me what to do when someone keeps on hurting me, and that is not to be around that person anymore."

"I know, and I get sad sometimes that my daddy is gone, but I like to see you happy," he said, and she hugged him tightly.

She checked the clock, and Terry would be there soon, so she told him to let her finish getting ready, and he went to his room. When Terry made it, she introduced him to C.J., and it went well. After she said good night to C.J., she went back down and joined Terry on the sofa.

"So I wanted to tell you how beautiful I think you are on the inside and out. I've enjoyed every moment we have shared, Cher, and I care for you," he said.

"Me too, Terry, and I want tonight to be special," she said and kissed his fingers.

"Are you sure you're ready to take our relationship to that level?"

"Yes, I'm ready," she said, and then they heard a big bang, and they both hopped off the sofa and ran to the door.

Terry snatched the door open, and Cortez was outside with a tire iron going crazy on Terry's car. Terry charged and knocked him to the ground, and they began rolling around. Cher stood paralyzed, afraid to move. Cortez scrambled to stand up, and when Terry came up, he took a clean blow across the side of his head from the tire iron, knocking him into the cement fountain in Cher's courtyard, rendering him unconscious.

Cortez headed for Cher, and she ran into the house and tried to lock the door, but he kicked it in before she could lock it. She searched for her cell phone, but it was upstairs. And she tried to go for the cordless, but Cortez caught her.

"You thought I was gon' let you go, huh, Cher?" he whispered in her ear, holding her by the neck with a firm grip.

"Cortez, please, C.J. is upstairs. Don't do this, please, just go. I won't call the cops. Please go," she pleaded.

He grabbed her by her hair and slammed Cher's face into the fridge, and she screamed in agony from the pain as her body involuntarily fell onto the table, knocking some of the contents off. Within seconds, C.J. entered the kitchen.

"Daddy, nooooo, leave my momma alone!" he yelled and tried to pull Cortez away.

"C.J., go back upstairs, baby. Go back into your room right now. Momma is fine," Cher said calmly as she tried to stand up from the table, blood oozing from her nose. She was dazed, still knocking over things on the table, trying her best to stand.

"Go upstairs to your room now!" Cortez's voice boomed, and C.J. ran up the steps.

"Cortez, whatever you want, I'll do it, I promise. Pleeeeeease don't do this. I'll be with you. I'll be with you, just please, don't hurt me no more, please," she begged, finally able to stand.

"Cher, I don't want your whore ass anymore. I want to choke the life outta you right now," he said, grabbing her by the hair again. His grip was so tight that Cher thought her scalp was bleeding. "And guess what, Cher, Terry ain't gon' want you either when I'm done with you," he said, pushing her down onto the floor and pulling out a blade. "We are going to see how beautiful he thinks you are once the doctor stitches up that pretty face," he said, walking toward her.

He got up on her, went down on one knee, grabbed her face, and brought the blade close to her cheek. She reached over, grabbed the empty bottle that somehow hit the floor in the madness, and whacked him across the head, dazing him a bit. She ran toward the steps, but he made it to her before she reached the top. He flipped her onto her back and tried to stab her, but she put up her hand to block him, and the blade caught her arm instead.

She struggled and clawed at him, trying to get away from him. She kicked and fought, and her knee caught him in his jewels just hard enough to allow her to break away. She ran into her room, crawled quickly across her bed, got the phone, and called 911, but he was approaching.

"911, what's your emergency?" the operator said, and he was still coming.

"Pleeeeease send somebody now. Pleeeeeease!" Cher yelled into the phone, and the lady tried to ask questions, but Cortez was standing in her doorway. She snatched her nightstand drawer open with her free hand and grabbed her gun, pointing at him.

"Don't come any closer, Cortez. Get outta my house now!" she screamed, and the operator was trying to ask her questions, but Cortez took a step, and Cher was trembling. "Don't come near me, Cortez. I will shoot you. I swear I will if you come any closer," she cried, shaking, and Cortez took another step.

"Put that gun down right now!" Cortez demanded.

"Cortez, please just go!" she begged and took the safety off, but he kept coming, and she couldn't back up anymore. He leaped onto her bed, and she pulled the trigger, and he fell back, and she dropped the gun.

"Ma'am, ma'am, ma'am," the operator kept saying, but Cher dropped the phone and slid down the wall.

She heard Cortez coughing, gurgling, and breathing hard like he was trying to catch his breath. He was on the other side of the bed, and Cher was afraid to move. She just began to sob loudly into her hands, and then Terry came in and rushed over to her. He went over, and Cortez was still trying to hang on to life. He grabbed Cher's phone, and not even five minutes later, they heard sirens. The police were downstairs in a flash, and Terry ran to the top of the stairs.

"Up here, and we need an ambulance!" he yelled.

The police rushed up and ordered them to put their hands up. They checked Cortez for a pulse. The officer radioed for the paramedics. They took Cher's gun, put her in handcuffs, and put her in the squad car. Cher told Terry to call Kennedy, and they hauled her to the station.

Chapter Forty-five

Cortez was pronounced dead at the scene, and after they allowed Cher to receive medical attention, they questioned her and Terry for six long hours. They finally released her, and Kennedy and Julian were waiting for her. When she saw Kennedy, she almost collapsed in her arms, and Terry helped Kennedy get her to the car. They went to Kennedy's house, and Cher was numb. She couldn't believe she had shot and killed C.J.'s father. How was she going to cope with that? Her son was going to hate her, she thought as she sobbed. Terry and Kennedy sat with her, and then Kennedy offered Terry something to shower with, and he said he'd go home to shower and change and come right back.

Cher couldn't stop shaking and was hurt by what she had done. Even though she had a broken nose and got eight stitches in her forearm, Cortez was dead, and she didn't intend to take his life when she shot him.

"Come on, Cher, let's get you a bath," Kennedy said, helping her up. She took her to the guest room, and Cher sat on the ottoman. Kennedy went into the bathroom and started the water. Cher sat in a daze, and Kennedy called her name three times before she answered.

"Is he dead? I killed him, Kennedy, I killed him, didn't I?" Cher cried loudly, and Kennedy held her and let her cry. "I didn't mean to. I didn't mean to do it," she cried louder.

"I know, Cher, I know," she said, holding on to her tight.

"C.J. is going to hate me. I killed his father. I killed my son's father," she wept, and Kennedy knew this would be harder than when her father died.

She had no idea how she was going to console her. Kennedy told herself that it would be impossible for her to help Cher through this, and it took her fifteen minutes to get her up and out of her clothes. She helped her bathe and gave her two pain pills Cher received from the doctor. She tried to fight it, but she was asleep within thirty minutes, and before Kennedy went into her bedroom with Julian, Terry rang her bell. She let him in and showed him to the guest room, and he climbed into bed with Cher.

Kennedy sobbed while Julian held her. All hell broke loose the next day. People were calling Cher's phone back-to-back, and when Cortez's parents showed up at the funeral home, they had no compassion for Cher. His mother saw the damage her son had done to Cher's face and knew the history of why Cher left him, but she shot a lump of her nasty spit out of her mouth onto Cher's face, and Kennedy pushed her old ass. Julian had to break them up. She kicked Cher out and told her she wasn't welcome at her son's funeral and told her if she dared to show up, she would kill her, and they left.

Cher had visits from the press, the paper, the news, and a couple more visits from Chicago's finest until they finally ruled it self-defense. She was grieving and hurting so badly behind the incident that she couldn't return to the house. The hardest thing for Cher was sitting down with her son to tell him why she killed his dad. He cried and didn't say much. He just held her hand and told her they were going to be all right.

A couple of weeks after the incident, she finally found the strength to go home. Terry and Kennedy were by her side, and when she went into her room where it happened, she managed to keep it together. She packed some of her belongings and some of C.J.'s things, and they went to Terry's.

She made arrangements for her house to be packed up and for new carpet and paint to go in her bedroom, and she put it on the market. It didn't take long for it to sell, and after a couple of months, Cher felt a little better, but she still had nightmares. It was evident that her nose had been broken, but Terry and everyone who knew her thought she was still beautiful. She could live with the fact that her face would never be the same. She couldn't deal with the fact that she had killed her son's father.

Chapter Forty-six

Summer was gone, and Christa was almost full term. Leila was going over the final details for her shower, balancing business, marriage, and being a wonderful mother to her kids. She had two planners on staff, and even though her business was booming, she always left the shop on time because she finally had help, and Rayshon was happy. No more late nights or bringing work to bed and no more fears of failure. Leila now had peace of mind.

"Can you call and confirm the cake delivery time?" Leila asked her assistant, and she was off. She walked around with her clipboard, double-checked everything, and checked her watch. The guests would arrive soon, and Leila had to ensure everything was in order. She was going over her checklist when Rayshon walked in.

"Hey," he said.

"Hey, baby, I'm so glad you're here. There is a bag in my truck with some games in there, and I need you to get it for me," she said and went to hand him her keys.

"Wait a minute, baby. I stopped by early because I have a surprise for you," he said, and Leila didn't have time to be romanced.

"Rayshon, I'm running out of time, and I don't have time for surprises, baby," she said, and he stepped to the side to let her see.

"Renee!" she yelled in shock.

"Leila!" she said and rushed over to hug her.

"It's so good to see you. It's been forever since I saw you. When did you get here?"

"I got here a couple of days ago, so here I am."

"Oh, my Lord, girl, it's been so long. How long are you here? We have to get together after this and catch up."

"Well, I moved back because my mom is not doing too well, so we had to pack up and move back to this cold-ass place," she said, and even though Leila wanted to continue their reunion, she had work to do.

"Oh, I'm so sorry about your mom, Renee. Please tell me you can stick around because I have a ton of things to do. This event starts in an hour."

"I just have to go and check on my mom, and I can be back, and I'll bring Derrick," she said, and they hugged again. She left, and Rayshon helped her finish up.

Soon everybody started to come, and to see all of their friends was so good. They played games and offered toasts and congratulations to Isaiah and Christa. As the guests started to leave, all of Leila's closest friends had instructions to stay. Leila was happy to see that Renee had made it back.

"I asked all of you to stay after the shower for a little party of my own. Ray and I wanted to just spend time with our close family and friends. Since we are all here, I thought today would be the perfect opportunity for us not only to celebrate our newest family member, Ivory Nicole Lawton, but to celebrate our lives. We are all here because somehow God allowed us to become connected to one another whether it was through tragedy, drama, or love. We somehow came to be friends. I would like to make a toast to," she said, raising her glass, calling each person out in the order they were sitting at their round tables, "Christa and Isaiah, Iyeshia and Craig, Katrina and Cordell, Janiece and K.P., Janelle and Greg, Kimberly and Rodney, Kennedy and Julian, Cher and

Terry, Teresa and Maxwell, Kenya and Tony," she said. Kenya had started hanging at Jay's, and she and Tony, Julian's manager/bartender, hit it off.

"Devon and Alicia, and my old friends Renee and Derrick," she continued, and everyone clinked glasses. "We've had our share of ups and downs, the ins and outs, but at the end of the day, we survived and finally made it to happy," she said, and everyone nodded in agreement with bright smiles.

"Now when everyone first arrived, there was a card and pen on your table that asked you guys to write down something important you wanted to share with your friends and family tonight, and I only got a few cards, so I will open them and read what special things you guys wanted to share tonight," she said and reached into the glass bowl and opened the first card.

"This one is from Alicia and Devon. 'We are pleased to announce that we finally set a wedding date, and we would love it if Leila would be our wedding planner,'" she read and laughed. "Devon, I thought you said no way to me planning your wedding," she said, looking at him.

"Well, I changed my mind," he said and smiled at her.

"It will be my pleasure," she said. Everyone applauded, and she went for the next card.

"This one is from Kennedy and Kenya," she said and opened it. "'We are happy to share that we will be opening Soul Sista's Karaoke Bar and Grill next year,'" Leila read, and Kennedy reached for Kenya's hand.

Her sister was now able to say she was a business owner, and Kennedy was happy that she could help her with at least one of her dreams, because going back in time and being with their late mom was not obtainable.

"Wow, ladies, that is great. I guess since the both of y'all can sing like Aretha and Patti, that will work out just fine," she joked, and everyone laughed.

"Let's see. We have one more. This one is from Greg and Janelle. 'We wanted to let everyone know that in about six months, we will have another addition to our growing family because we are pregnant,'" she said, and Janiece's mouth dropped.

"That's why you've been making me drink alone lately. I knew your ass wasn't on no medications," she exclaimed, and everyone laughed. She stood and hugged Janelle, hugged Greg, and took her seat while everyone yelled out congratulations to them too.

"Okay, you guys, that is it, unless someone else has something they want to share," she said.

"I do," Rayshon said out of nowhere.

"Okay," she said, wondering what news he had and why this was her first time hearing it. "Come on over and share," she said, and he approached, and she handed him the mic.

"Hey, everyone, and congrats to you all," he said. He turned to Leila and took her hand. "This is something I want to do, or should I say I've wanted to do for a while now," he said and went down on one knee, and Leila thought he was crazy because they had been married for thirteen years.

"Ray, what are you doing?" she asked, and he pulled out a ring box.

"When we got married the first time, we went to city hall and hid our marriage from Devon for three weeks," he said, and Devon laughed.

"I remember that," he added, and everyone laughed.

"We all do," Leila confirmed, putting her eyes back on her husband.

Ray continued, "At that time, everything was rush, rush, so in front of our close friends and family, will you marry me again?" he said, flashing a ring twice the size as the one she had on. "This time, I want to vow my love to you in front of our family, friends, and more importantly, our children," he said, and she blushed.

"Of course I will," she said, and he stood to kiss her.

"Let's get this party started!" Ray yelled, and everyone applauded.

They got the music going and started popping bottles, and they danced and had a good time. Christa had a round eight-month belly in front of her, but she still went down the Soul Train line shaking what her daddy gave her because her Korean mom's ass was flat as a board. They had a great evening, and everyone exchanged hugs, kisses, and love before they headed home.

After that night, Ray and Lei had a small intimate wedding a couple of months later with all of their family and friends. Leila's business grew, and Rayshon opened a chain of Johnson's Physical around Chicago and the suburban areas. When Deja went to college, Rayshon decided to retire from physical fitness and enjoy his family. They got updates on Karen and were grateful to God that her doctor never signed off on her release. They decided they'd wait until Shon's eighteenth birthday or if and when he asked to tell him the truth. Whichever came first, they promised to tell him about his mother and left the choice up to him if he wanted to see her. They loved each other and their kids and had their perfect endings.

The following year Devon gave up his condo. He and Alicia got married, and not long after that, Alicia got her son back. She didn't have to fight Anthony because he chose to go overseas as a military contractor, and A.J. couldn't go with him. It was a rough adjustment at first, and A.J. couldn't stand Devon, but after a little push and pull, they got it together. Devon thought he'd never have a love as he had with Leila, and it was true because his and Alicia's love was what it was—his and Alicia's. Devon knew not ever to try to compare anything to it. Devon finally had his perfect through all the pain he caused and the pain he went through with Alicia.

Kennedy and Kenya opened their karaoke bar and grill, which quickly grew in business. She and Julian still worked hard as a power couple but decided to promote a couple of people to manage so they could spend more time together and with their children. Kennedy missed her dad but was no longer angry at him for keeping her mother's secret. She figured all things happened the way they were supposed to. After Kenya's success, Rob attempted to work it out, but Kenya and Tony were inseparable, so Rob didn't have a chance. After the abandonment, secrets, and loss, Kennedy, Julian, and Kenya finally had their perfect.

After asking Cher to marry him ten times, Cher finally said yes to Terry. It took her a long time to stop having nightmares about the shooting, and since her son forgave her and didn't hate her, she allowed her wounds to heal from that marriage and let Terry become her husband. He promised he'd spend the rest of their lives making her feel like a queen, and Cher believed that he would, and not long after she gave Terry her hand in marriage, she gave him his first child. Everyone was shocked when she announced that she was pregnant at 44, but she was healthy and gave birth to another little boy. Holding her newborn in one arm, holding C.J.'s hand with her other hand, and smiling at Terry while he snapped a picture, Cher finally had her perfect.

After the Robin incident, K.P. went through a dozen temps trying to find the right fit for his assistant, and it hit him to ask Janiece. It was weird at first going to work every morning with her and then going home, but it was fun to get a quickie in on his desk at the office with his wife, who was also his hot-ass assistant. Janiece realized her insecurities weren't K.P.'s fault, so she did join the gym and got active, and now that she looked and felt better about herself, she no longer felt insecure around gorgeous women because she also had a spot in the gorgeous category. After a couple of years of being her husband's assistant, she called it quits but ensured he hired a male assistant. She was confident but not stupid, and after making the changes about herself that she didn't like, she went back to being a normal wife, not the jealous wife, and K.P. and Janiece finally had their perfect.

Greg and Janelle had a little girl and never mentioned or talked about Janelle's affair again. It was weird for the first few encounters with Devon, but they handled things like adults should and let it go. Greg no longer had visions of knocking Devon out, and Janelle no longer had moments of thinking about what it would have been like if she and Devon had gotten together. She was in love with Greg and her three children, and they had their perfect.

After Christa had Ivory, she wanted to get pregnant again right away. Isaiah was excited that she was excited because he wanted a big family too, but after baby number two, Christa wanted to have another one. He was all for it, but it didn't happen immediately with the third baby. They were not sure why it took three years to conceive the third baby, but it did, and after that, they were content. Isaiah finally took over the dealership because his dad was getting older, and it wasn't as awful as he thought it would be. He had a wife who adored him, four beautiful, healthy kids, and he and Christa had their perfect.

The End

These final chapters are: *Now You Wanna Come Back, My Best Friend & My Man,* and *Who Do I Run To?* I hope you enjoyed this novel, and I asked that you please post a review. I have a lot of new characters and story lines coming soon, so although this is a farewell to some of your favorite characters, I am excited to introduce you to some interesting new ones I hope you will enjoy. Thank you for your support, and please tell a reader, a family member, or a friend to try my novels.

Happy Reading!